MY DEAR AUNT FLORA

At Rushing Farm, the Manning household — with Aunt Flora at its head — lives in harmony. With the appearance of George Manning, however, peace is at an end. George is a successful actor, spoilt and selfish. He sees nothing at Rushing but discomfort and boredom, and his relations hope that he will carry out his repeated threat of departing by the next train. But with the arrival of Brian Lorimer and the enchanting Angela Reynolds, George finds something at Rushing which proves a greater attraction than his comfortable existence in London.

Books by Elizabeth Cadell
in the Ulverscroft Large Print Series:

ELIZABETH CADELL

MY DEAR AUNT FLORA

Complete and Unabridged

ULVERSCROFT
Leicester

This edition published in Great Britain
in 1982 by
Robert Hale Limited
London

First Large Print Edition
published 1996
by arrangement with
Robert Hale Limited
London

British Library CIP Data

Cadell, Elizabeth
My dear Aunt Flora.—Large print ed.—
Ulverscroft large print series: romance
1. English fiction—20th century
I. Title
823.9′12 [F]

ISBN 0–7089–3512–5

Published by
F. A. Thorpe (Publishing) Ltd.
Anstey, Leicestershire
Set by Words & Graphics Ltd.
Anstey, Leicestershire
Printed and bound in Great Britain by
T. J. Press (Padstow) Ltd., Padstow, Cornwall

This book is printed on acid-free paper

TO
MY BROTHER-IN-LAW
GEORGE MACKENZIE MARTIN

1

"HAS it ever struck you," asked my sister-in-law, following me into the kitchen and watching me absently while I washed up a pile of crockery, "that we might go down and live at that farm that Uncle Herbert left you?"

"It isn't a farm — it's a house and two fields," I said, "and we couldn't live there."

"Why not?" asked Phyl. "Have you ever seen it?"

"Not properly," I replied. "Hugh and I drove over and looked at it once when we were motoring in the district but I don't remember anything about it except that it was large and miles from anywhere."

"Sounds lovely," murmured Phyl. "Large and miles from anywhere." She looked round the tiny kitchen and leaned dejectedly against the draining-board. "Don't you," she said fretfully, "loathe this beastly little place?"

"Yes," I said, trailing my hands in the water and pausing for a moment. "I loathe it as much as you do and we were fools ever to come here."

"I suppose we were," said Phyl slowly, one white finger following a drop of water down the sloping groove of the draining-board. "It was a bad move, but we did it at a bad time. But mistakes can be put right, can't they?"

"Some can," I said, going back to work, "but we have to be careful about not being wrong a second time. We've been here nearly two years," I pointed out, "and it hasn't killed us."

"Not entirely, but it's getting on my nerves more and more," said Phyl, "and you look frightfully thin and you're not happy, Jonny."

This was the abbreviated form of the only name my parents thought fit to give me. I was named Jonquil, which was a little unfortunate, as I am not at all like a jonquil or any other flower.

I smiled at Phyl.

"If you're going to stay in here and make me waste time talking," I said, "you'll have to work. The drying-up

2

thing is behind you."

Phyl turned and took down the cloth obediently, but made no move to use it.

"Will you promise, Jonny," she said urgently, "that you won't let the landlord talk you into renewing the lease at the end of the two years?"

"I promise," I answered unhesitatingly. "I'm as keen as you are to get out, but we're going to be more careful this time. — Is this farm the last of Uncle Herbert's legacies?" I asked after a while.

"Yes," said Phyl. "You and Hugh got it because it was the biggest, I think. I got a cottage near Bath, and Tommy and I sold it almost at once. George did very well out of his — it was near Staines and he did it up and sold it to a theatrical magnate and made a very good thing out of it."

"George would, of course," I replied.

Uncle Herbert had made a great deal of money in his time by buying up derelict houses and transforming them into desirable residences. None of his ventures turned out badly except the three houses which he had kindly bequeathed

3

to his nephews Hugh and George and his niece Phyl. He had lived for a time in the house in Rushing which Phyl was now proposing we should occupy, but had not succeeded in making it desirable enough to offset its remote situation, nor had we ever succeeded in letting the house.

"If you'd come down to Rushing," said Phyl, returning to the attack, "you might find yourself looking at it with different eyes."

"It isn't a case of eyes, but of hands and feet, Phyl," I said firmly. "It's a large, rambling house, with big rooms and lots of them and I couldn't manage it alone — and you wouldn't do anything," I added without rancour.

This was such an accepted fact in the family that we had long ago ceased to comment on it. Phyl just didn't work. She kept her room in perfect order, looked after her clothes, amused the children and arranged the flowers. Everything she did was done, however, very slowly, painstakingly and thoroughly, and she proved, in double harness, a serious drag. She had a gift of coolness and restfulness, and whatever outsiders thought of her inactivity and whatever uncharitable label they attached to it, we in the family were used to a languid, beautiful, lounging Phyl, and we liked her that way.

I finished the washing up, retrieved the drying-up cloth from Phyl's idle hands, and proceeded to dry the dishes.

"Tell me, Jonny," said Phyl, coming out of a long reverie, "would you consider living at Rushing if Aunt Flora could come and live with us?"

This, I felt, was such an unnecessary question that for a few moments I could only stare at Phyl in surprise.

"Of course," I said at last. "That would be quite different. Carrie would be there to do the cooking, for one thing, and the place wouldn't seem too big with Aunt Flora in it, if you understand" — Phyl understood perfectly — "and — " I broke off impatiently. "It isn't in the least use discussing it," I said. "Aunt Flora isn't free and she can't come."

"She could," said Phyl, "if she wasn't looking after that beastly old man."

This was true, if a little strong. Aunt Flora was born to look after somebody, and almost as soon as we had left her and moved into homes of our own, leaving her free from the responsibility of our welfare, a new burden had been thrust on her. Her brother Edward's wife died, and the old man, after a lifetime's excess in almost every type of pleasure known to the world and the flesh, was in no state to end his days alone. Aunt Flora surveyed the melancholy wreck and without hesitation took over the arrangements for its salvage. She installed him at Burnton, a large house owned by her brother Bruce and in which we had been brought up, and all our efforts to dissuade her from this course were unavailing. Phyl's brother George, rapidly rising to great heights as an actor, had made strenuous efforts to persuade her to live with him in London, but she considered that Uncle Eddie would, of the two, be less trying. When we found that the new life had only the most beneficial effect on her health and spirits, we looked at the other side of the matter and came to the unexpected conclusion that Uncle Eddie had only got what he deserved. Aunt Flora left him occasionally to stay with one or other of us, and regaled us with stories of her struggles to keep the old reprobate away from his wine and women. The tales were wildly exaggerated, but we knew Aunt Flora and were able to disentangle the imaginative flights from the facts.

But it was her adoption of Uncle Eddie which prevented her from coming to us now, and I understood Phyl's feelings, although I deplored the frankness with which she voiced them.

"You shouldn't call him a beastly old man," I said.

"Why not?" asked Phyl in surprise. "He is."

"Well, don't let's discuss it," I said. "Aunt Flora can't come, and it's no use abusing the poor old fellow."

"Don't call him a poor old fellow," said Phyl impatiently. "He's mean, depraved, selfish and inconsiderate — oh, well," she ended with a sigh, "let's forget him."

Uncle Edward may have deserved some of the epithets Phyl bestowed upon him, but that he was by no means inconsiderate was proved late the same night when the telephone rang just as I was in bed and on the edge of sleep. I reached for a dressing-gown, but heard Phyl speaking, and waited to hear who could be ringing up at that late hour. A few minutes later she rang off and came into my room looking flushed and excited.

"That was Aunt Flora," she said, sitting on my bed and tucking her bare feet under her. "Extraordinary, isn't it, after our conversation this morning about that place and her not being able to come . . . "

"Is Uncle Edward worse?" I put in anxiously.

"Dead," said Phyl simply. "You needn't have refused to talk about her not being able to come. She's free and she'll come and everything's going to be all right and we're all going to be frightfully happy."

"What about Uncle Edward?" I asked, trying to recall her to the decencies.

"Should I go to Burnton, do you think?" said Phyl, pursuing her train of thought. "Aunt Flora's sure to ring George up, and he'll be on to her at once trying to get her to go and live with him, and . . . Who would have guessed," she mused, "that she'd be free so soon?"

"Not Uncle Edward," I said thoughtfully.

"The danger is, Jonny," went on Phyl urgently, "that Aunt Flora hasn't ever realized how we've loathed living here. We've got to tell her and explain that we couldn't tell her before for fear of worrying her. Once George begins to work on her feelings — you see what I mean?"

"Uncle Edward," I said, "is . . ."

Phyl frowned irritably.

"What on earth," she demanded, "do you keep chanting 'Uncle Edward' like that for?"

"He's dead," I replied, "and — "

"That's what I've been trying to tell you," said Phyl. "Move up, Jonny, and let me come in for a few minutes — my feet are frozen." She snuggled against me and warmed her chilled feet by the simple process of resting them on my warm ones.

"Let's talk about the future," she said. "Life at that farm place with Aunt Flora and Carrie and the children and lots of dogs. No cows — Aunt Flora doesn't like them — and — "

"Aunt Flora hasn't come yet," I reminded her.

"She'll come," said Phyl confidently, "unless that beast George deludes her into thinking he needs her. Just the sort of thing he'd do. I'll go up for the funeral and keep an eye on him," she went on, "and afterwards you and I and Aunt Flora can go down and look at the farm and see about putting it in order."

"I wish you wouldn't discuss the future over Uncle Eddie's deathbed," I said. "It isn't decent and you haven't said a word of regret. I know," I added after a little thought, "that he was a dreadful old" — the family name for him was 'Old Soaker' but under the circumstances I sought for a milder term — "old drunkard, but you oughtn't to use his deathbed as a — as a springboard for a happy future." I paused to watch the effect of this brilliant phrase on Phyl, and found that she was asleep, lying snug with the blankets tucked under her chin. I looked at her with disgust and saw that she occupied the whole of the bed with the exception of the four inches on which I was precariously perched. It was impossible to disturb that sweet, deep-breathing calm. I tucked the blankets round her and padded to her room, where I climbed between her cold sheets and tried to warm myself on the luke-warm bottle. I thought, shiveringly and gloomily, of telephones ringing in the middle of the night and bringing sad news; of people who employed cuckoo tactics and turned other people out of warm beds; of poor Uncle Edward, who would now be trying to explain away nearly seventy years of concentrated wicked living . . . I wished I could get warm . . . But there was a distant gleam which got brighter every moment — a happy thought that filled my mind and warmed me at last. Uncle Edward had gone where a good nurse could do nothing for him, and he had left us Aunt Flora . . .

* * *

Aunt Flora was my aunt in name only. My mother, who died in Bermuda when I was five, had been her greatest friend, and my father had sent me to England to remain under Aunt Flora's care until he could come and make a home for me. He died a year later, and Aunt Flora, assisted by the faithful Carrie, who was cook, housemaid and nurse, had brought me up. Until I was ten, we lived in a small cottage in Cornwall within sound of the Atlantic, devoted to one another and as happy as any household in England. Then came a change which increased our number and also our happiness. Aunt Flora's younger brother and his wife had been killed in a train accident, and their three children — Hugh, aged twelve, Phyl eight, and George six, were added to Aunt Flora's family. She moved to Burnton, owned by her eldest brother Bruce, who did not wish to live in the house owing to his wife's preference for being near London. At Burnton we were brought up — the three good-looking, charming Manning children and my more ordinary self. I married Hugh when he was twenty-two, and we had two children, Paul and Polly. George embarked upon what was to prove a brilliant and successful career as an actor, and Phyl married Tommy Blair, the best Rugger forward in England and Hugh's greatest friend. Apart from our anxiety on Aunt Flora's — or Uncle Eddie's — account, there was no cloud anywhere in our sky.

Life was perfect — for a time. Then, on a flawless, exhilarating Christmas Eve, the whole family met as usual for the annual reunion at the lovely house Hugh and I had bought in a Sussex village. Everyone was there — Aunt Flora, released for a while from the delighted Eddie; George, now famous on stage and screen; Paul and Polly and the beautiful, happy Phyl. Hugh and Tommy were to come down from London in Tommy's car.

They never came. The car overturned on a treacherous piece of road fifteen miles out of London, and the bodies of both men were brought home on Christmas Day.

A month later, Phyl and I, with Paul and Polly, had moved into a small flat in a seaside town and attempted to begin life again in entirely new surroundings. It was a hasty and unwise decision, and we had both regretted it almost as soon as we had moved into the flat. When we were able to think clearly, and discovered how cramped and unsuitable were our new surroundings, we realized how ill-equipped we had been to make any reasoned decisions. There had been nobody to turn to for advice. Aunt Flora, though torn with love and anxiety for us, had been summoned to Burnton to deal with a particularly bad outbreak on the part of Uncle Edward. George had been kind and helpful and did his best to dissuade us from making hasty plans, but we had been feverishly eager for any kind of change.

We had, however, been happy in being together. The children had kept well and had, at first, been contented in their cramped surroundings, although they both felt the need for more space now. If — there were many ifs — if Aunt Flora would come to us; if we liked the farm; if we could live there together . . . Warmed and comforted by the thought of a new life ahead, I drifted into sleep.

2

THREE weeks later, Aunt Flora, Phyl and I went on a visit of inspection to Rushing Farm, in the village of Rushing under-Felling.

A train from London took us to a junction with the imposing name of Clinton Overway, and at this point one left behind the ordered, busy life of cities and towns and adjusted one's pace to the slow, unhurried ways of the unspoiled countryside. An engine which looked like one of the earliest models puffed its way into the junction fifty minutes after the London train had left, and after resting for some time, took us without any sign of haste through beautiful country, stopping at three or four intermediate stations and coming to rest at the terminus of Felling.

We alighted and looked round with interest. This was to be our nearest town; our shops, our library, and our cinema.

15

It looked too small to contain all these amenities, consisting of little more than one street and a few outlying houses of varying sizes.

There were buses in the station yard with boards indicating their destinations, but none of them offered Rushing. After seeking information from several of the drivers and getting none beyond what we already knew — that the Rushing bus was not there — we went to the station master and inquired about alternative transport to Rushing.

There was, it appeared, no alternative transport. There was one bus and one only which ran between Felling and Rushing, and this was owned by a certain Mr. Alfred Duff who was, the stationmaster told us, fairly regular in his journeys to and fro except on the occasions when his domestic affairs got out of control. Mrs. Duff had fits of ill-temper; when her fits were on she cooked no food for Mr. Duff and Mr. Duff, unfed, could not be expected to attend to his duties.

Aunt Flora looked enchanted with this recital. Tall and white-haired, she looked at the stationmaster with a charming smile.

"I see — if Mrs. Duff says we ride, we ride. Is that it?"

The stationmaster thought this summed it up very well.

As it was clear that there was nothing else to be done, we took our seats on the platform with many others who, like ourselves, were awaiting Mr. Duff's pleasure. Nobody displayed the slightest impatience and there seemed to be a general expectation that the bus would turn up before nightfall.

We would have liked some tea, but we were afraid to go into the little village street and look for a café in case the bus arrived during our absence and vanished Rushing-wards without us. We walked up and down the platform to keep ourselves warm, sometimes seeking the shelter of the tiny waiting-room with its fire.

About two hours after our arrival there was a general move on the part of those waiting, and we followed the little crowd into the station yard, stopping in astonishment at the sight that met our eyes.

17

The Rushing bus was without exception the most dilapidated piece of coachwork we had ever seen. Paintless, dusty, mud-streaked, with two windows completely missing, it stood in the yard, its engine running and the entire framework bobbing up and down in a frenzied, palpitating manner that made us feel rather sick. I shuddered at the thought of three miles of that bone-shaking movement. We gazed at the vehicle in dismay, and presently Phyl sugggested that if we wished to get seats we had better hasten into the unattractive interior.

Aunt Flora, however, was in no hurry. She had waited two hours for Mr. Duff and she was anxious to become acquainted with the seedy individual who controlled the movements of some twenty persons, including, on this occasion, herself. She walked up to where he stood, door-handle in hand, waiting until the last passenger should have mounted.

"I'm very glad to see you," she said warmly. She surveyed the bus with interest. "Shocking thing, isn't it?" she continued sympathetically. "I wonder you got here at all. I don't think" — she poked her head into a windowless aperture — "I don't think I should like the inside — I'll get up on that seat beside you, and I shall be able to ask you about the country as we go along."

Mr. Duff seemed too surprised to do more than hand her up, and having done so, he sprang into the driver's seat and proceeded in the direction of Rushing. Phyl and I took our places on one of the seats that ran the length of the bus and I found myself next to a pleasant-looking woman who gave me a shy smile and asked me whether I had ever visited Rushing before.

"Only once, for about ten minutes," I said, "but not by this route."

She smiled. "It isn't very convenient, is it?" she said, "and it's a dreadful bus. Poor Duff isn't entirely to blame. His wife is a woman of extremely narrow views, and if he displeases her in any way by refusing to go to church or by" — she leaned closer and lowered her voice — "by drinking too much, she won't give him any food. The poor fellow doesn't really have much of a life."

I looked out at the really beautiful scenery through which we were passing, but the erratic course pursued by Mr. Duff filled me with dread, and I turned back to my neighbour.

"There's really nothing to be alarmed about," she assured me. "He goes round corners in a very reckless way, but he has done the same for fifteen years without one accident."

I somehow failed to find comfort in this. Phyl looked as if she was enjoying herself and Aunt Flora and the driver were chatting together in a way which did not help to keep Mr. Duff's eye on the road.

We drew up at last before a delightful-looking inn whose sign read 'The Gentle Fawn,' and the name suited the quiet, peaceful scene. Phyl and I hurried out of the bus thankfully and went round to the front to help Aunt Flora down. Mr. Duff, however, was already doing this, and it was clear that the two had become good friends.

"She's waiting for me," he said in a mournful undertone to Aunt Flora.

20

"There she is now, watching to see I don't go in and have one."

We looked with interest at the small, thin woman standing at the door of a cottage opposite. Tiny though she was, she looked formidable, and we sighed for Mr. Duff.

"If he drinks," said Aunt Flora, who had obviously heard the tragedy from the lips of the victim, "he doesn't eat. I wonder," she added, staring thoughtfully at the Duff residence, "how it would have worked with your Uncle Edward?"

"You'll be Mrs. Manning," said a voice behind us, and the landlord of the inn, as calm and restful as his own sign, bowed to us from the doorway.

"This is Mrs. Manning," said Aunt Flora. "I'm Miss Manning, and I'm afraid we're rather later than I said we'd be, but I suppose you know the habits of the bus better than we do?"

"Indeed, yes," smiled Mr. Pollitt. "You'll have a bad impression of the place."

"Quite the contrary," Aunt Flora assured him sincerely. "It was most interesting. There isn't," she continued, looking round, "very much of Rushing, is there?"

"Only just what you see," said Mr. Pollitt, stepping out and joining us.

"About nine cottages, the inn and the church — and a few houses on that hill. Isn't it unusual to have a church in such a tiny village?" asked Aunt Flora.

The church and the inn, Mr. Pollitt explained, were both built in expectation of the railway extending as far as Rushing. The line had, however, stopped at Felling, and though the Church was a little too large for the size of the village, the inn had prospered and was almost always full.

"Once people get as far as Rushing — if they can manage the journey," said Mr. Pollitt, "there's something about the place that seems to charm them all."

We were to see this proved many times in later years, but our immediate concern was to see our house. The landlord was deeply interested to hear that we hoped to become residents, and led us out of the cold air into the snug little inn parlour.

"It'll be too late to look at the place to-night," he said. "It's a fine house, but it wouldn't let — too big, I reckon, for occasional visitors."

He remembered Uncle Herbert and his brief residence there, and thought he had improved the place a good deal.

"But that's some time back — a matter of ten years or so," he said. He led us to a side window and pulled aside the curtain. "You can see a green gate a little way up that hill — the house stands on a bit of a ridge amongst those trees. Fine views."

He dropped the curtain and set chairs for us in front of the fire.

"This place isn't as out of the way as some," he said. "We've got electric light and a good water supply. The rest of the new gadgets haven't come our way yet, barring telephones, but you'll get your morning paper by eight-thirty and your letters by nine, and that's pretty good, considering."

Phyl and I would have liked to go, dark as it was, and make a preliminary survey, but both Aunt Flora and Mr. Pollitt pronounced this foolish, and when we found that it had begun to rain heavily, the matter ended.

Mr. Pollitt's remarks on electricity and

water had recalled to my mind the chief objection Hugh had raised against the house, and I confided to Phyl when saying good night that the sanitation on the farm was of a rather primitive type.

"What's it like?" she asked.

"Al fresco," I said briefly.

Phyl considered this. "Well, don't mention it to Aunt Flora," she said after a time. "It'll only prejudice her, and" — she smiled mischievously — "we must let her form her own opinions fairly."

I agreed to this with great relief, and spent a rather restless night dreaming of Mr. Duff and his bus.

It was still raining heavily the next morning, but it was warmer. Immediately after breakfast Phyl and I hurried the protesting Aunt Flora across the road and up the slope towards the green gate. She argued quite reasonably that the house would still be there when the rain had ceased, but our impatience was too great to be borne, and we buttoned her firmly into her mackintosh and handed her her large umbrella. We reached the gate and, turning into it, walked up the drive and stopped in front of the house.

I had spoken truthfully when I told Phyl that I had scarcely taken in any details on my first visit. I had not been interested in derelict houses miles from anywhere, and had come simply to stand by while Hugh decided whether the place could serve as a holiday house for the family. I saw now a pleasant, solid-looking house with large windows and green shutters and a spacious covered verandah running round it on two sides, railed, and with three wide wooden steps leading down to the garden. I looked at the house. I saw polished furniture, a shining kitchen, children's bedrooms. Phyl looked at the verandah, seeing a long, comfortable chair, and Aunt Flora's eyes roamed round the large garden and saw beautiful roses blooming on a June day. The matter was almost settled before anybody spoke.

"You didn't tell me," said Aunt Flora resentfully, "that there was a garden like this — although I might have known. Your Uncle Herbert wouldn't have lived here. He was a silly fellow, but he was a prince of gardeners. Thank God he can't see what a wilderness it is now."

She stepped across ancient flower beds on to what was once a splendid lawn. "Look at it," she said, oblivious of rain falling on her and damp soaking into her stockings. "Look at it — can you imagine anybody letting a place get into such a state?" She made her way across the grass, looking round her and seeing immense possibilities opening before her eyes, and we followed her exploratory journey with almost equal interest.

The lawn sloped gently from the side of the house to a low wall which separated it from the field beyond. In the middle was a magnificent beech tree. Ruins of flower beds, overgrown paths and a neglected orchard lay beyond on one side. On the other, a little gate led into what had once been vegetable gardens. Of the farm nothing remained except a small cowshed with room for three animals. It was roomy and stone-floored and would, I thought, make a good outdoor retreat for the children. There were two good sheds and a tomato house which looked like one of Uncle Herbert's improvements, and a large cucumber frame.

We stood in the rain and surveyed the scene, and Aunt Flora stalked over the disorder, her umbrella bobbing and her mind racing with plans for restoring the gardens to their former loveliness.

"Come and look at it from the verandah, darling," urged Phyl at last. "You'll be swamped if you don't take shelter."

"My dear Phyl," said Aunt Flora tartly, "you insisted on my coming out in the rain and now I insist on staying out in it. Look at this," she went on, opening a small gate and going through — "acres of vegetables."

We followed and saw acres of mud, but she was looking into a future filled with salad.

"Not at all a bad shed," she said, opening the door and peering in. "How much of this land do we own, Jonny?"

I took heart at the plural.

"Only two fields," I said. "It isn't really a farm."

"Well, the name's nice, anyhow," said Aunt Flora. "We won't change it."

"Come and look at the inside," I begged.

27

"Not yet — you go if you want to," she replied, walking along a new path and inspecting bedraggled bushes. "This poor garden makes me feel wretched."

She stopped and pointed to a small ivy-covered building standing about fifty yards from the house.

"What's that?" she inquired.

"That," said Phyl gloomily, "represents the Usual Offices."

"You mean the outside ones," said Aunt Flora.

"The only ones," said Phyl.

"You mean there's no other?" asked Aunt Flora in astonishment. "Nothing inside whatsoever?"

"Nothing," said Phyl glumly.

"How extraordinary," exclaimed Aunt Flora, pausing to consider the situation. "Can't you imagine," she went on, "groping out here on a black, stormy night and ending up by falling into those raspberry canes?"

The prospect obviously had no terrors for her, and Phyl and I breathed more easily. Aunt Flora went forward to make a closer inspection and pronounced everything to be in quite good order, and we proceeded with light hearts into the house.

We stood in the hall, and it was my turn to make discoveries. Some of them were pleasant, and we exclaimed joyfully at bedrooms with lovely views, a roomy bathroom, a beautifully-proportioned drawing-room with doors opening on to the verandah, and large, airy attics. There were less delightful surprises: the stairs were uneven and rather dangerous, the dining-room had two doors leading into the hall and one into a small pantry and promised to be draughty. Every room in the house would require redecorating and the kitchen had what we considered most inadequate cooking facilities.

We walked upstairs and downstairs until we were exhausted, and then sat on the top step of the verandah and summed up.

"What do you think?" I asked Aunt Flora anxiously.

"Does it matter what I think?" she replied, smiling at us. "You've made up your minds to love it all and you'd be just as delighted if it were ugly and poky and falling to pieces."

"That's not quite true," said Phyl slowly, leaning against the railing and staring out at the wet garden. "I must say Jonny rather understated its possibilities, but I can understand what she meant when she said she wouldn't come here without you. It would be" — she paused to find the word — "homey with us all, but Jonny and I would be lost alone."

"Carrie won't be able to do more than the cooking," said Aunt Flora. "I'll expend my failing strength on the garden — not all the time, of course, but it still leaves rather a lot for Jonny. You," she said to Phyl as calmly as I had said it weeks earlier, "won't do anything at all."

Phyl looked depressed.

"I'll do my room," she said defensively, "and my washing and ironing and Jonny's ironing too — "

"And the flowers, of course," said Aunt Flora with sarcasm.

"If we ever have any," replied Phyl sweetly. She turned and looked earnestly at Aunt Flora. "You will come, won't you?" she begged.

There was a long pause while Aunt

Flora turned the matter over in her mind. As always when she was thinking deeply, she put her hands on her knees and played five finger exercises absently, and we fixed our eyes on the busy fingers and would not have dreamed of saying a word until they had come to rest. Phyl and I waited for the exercises to stop, and spoke in the same instant.

"Well?"

Aunt Flora looked at us both musingly.

"Do you think there was any truth in what George said about needing someone to run his home?" she asked.

"Not one word," said Phyl, who had no idea what he had said.

"I don't know what he said," I added more honestly, "but you know he's been wanting to have you for years, and he knows this is his chance." I could have added that she would hate life in a London flat, but this would have aroused her sympathy for poor George's having to endure this hardship, so I held my tongue.

"I like the look of the place and I like what we've seen of our neighbours. We ought to find," said Aunt Flora reflectively, "a good many People Like Ourselves."

We knew this expression of old. It had no reference whatever to social grades — it meant, simply, anybody who was charming, interesting, clever, amusing or of outstanding personality.

"We could be happy here," I said. "Think of it — you and Phyl and Carrie and the children and — "

This list of loved ones proved too much for me in my excited state, and I fumbled for my handkerchief, muttering angrily at my foolishness.

Aunt Flora studied me.

"You're overtired," she said, "and you're as thin as a rail. God knows why you both stuffed yourselves into a poky little flat in a wretched little town, but you wouldn't take anybody's advice. Now dry your eyes and listen to me. Are you both absolutely sure," she continued, looking from one to the other, "that you're not going to feel too cut-off — too isolated — down here? You're both comparatively young women, and I haven't seen anything in the way of diversions in Rushing."

"We're not cut off at all," said Phyl, "and nobody could want diversions in a place like this. The only thing that worried me was that Outer Hebrides place" — she waved a hand in the direction of the ivy-covered outhouse — "but apart from that, it's all perfect. Can't you imagine Paul and Polly here?"

"I can't imagine George here," replied Aunt Flora. "He wouldn't — God bless my soul," she ended in astonishment — "Jonny's still howling."

Phyl leaned over and gazed at me anxiously.

"What's the matter?" she asked.

"You mentioned the children," I said tearfully, "and it reminded me — Polly — there's no school."

Aunt Flora sat upright and gazed at me with disgust.

"Do you mean to tell me," she said, "that you came down here with your mind made up to live in this house before you had even made any kind of inquiry about educational facilities?"

My tears fell faster than the rain and Aunt Flora, who loathed tearful women, folded her hands and waited for me to recover. There was a heavy silence and I saw all my hopes fading. I could not afford a boarding-school for Polly, and I had not given a thought to the impossibility of there being a suitable day-school in a remote country district.

"I was a fool," I said at last. "I never dreamt there'd be no school at all."

"There is a school," said Aunt Flora, "and a very good one. You must both be in an extraordinary state of mind not to have remembered that Connie Duncan's girl is at a school at Rosing Grange, which you passed half a mile this side of Felling. I can't think how you missed it."

"We weren't sitting by the driver, darling, and so he couldn't point it out to us," said Phyl.

"Will they take a day-girl?" I asked.

"I shall ask them," said Aunt Flora majestically, and we all knew they would. "I can't imagine," she ended, "how you two ever got along by your two senseless selves. This may be your house, Jonny, but thank God there's going to be one woman in it with a head on her shoulders."

"Would that," inquired Phyl, "be you, by any chance?"

"Will you come?" I asked in the same instant.

Aunt Flora looked with amusement at my tear-stained face and pink nose.

"Try and stop me," she invited.

3

WE had been at Rushing for a year, and Aunt Flora was still trying to persuade old Barnes, the handyman-gardener, that it was her garden and that she wanted a hand in its lay-out.

He was a tantalizing old fellow and I felt sorry for her. Vegetables and flowers popped up, in due season, in the oddest places. Aunt Flora was losing sleep at nights wondering what new green shoot would appear a quarter of a mile from the place she had told Barnes to put it. Her roars of rage had no effect on him — he merely gazed stolidly at the offending plant, scratched his head and repeated the last two words of every one of Aunt Flora's furious sentences in a lunatic way. To-day Aunt Flora was roaring again — and I was more sorry for her than usual, for it was a beautiful, hot sunny morning and no weather for exertion. I sat on the verandah, shifting my chair from time to time as the sun moved round, and dealt with a pile of the children's mending. A little way away, in her favourite long wicker chair, lounged Phyl in immaculate shorts and a pale lemon shirt. A book lay face downwards on her knees and her arms were clasped behind her head. Her eyes were half-closed and she watched me lazily, saying nothing, and smiling now and again as the sounds of the contest from the flowerbed came to our ears. Carrie was moving about indoors, and the sixty-year-old Mrs. Watt from the village who came in to help her twice a week was hovering round waiting for a lull in Aunt Flora's wrath in order to ask for some vegetables for lunch.

"Go and give the basket to Barnes," I said, taking pity on her. "He'll take the stuff in later. And Mrs. Watt — I suppose there wouldn't be a nice cool drink of some kind, would there?"

Apparently there would, and presently she reappeared with a tall jug and three glasses.

"Better make it four," I told her. "I hear the Colonel." Her face stretched into a delighted toothless grin, and she produced the fourth glass, and a medley of barks, whistles and calls heralded the appearance of our nearest neighbour, Colonel Bainsley. He stepped on to the verandah and removed a meek and drooping panama.

"Good morning," he said, settling himself comfortably and lifting the smallest of his three beautiful dogs on to his knee. "And by jove, it *is* a good morning, and what's Miss Manning shouting out there for in this heat? More misplaced flora?"

Phyl smiled her appreciation, and the Colonel looked as pleased as though he had led a successful charge. He glanced suspiciously at the jug. "That looks nice and cool," he remarked, "but what would it do to the legs of an old war-horse?"

"Practically nothing," I said, "but you know where the real stuff is kept and it isn't too hot to go and fetch it."

"You're right," he said. "But keep this chair empty until I come back — I passed Miss Peel on my way here and I think she was making for these parts." He stood up and looked round appreciatively. "Funny thing," he said, "I completely missed the

38

possibilities of this place. We all did. I've shown people round it scores of times, and it just looked like a glorified barn. I even" — he looked at me and chuckled — "I even put one or two people off it."

"And did me out of years of profit," I remarked.

"Yes — I'm sorry," smiled the Colonel with no sign of remorse. "But I don't think anyone else would have turned it into anything like this, so I'm glad I saved it for you."

He went round the outside of the house and met Aunt Flora, her roars now sunk to a low muttering, on her way indoors with the vegetables, and the two went on together, discussing the morning's tragedy.

I poured a drink and handed it to Phyl. She didn't look at all as though she needed a cool drink. I sipped mine and then went on with my sewing. It was dull mending, but necessary.

I looked up at intervals and gazed with pleasure at Phyl's cool, lovely figure and felt, as I always did, rested and refreshed at the sight. I could never understand why the unthinking could accuse her of being a useless woman, for the sight of her, a series of pictures of beauty in repose, was an unfailing spur to others. In the family we made greater efforts from the knowledge that we were privileged to do her share of the work. Outside it, breathless, bustling women, already exhausted by the effort of telescoping two days' work or pleasure into one, would be goaded to a frenzy of irritation at the sight of the languorous Phyl, and lash themselves into more fevered activity than before. Kindly village women, charmed by her gentle ways and convinced that her hours in the long, comfortable chair betokened some kind of decline, called frequently with little offerings from their gardens and spent happy half-hours snatched from their busy days, talking to her on the verandah. Aunt Flora thought that her most useful attribute was in always being on hand in her chair to entertain callers, thus enabling us to get on with our work in the house and garden without interruptions.

Little Miss Peel came hurriedly up the

drive and paused at the verandah steps.

"I haven't a moment," she panted, "Duff is getting ready to go. I promised to match some wool for Miss Manning in Felling — could you let me have the pattern?"

I begged her to have a hasty drink and went indoors for the wool sample. I gave it to her and took her basket and library books.

"I'll walk to the bus with you," I said. "Why can't you rest quietly like Phyl on a hot day like this?"

Miss Peel puffed at my side like a toy engine. "I don't know," she said, "it's just that if I'm not doing something all the time I feel uneasy. I think it's the result of being brought up in deadly fear of the word 'sloth'. There's really nothing to go into Felling for to-day. Miss Manning isn't in a hurry for the wool, but one gets into the habit of running to and fro . . . "

"Why not sit with Phyl and have a nice restful morning?" I said persuasively, slackening my pace for a moment.

Miss Peel prodded me urgently through the gate and hurried down the hill, slowing to an easier pace as she saw Duff in conversation with his formidable spouse.

"We live in such a rush," she said. "Perhaps it isn't quite right, but somehow we get mixed up between laziness and leisure. We feel guilty if we aren't doing something. I think when I get home to-day — perhaps after lunch — I'll sit down for half an hour by the clock and do nothing — just fold my arms. I don't think I'll last the half-hour, but I shall try."

We began to laugh, but Miss Peel heard the bus's preliminary warning hoot, seized her basket and books and took to her heels, achieving a wobbly and wavering course and looking smaller, but somehow even plumper as she disappeared into the bus.

I went back to the verandah and took up my sewing. Aunt Flora brought out a basket of beans and a basin and sat slicing the beans into incredibly thin, long slices. Carrie could never give the time to preparing them as Aunt Flora loved them. The Colonel, beer in hand, looked a little cooler. He gazed out at the shimmering heat and remarked: "If the clerk of the weather is entering this one, it'll have to go down as a scorcher."

"I hope it's a lady clerk," remarked Aunt Flora, "for he or she has a pretty good idea of what goes on — or off. Every time I shed a garment the temperature drops ten degrees."

"Seems a wicked piece of ingratitude," said the Colonel, taking out a handkerchief and mopping his brow, "but I wouldn't mind if it dropped a few degrees now. It's an extraordinary thing — one longs for such days, and then finds them rather overpowering."

"This sort of weather always makes me wonder where those hot Southern natives get all their passion from," said Aunt Flora. "I can't imagine working up any sort of frenzy when it's ninety in the shade."

"Nice cool nights," remarked Phyl, without opening her eyes.

"What was that you were having out there with Barnes?" I inquired. "Wasn't that a frenzy?"

"It was not," denied Aunt Flora. "When you're saying the same thing to the same person for the fortieth time without effect, you find yourself becoming a little emphatic."

"Quite so," said the Colonel. "Annoying fellow, old Barnes. He used to work for some people called Rowley who lived in our cottage for a time. They rigged up a scarecrow with some old clothes Rowley was going to get rid of. The next morning they found Barnes looking rather smart in the scarecrow's outfit, while his own castoffs were arrayed on the scarecrow. He didn't say a word to the Rowleys — and they felt a bit delicate about bringing up the subject."

Aunt Flora looked uneasy — some of her working garments were a little odd and she could look like a scarecrow as easily as anybody.

The Colonel shifted a little in his chair and regarded the graceful form of Phyl. She looked asleep, but one hand moved in a slow caress on the head of the largest dog as it lay beside the chair.

He turned to me.

"Do you think you'll be able to wake Mrs. Blair up in time for tea?" he inquired. "My sisters are expecting you all."

"I'll get her there," I promised, trying to look cheerful at the prospect of a visit to what we all called the Colonel's Misses. They were a pair of unlovely spinsters, and a great deal of our liking for the Colonel sprang from our admiration and amazement at his unfailing cheerfulness in spite of his dreary little house, lack of companionship, and the constant friction that waged between his two ugly sisters. He was a man who loved his fellow men, and would have loved to pass his time among them, eating and drinking and whenever chance offered, making merry. His fellow men, however, had one by one wilted and fallen away before the vinegary and hostile attitude of May and Claudia. Claudia, the younger, had gone out to India for a year in the long-distant past to keep house for her brother just prior to his retirement; the Colonel perhaps hoped that, taken singly, they might have a chance. However, no handsome captain, no dashing major came forward to relieve the Colonel of this half of his wretched fate, and Claudia came home as simple and unspoiled, as she often explained to us, as when she left. If she brought any happy memories back with her, they were soon poisoned by the jealous attitude of May.

Whenever the tactless Claudia began a story about her life abroad, May's jealousy and sarcasm would break forth, and the fight was on. Very few people visited them, but we went whenever they asked us, Aunt Flora because she had never met anybody like them and couldn't bear to miss a minute of it, and I because Phyl wouldn't make the effort unless I made it too — and I think that they really loved Phyl.

"Why don't you stay and lunch with us?" Aunt Flora asked the Colonel. "The children are all away swimming, and they've taken their food, and Jonny's lunching with the Exleys. I've been slicing these beans for hours and you ought to stay and help us eat them. Jonny'll telephone for you and you can walk back with us at tea time."

This arrangement suited the Colonel to perfection, especially when it was explained to him that Phyl and Aunt

Flora would retire to their rooms after lunch, leaving the long chair and the verandah to him.

I folded up my sewing, most of which could now be called mended, and went indoors to telephone to May and explain that we had persuaded the Colonel to avoid the hot walk home in the heat and stay to lunch. Then I went through the hall into the little dairy, blessedly cool to-day, and filled a bowl full of cream and left it ready for lunch. I went into the kitchen and told Carrie the Colonel would be staying, at which she looked pleased and remarked that I'd better leave out some more cooling drink for him. I remembered the beans, and fetched them from the verandah, and then went upstairs to change into a fresh frock. It was so warm up there that I closed the green shutters of my bedroom and wished I had done so before going down earlier in the morning. I undressed and went into the bathroom, which looked cool and green and pleasant, and slipped into the collar shower which Aunt Flora had bought years before at a Modern Homes Exhibition and had been unable to fix at

Burnton as all the bathrooms there were already equipped with showers. This was a good one when the double-water system worked and there was a steady water temperature, but sometimes one or other of the upper taps jammed and one was squirted with boiling hot, or alternatively icy cold water. I hoped that if there was to be any trouble to-day, it would jam the hot and not the cold. I slipped into a cool pale blue linen dress, and, with a shady straw hat and white sandals, felt ready to face the heat of the road.

I went into the dairy again and carried the bowl of cream on to the dining-room side-board, and looked round with love and pride at the lovely, simply-furnished room with its long shining table, a gleam of silver here and there, our pictures, the sideboard with its attractive china and the brown bowl filled with thick yellow cream. I wanted to stay at home here in this low, long room instead of going through the hot, dusty street to someone else's not-half-so-lovely house. Perhaps other people's floors were not so uneven, perhaps their staircases didn't have a treacherous stair half-way up

which tripped people if they weren't
warned. Maybe other people had richer
appointments, and an inside lavatory, and
running h. and c. in all the bedrooms.
They could have all those, and leave me
Rushing.

After one look at the road, hot
and uninviting, I turned back and
walked through Aunt Flora's flourishing
vegetable garden, past the small cowshed,
and into the field. This way was rather
longer, but I would get shade and cool
green grass under my feet. I missed the
dogs, but all three were at the sea with
the children. I came in sight of the Exleys'
outhouses and saw a haycart, empty of
hay but filled with village children going
down to a distant field for another load.
The farm was unusually quiet, most of
the hands being down at the hayfield, and
I made my way round the house and into
the hall, rather over full of beautiful old
furniture, its polish gleaming attractively
in the dim light. The house, and most
of what was in it, was very old, very
solid and very good. Exleys had lived
and farmed here for generations. The
present owner looked anything but a

farmer, being small, slight and rather studious-looking, but he ran the place even better than his father, the late 'Bottle' Exley, lurid stories of whom were still told in the village, and who had broken records both in the farming world and in countless pubs within a radius of ten miles. His son was respected and liked, but those of the older generation who could remember the old man, felt that young Will would never fill his father's shoes. In the more spectacular ways, Will was not anxious to. He was a pleasant, quiet man, though extraordinarily ugly, and unfortunately his son had inherited and even improved upon the Simian cast of his countenance, so that strangers coming suddenly upon Ivan Exley, now aged ten, would feel confused and bewildered at thus being confronted by a well-grown monkey in grey flannels and a sports jacket. There had been no more young Exleys, and no wonder, said Aunt Flora, who considered that after so lamentable a first performance the parents were well advised to refrain from further production. Nor was the behaviour of the young Ivan, universally known as Ivan the Terrible, calculated to offset the first impression he made upon people. His cunning and his gift for monkey business had to be experienced to be believed, and by this time everybody in the village was an ardent believer. He cost his father a good deal in damages every school holiday. Booby traps, laid presumably for his young friends, were fallen into by his adult enemies. Children for miles round, feeling bored or finding time hanging on their hands, would suddenly remember Ivan, and come in search of him and trouble. He liked Paul and obeyed him, and most of his mischief was done out of Paul's reach. So far I had escaped booby traps, due to Paul's warning to "lay off my Mother, or else . . . " Polly loved him. "You're a monkey," she said with childhood's candour, "and you look like a monkey and you behave like a monkey and I like monkeys." So did Aunt Flora. She loved the terrible Ivan dearly, and the two of them spent long hours together in our garden, where he sought and found refuge after many of his scrapes.

His mother called to me from the

kitchen, and I went in to find her lifting delicious cold food out of a frigidaire on to a tray, to be carried into the dining-room. There were no indoor servants, and Will Exley boasted, not without justification, that his wife was the best cook in the county.

"We shall be alone," she said. "I sent Will's lunch to the hayfield, and of course Ivan is with your family." She handed me a tray, picked up another, and indicated by a movement of her chin that I was to go into the dining-room.

We laid the things on the table and presently sat down to a quiet, pleasant meal. I looked across at her and wondered how so good-looking a woman had produced a zoological specimen as a son. One couldn't help feeling that the terrible Ivan had somehow done it on purpose.

After lunch we washed and put away the dishes and walked out into the little square of garden tended by Mrs. Exley. The heat was so great by now that one's eyes could hardly stand the glare outside.

"Come down to the stables," said Mrs.

Exley, "I've a surprise for you."

It was a relief to enter the semi-darkness, and my eyes unscrewed themselves so that I was able to see what Mrs. Exley stooped to pick up. It was the most beautiful Great Dane pup, not more than nine or ten weeks old, fat, large even now, and altogether adorable. I gave a gasp of wonder and admiration, and we stroked the beautiful fellow and endured his affectionate licks. I had never seen, or at least had never handled, a Great Dane puppy, and fell in love with him at once.

"Is it Ivan's," I asked, "or Will's?"

"It's Ivan's," replied Ruth Exley. "His uncle Robert breeds them, and promised him one some time ago, and this is it. But Ivan's heart is set on giving it to Miss Manning."

"D'you mean Aunt Flora?" I asked idiotically, since there is only one Miss Manning in Rushing.

"Yes, Aunt Flora. Do you think she'd like it?"

"Like it? — she'd adore it," I said. "But you're surely not going to let him give it away, are you? It's a sweet thought and she'll be stunned at the very idea of his thinking of it, but the poor fellow would regret it and I don't think you ought to let him do it."

"Well," she said, "it isn't just an impulse — he's been thinking about it for a long time. I thought he might waver when he had seen it, but he didn't. He has four dogs already, to say nothing of his other things like the marmoset and his frightful white mice, and if Miss Manning feels that a thing as enormous as this is going to be won't get round her legs all the time, I hope she'll accept it."

"Accept it!" I cried, knowing Aunt Flora's predilection for dogs, the larger the better, "She'll go quite mad."

"Won't it ruin her lovely garden?" asked Mrs. Exley.

I hesitated over this. Training the other dogs had been a comparatively simple matter, but I thought of this huge awkward puppy lolloping across the flowers, devastating whole beds with a mere playful flick of a gargantuan paw. "Well, it'll be something to think about, but if she sees this first, I think the rose beds will fade completely out of her mind," I said.

"Don't say anything about it," Ruth requested. "I suppose Ivan will take it up in a day or two and make a formal presentation."

We left the stables and went out into the hot sunshine.

"Do you want to go indoors," asked Mrs. Exley, "or stay out?" I wanted to stay out and I wanted to find a shady tree and relax under it. Mrs. Exley fetched a rug and spread it under a tree on a smooth slope running down to a gurgling little brook. She sat and looked at the cows on the other bank and I lay and gazed up at the green branches above us.

"This must be almost perfection," I said after a long silence. "Blue, blue sky, green grass, red cows, yellow buttercups — and I've got to leave it all and go and have tea with May and Claudia."

Ruth Exley made a sound suggestive of sympathy.

"We haven't been invited for a long time," she said, "and they refused to dine here last week when Will's brother was here — he brought Ivan the dog and stayed a few days. I rather hoped the Colonel would accept for himself, but he didn't."

"Probably couldn't," I answered, "I'm sure they wouldn't let him out to one of your dinners by himself! They dread his imbibing the spirit of the deceased grandfather Exley."

Ruth laughed. "Perhaps. But I think they're really a little frightened of Ivan."

"And no wonder," I put in.

She smiled. "Yes, and no wonder," she repeated. "But I don't think they have any reason to be. The Colonel helped the children to put a new roof on their tree house when the old one blew off, and when Ivan came home that evening he looked a little thoughtful. I think he was wondering whether his feud against the sisters made things any more difficult for the poor man."

"Have May and Claudia always been as bad as this?" I asked.

Ruth considered for a few moments. "I don't think so," she said finally. "They were always apt to make things unpleasant at parties — they created a sort of tension and we all used to pray that they wouldn't do anything to discredit the Colonel, for we liked him so much. I have a feeling that things are a little more difficult for them lately in a financial way, but that trouble, of course, is with most of us these days."

We left the Colonel's problem and turned to minor ones of our own. The tree house was one. It was built on a strong though rather high fork of a tree in one of the two fields belonging to me, and adjoining our small orchard. I could see it from my bedroom window, but it was out of call of the farm and indeed of any of the houses in or round the village. It was a fine piece of work and nearly every child in the village between nine and fourteen had had a hand in the building of it. It was now the headquarters of a sort of summer camp and a rallying point for the children of Rushing. Two tents had sprung up under the tree, and except on the days the children decided to go swimming, the field swarmed with a highly organized and well-disciplined band of brothers. Paul, as owner of the ground, was the Headman. On his orders the band assembled. Without orders no child, not even Ivan, not even Polly, went into the field. Ivan was Lieutenant No. 1, and No. 2 was a newcomer to the village, a really dreadful-looking boy who, it was rumoured, had been too much for his parents at Battersea and had been sent to his uncle, our village postman. The postman seemed hardly the person to choose as a disciplinarian, being very small and very mild, and although I had never interfered with the children's choice of companions, I was a little uneasy now.

I asked Ruth what she thought of No. 2, and she laughed.

"Isn't he frightful?" she said. "The poor child looks like a miniature prize-fighter. But it's no use worrying, Jonny. He's elected, and apart from his appearance and a few rumours we've really nothing against him."

"No," I admitted grudgingly, "but do you honestly think that anyone could look like that without having criminal tendencies?"

Ruth laughed.

"Let's wait a bit, and see how he settles here," she said.

This was unsatisfactory, especially as Polly had constituted herself the boy's guide to the country, and led him on personally conducted tours all over her favourite haunts, dragging him along streams, up and down hills, and finally bringing him panting and drenched in perspiration to the house for a cooling drink and one of Carrie's buns. I comforted myself by remembering that Paul had always been able to weigh his fellows up pretty well, and he also had a well-developed sense of responsibility with regard to the excitable Polly.

"Have you had any complaint about the bells?" asked Ruth.

"None so far — but the noise is appalling," I said. "First your gong, then Lady Wheeler's bell, then toots and whistles from the village, and of course — "

"Yes!" The placid Mrs. Exley gave an excited little jump which brought her round facing me. "What is that other noise?"

"It's Aunt Flora's Swiss cow-horn," I

said with pride. "It was packed away in one of her trunks in one of the attics and she couldn't find it at first, but she came across it eventually and now she lives for the moment when she can blow it. It's a terrible noise — it blows all the birds out of their nests."

This was almost literally true. But it also fetched the children home. We had been forced to institute some form of signal to communicate with the distant band of brothers, in sheer pity for the weary, hot and irritated mothers who had previously tramped over the fields bleating plaintively for their young. The new signals, though momentarily shattering the peace of the countryside, were excellent. Each child recognized the individual summons, and came instantly.

I went into a pleasant reverie, and thought drowsily of Aunt Flora's surpassing skill on her horn, but it was time I was going back, and with the greatest reluctance I sat up and, stretching luxuriously, prepared to depart.

"It's lovely and I can't bear going," I said, "and thank you for the delicious lunch and the lovely rest. Don't come to the gate — you'll get hot again."

"Of course I'll come," said Ruth. "I'll go a bit of the way with you."

She left me in sight of Rushing and I found perfect peace there too. The Colonel slept peacefully on Phyl's chair, the three dogs panting in shady corners nearby. I went into the kitchen and prepared some tea, and treading softly, carried some to a small table by the Colonel's side. I then went upstairs as noisily as possible, carrying a tray with cups of tea for Aunt Flora, Phyl and myself. I stopped outside Aunt Flora's door and called to her.

"What's the rattle?" she called. "Not a cup of tea by any chance?"

"A cup of tea," I assured her, going in and giving it to her. "To wake you up. I've left some by the Colonel, and I heard him stirring as I came up."

I went towards Phyl's room, meeting her coming out of the bathroom, and Aunt Flora followed me on her way in. She looked admiringly at Phyl's elegant white bathrobe. "What the farming women will wear to this season's shower," she said, drawing her own faded dressing-gown around her with a queenly gesture, and disappearing into the bathroom.

I threw my hat on a chair and lay on my back on Phyl's bed, watching her as she got into dainty under-garments and a beautifully-tailored white pique frock. Her room was a picture of orderliness, charmingly furnished, and beautifully kept. Nobody ever touched it but Phyl. She never came downstairs until eleven, but before she left, she put her room into perfect order, except on Mondays when Carrie went in and gave it what she called a thorough go-over. Unlike most languid or lazy people, Phyl loathed the least disorder round her.

When she was almost ready I went to my room, and freshened up and joined the Colonel on the verandah. He had washed in our downstairs cloakroom and was looking fresh and more or less cool.

"Thank you for the tea," he said gratefully. "I feel grand, but hardly equal to going out into that." He indicated the scorching outdoors.

Aunt Flora came down, in a light coat and skirt with a shady straw hat on top of her head and an enormous sunshade.

"We'll go ahead and take it slowly, Colonel. How do I look, Jonny?"

"You look sweet," I said obligingly.

"I thought so," said Aunt Flora. "Come on, Colonel, it won't be so bad if you come under this tent of mine." She unfurled the sunshade, which indeed looked like a small marquee; the Colonel crept gratefully under it, and they set off.

Phyl was smiling as we followed a little way behind the others.

"Something funny?" I asked, tucking her arm under mine.

"Aunt Flora," she said. "She says there'll be trouble — this heat will remind Claudia of India and, she says her sunshade'll be useful if it comes to an all-in."

"There won't be any rows to-day," I prophesied. "Nobody could fight in this heat."

We walked slowly, and the bobbing tent ahead of us disappeared round the corner of the lane leading to the Colonel's house.

"I've got to go up to London next

week," said Phyl. "Can you come too, Jonny?"

"Oh, Phyl, not during the holidays," I protested. "Couldn't you put it off for a bit?"

"No," said Phyl. "I didn't think you'd be able to manage it, and I would have preferred to wait, but I promised Brian I'd meet him and there's only another week of George's play, and I haven't seen it. He'll rave if I miss it."

"Let him," I said. "Still, you ought to go. Don't stay away longer than you can help — Paul likes to have you about when he's home."

I was sorry not to be able to go, for Phyl and I enjoyed our mild jaunts to Town together, but holidays were busy times. And so I thought no more about the matter, and later even helped Phyl to pack, and saw her off lightheartedly on the Felling bus, with no foreboding of what she was going to let us in for. If I had had the smallest suspicion of what was to come, I would have left the house to Aunt Flora and Carrie, put the children into an orphanage and clung to

Phyl until I had got her safely out of George's way.

But I had no premonition, only an increasing desire for some tea and a mounting unwillingness to have it with May and Claudia.

"You don't suppose," I asked Phyl without much hope, "that they'll carry a table into the garden and give us tea out of doors under that big tree?"

Phyl didn't think they would, and when we went through the little iron gate there was no sign of any tea under any tree.

Inside, there were more people than one usually found assembled at one time beneath the Colonel's roof. Aunt Flora sat, back to the window, in a chair which commanded the best view of the room, and looked about her expectantly, waiting for hostilities to begin. But I was right. Nobody had any energy for skirmishing. Both May and Claudia had lost their usual air of sharpness and watchfulness, and May waved us to chairs with unwonted languor.

"It's nice to see you," she said. "I nearly telephoned telling you all not to come to-day, and save yourselves that hot walk, but I was selfish."

There was a pause, during which everyone waited tensely for one of Claudia's remarks about the temperature at Jubblepore in May of '92, but mercifully she was looking after old Mrs. Sayers and moving a chair to accommodate the old lady's god-daughter, who was down on one of her frequent visits to her godmother. She was a young woman with a gay and roving eye, and worked in an office in London. The security of her financial future depended chiefly upon what her godmother would bequeath her — and it ought to be a great deal, for old Mrs. Sayers had substantial means and simple tastes — and Miss Stafford thought it expedient to accept the old lady's invitations. Even without makeup, which she wisely left off during her visits, she was rather flashy. She came frequently to Rushing, and confided to Phyl that she didn't really mind the visits.

"In small doses they might be a nice rest," she said, "but it's the hellish effort to pretend I like it that makes it so exhausting."

None of us liked her very much, but her stout efforts in however unworthy a cause compelled our admiration. I knew something of her life in Town, and an existence of even a week without cigarettes, drinks and even one of her young men must have been purgatory for the poor girl. Aunt Flora eyed her pityingly as she sat between Claudia and old Mrs. Sayers, listening to a long discussion on the merits of various poultices.

May pulled her chair away from the table where she had been pouring tea.

"Haven't you got an extra child these holidays, Mrs. Manning?" she asked. "I would have thought you had enough on your hands with your own two, and the entire village in and out of your grounds all day."

"Yes, a rather nice child," I said. "The Headmistress couldn't have her at the school these holidays as she was going away herself. Her parents are theatrical people — dancers, I think — by the name of Kemp."

"D'you mean Malcolm and Eileen Kemp?" asked Miss Stafford, looking suddenly animated. "I've met them — didn't know they had a daughter."

"I believe they came down last Christmas and took her up to London for a week," I said, "but from what she tells me now and again she doesn't care for journeying round England in the wake of Father and Mother."

"She's a nice child," put in the Colonel. "Good head on her shoulders."

I had not been keen on having the child, but I knew Miss Crompton would sacrifice her own holiday rather than leave her, as the parents proposed she should do, in the charge of the school housekeeper, an excellent but rather aged woman. So I had offered to have her, and Miss Crompton had looked at me in almost tearful gratitude, which affected me so much that I left the school glowing with the unusual feeling of having done much good.

I had, in fact, cast my bread upon the waters, and they were shortly to come back to me several thousand-fold.

I rose to leave before the others, being anxious to be home before the children and see to their supper. I was a little late, and arrived to hear Carrie stating that: "Not a bite will there be until you all take them wet things off the hall table and hang 'em in the boiler-room." The hall table was indeed a litter of towels, bathing suits, Polly's bucket full of shells, and over everything was a liberal sprinkling of sand. The mess was duly cleared and Carrie set supper before the famished trio.

"I hope you haven't taken the skin off yourselves," I said anxiously. "Did you rub any lotion on yourself before sunbathing, Diana?"

"I forgot the first time," said Diana, whose fair skin burnt easily. "I don't think I've actually caught or anything."

"I'll rub some in when you're undressed," I said.

They looked a nice trio. Paul, enormous for his fourteen years, dark, quiet and humorous; Polly, also dark and ready to laugh but built, fortunately, on daintier lines. Diana, in age between the other two, slender, long-legged and rather serious.

The two girls were asleep almost as soon as they got into bed, having had a full day. I was glad when the chatter, laughter and noise ceased, and I went round clearing up clothes, folding and sorting, and sweeping up sand from the bathroom floor. I met Paul on his way up to bed; he sat in the middle of the stairs, clasped my ankles firmly in the circle of his arms, and pretended to go into a sound sleep, snoring loudly.

"Shut up, Paul — you'll wake the others," I protested. "And let my feet go before I fall downstairs. Paul — Paul you idiot!"

With grunts, groans and stretches, as one newly awakened, Paul turned and continued his progress upstairs on all fours, sinking into another deep slumber on the top step.

"All right, stay there," I said, "but don't snore or you'll catch it. I'll be up to say good night."

When I went up later he was fast asleep, really asleep this time, lying on top of his bed covers, and clad only in pyjama legs. Settling him in was rather like trying to move a mountain, but I managed it, drew the curtains and went downstairs in time to join Aunt Flora and Phyl going into supper. This was a meal at which we always served ourselves, clearing away afterwards and washing-up. Carrie's working day came to an end at seven o'clock, and we made it a point not to ask her for anything after that hour.

It was growing cooler as we sat down, and later we sat on chairs outside on the verandah, saying nothing and looking across at the near-by hills. It was peace itself, and I thought it was wonderful, and had not the faintest idea that soon it was to be shattered, and that into the smooth-running machinery Providence was preparing to hurl a spanner. But so it was, and in less than a fortnight the projectile landed in our midst, in the picturesque form of George Manning.

4

PHYL was away for five days. She wired to Paul, asking him to go up for her last day, and they returned together the following morning, Paul in high spirits and Phyl, I thought, a little distrait. I was busy in various domestic ways and could not find time for more than an affectionate greeting, but I noted her abstraction and wondered if she had at last agreed to marry Brian. I rather hoped so, for I thought him a fine fellow and almost good enough for Phyl.

As the morning wore on I was dismayed to discover evidences here and there that Phyl was trying to help me. A pile of Polly's clothes which I had selected for repair and piled carelessly on my bed was spirited away, and I found the garments carefully folded and put away in their drawers. The vacuum cleaner, which is in parts and takes a good deal of putting together, and which I had assembled laboriously and left at the foot of the stairs, disappeared, and I traced it to its box in the broom cupboard, once again dismembered. I had left Diana's bed unmade, as I meant to do a small repair in the mattress, but the sheets and blankets arranged themselves smoothly and correctly while I was downstairs searching for the vacuum cleaner. I began to feel a little giddy, and decided that if the Brownies were really on the job, I might just as well take a book and go and read in the garden. The children were out; I could see Aunt Flora perched on her little steps working industriously on her ramblers, and Carrie's hymns were ascending from the kitchen. I realized with a sinking sensation that Phyl was helping me.

From earliest childhood, Phyl's helpful periods had been a sign of trouble. If she did wrong and was sorry, she had only one way of showing her regret, and that was by spending a day or so performing what she judged helpful acts for the person she had wronged. Something had always gone wrong when Phyl helped — and now she was helping me!

I felt a sudden desire for Aunt Flora's

steadying company, and went out into the garden, to find the steps rocking perilously as Aunt Flora tied up a high shoot.

"Phyl's helping me," I said simply and adequately.

"Good Lord," exclaimed Aunt Flora. "What has she done?"

"I don't know," I said. "I came to find out whether she had said anything to you."

"I've hardly seen her," said Aunt Flora. "I was wondering why she was staying inside all the morning, and thought she must have a good bit of unpacking to do."

"Do you think it's anything to do with Brian?" I asked.

"Shouldn't think so," replied Aunt Flora. "More likely some crime connected with Paul. She probably let him stay up too late or overfed him, or took him to a wicked play or one of those strong A films."

"Paul would have told me," I said.

"Well, it must be George," said Aunt Flora, holding out a hand for my support and making a dignified descent down the steps. "Why are you worrying? — she'll probably tell us to-night and in the meantime you'd better give her something really useful to do — harness the power while you've got it. You won't have it long."

And still I had no premonition.

The blow fell after supper, when we decided to go and sit outside. There was a light, cool breeze, and Paul, who had ten minutes or so to put in before his bedtime, lay flat on a rug at my feet and played lazily with one of the dogs. He groaned when I told him it was time to go up, and in a squeaky imitation of a baby's voice, begged for an extra few minutes.

"Not one extra minute," said Aunt Flora. "Get thee hence, and pretty quick, too! Otherwise I'll — "

"Otherwise you'll — " prompted Paul, getting up and settling his enormous form on her knee and rubbing his nose gently against hers. "What'll you do to your great-little nephew?"

"This," said Aunt Flora, with a dexterous movement spilling him off her lap on to the ground. There was

75

a roar of mingled rage and laughter from Paul, and Aunt Flora scurried round the garden pursued by the enemy yelling for vengeance and blood. She was panting when she returned to her chair, and Paul kissed us lightly and departed upstairs.

Aunt Flora rested after her exertions, while I knitted and Phyl watched us both. Finally Aunt Flora turned to her.

"Phyllis Blair," she said abruptly, "what have you done?"

There was a long pause. Phyl looked troubled. "I haven't done anything," she said after a while, "but there is something — "

"I thought so," said Aunt Flora. "How bad is it?"

"Well, it's George," said Phyl. "I saw him, of course, and he hasn't been well. The play finishes this week and the doctors have said he's to leave London at once and have absolute rest."

"What's the matter with him?" asked Aunt Flora anxiously.

"Well, just overstrain at present, but they must have warned him seriously, or I don't think George would carry out orders so promptly. He admits he has been going too hard."

"Has he chosen a nice quiet place to go to?" asked Aunt Flora.

"Y . . . yes," said Phyl.

"Well, that's all right," said Aunt Flora. "You gave us a fright to-day, mooning about and making us imagine something had happened. I'll go and look over George as soon as he's settled. Where's he going?"

Phyl murmured indistinctly.

"Can't hear," said Aunt Flora. "Don't mumble so."

Phyl gave an unhappy little sigh and then spoke.

"Here," she said.

There was a terrible silence. Aunt Flora, her mouth slightly open and her eyes staring, looked from me to Phyl and for once had nothing to say. At last she found her voice.

"Good heavens, Phyl, what on earth are you thinking of? George coming here for a rest cure!"

She pondered the dreadful possibility for a moment and then continued.

"Didn't you tell him about the — the

raspberry canes and so on?"

"I didn't remember myself," said Phyl — "only afterwards, when I was nearly home. It seems awful now, but I think I actually asked him to come here, and told him he'd like it."

"Like it!" I said in amazement and horror. "George like this? Why Phyl, he'll go mad — he'll loathe it."

"Of course he will," said Aunt Flora. "How *could* you, Phyl — you know he likes everything chromium plated, or gold plated, and a twenty four-hour valet service — Didn't you tell him the snags? — *any* of the snags," she repeated, with a glance in the direction of our distant little outhouse.

"No," said Phyl. "I — perhaps I was worried — I just said it was lovely and he wants to come."

Her voice faltered, and to my horror I saw two tears rolling down her cheeks. I dropped my knitting on the ground and flung myself down beside her chair.

"You idiot, Phyl," I said. "Stop it — *please* stop it. There's nothing to cry about. George can come and he can stay as long as he likes and perhaps he will like it, and there isn't a thing to worry about."

"Not a thing," said Aunt Flora. "He can come, and he can stay as long as he likes, and he'll have a real breakdown the first moment he sees the plumbing, and we'll have him raving on our hands."

"Don't be a bully, Aunt Flora," I said furiously. "He knows what a farm's like — he isn't half-witted."

"Not yet," said Aunt Flora. She unfolded a handkerchief of more adequate proportions and passed it across to Phyl. "The thing to do," she went on judicially, "is to get a letter off to George — you can write it, Jonny. Start with the welcome and then add a short list of the little improvements we mean to put in as soon as the plans are passed. We'll get a wire from George, and then he can choose one of the nicer ducal residences at his disposal and the duchess can nurse him back to health in the rose gardens. I'm rather surprised at you, Phyl — you're usually quite sensible. Stop wetting my handkerchief, and think what a let-off we're all going to have."

I composed several suitable letters in

bed that night and wrote one of them out next morning, addressed it to George's flat in London and sent Polly off on her bicycle to catch the early post. The morning letters came a little later, among them a brief note from George telling me how nice it was going to be to relax in the bosom of the family.

I distributed the letters and met the terrible Ivan lurking mysteriously behind a corner of the verandah. "Ss," he hissed, beckoning with a small forefinger. I assumed a conspiratorial air, looked to right and left and strode across to him on tiptoe.

"What's afoot?" I whispered.

"I've brought you-know-what," said Ivan, grasping my sleeve and leading me towards the field gate. Tied to a bar was the Great Dane pup, looking preposterously large, and tying himself into knots round Ivan's feet. He wore a collar, to which was attached a label reading 'To Aunt Flora, with love from Ivan the terrible.' "Will you please give it to her," he asked, "or leave it somewhere where she'll see it?"

"But Ivan," I protested, "you must

give it to her yourself — you've got to see how much she likes it, and you've got to tell her his name and all about him."

"Oh, no," said Ivan hastily, turning a deep red. "I'll come back later and see her. I forgot about his name. He's a pedigree dog," he explained kindly, "and they've got proper names. I can't remember exactly what Rex's is — part of it is Rex and I called him that just for now."

Aunt Flora was heard descending the stairs, and Ivan disappeared. The puppy dashed after him and I found myself almost carried off my feet by the strong and sudden pull on the lead. I was recovering my balance when Aunt Flora saw me from the long window in the drawing-room and stared in amazement.

"Great heavens, what have you got there?" she asked.

"You'd better come — it's yours," I said.

"Mine? — don't be ridiculous. I never saw the thing before," said Aunt Flora. She left the window and reappeared presently on the path. Her glance fell on the label and she stooped to read the words, straightening herself again with a face flushed from reasons other than that of stooping. She said not a word, but stared at the young animal, which was still making frantic attempts to follow Ivan through the field.

"Here you are," I said, handing her the lead. "He's yours, so why should he pull my arm out of its socket?"

Aunt Flora took the lead and rallied a little. "The silly, silly little boy," she said tenderly. "The young idiot. The — " She paused and looked thoughtfully at me. "Tell me," she said anxiously, "how many miles a day do I have to take this to exercise it?"

"I can't give you the exact mileage," I replied, "but I should think if you ran him to Felling and back before breakfast every morning — "

"Pish," said Aunt Flora irritably. "Come on, then good feller — what's his name, did you say?"

"I didn't say and I don't know," I replied "Details to follow, Ivan said, and I think there's a Rex in it."

The rest of the morning was passed by

Aunt Flora and the children accustoming the dog to his new quarters. The other dogs were suspicious but not unfriendly. Carrie stared at the newcomer unbelievingly when he was taken into the kitchen to be introduced to her.

"You'll have to be putting my table on stilts," she remarked. "That dog'll have his whiskers in my mixing bowl in next to no time."

The arrival of Rex and the subsequent discussion on his training, exercise and housing had driven the thought of George out of all minds but mine. I watched the preparations for the building of a vast kennel and speculated on whether my letter would reach London by the night's post, and if so, whether George would at once telephone his change of plan. We heard nothing from him that night, however, and I woke the next day to the certainty of getting word before nightfall. But the day wore on and we heard nothing.

After lunch I went into Phyl's room and watched her pressing one of her frocks into beautiful pleats. "There's no word from George yet, Phyl," I said. "I know it's early, but I was worried about my letter — I sent it to his flat. Do you know whether he's there?"

Phyl looked thoughtful, the iron suspended in midair.

"I don't know," she said doubtfully. "I only saw him at the theatre and at my hotel, but he didn't say he wasn't at his flat. They'd forward letters, wouldn't they?"

"I suppose so," I said. "But I feel certain that the moment George reads my letter he'll reach for a 'phone — so he couldn't have got it this morning."

Phyl leaned over and switched the heat off and hung her dress carefully on a hanger.

"If you're worried, Jonny, and nothing comes to-day I'll ring him up after supper." She smiled apologetically at me. "I was an awful fool," she said, "and of course he won't come."

"I'm the fool," I said, "to let George get on my nerves. It's time we buried that ancient hatchet. I'm really quite fond of him, Phyl — it's just that he's so abominable at home."

"I know," Phyl said soothingly. "He's

a beast and you ought to be like the rest of us and not take him seriously." She hung the hanger in her wardrobe and turned to me. "I've been thinking," she said. "I love living here so much, awkward as it is in many ways, that if George ever came and began criticizing, I'd stab him myself."

We both laughed at the idea of her doing anything so energetic and decisive, and Aunt Flora put her head round the door to ask what the joke was.

"Bring a book and rest in here with me, Jonny," coaxed Phyl. "It's too hot to work."

"It isn't too hot to saw wood for my kennel," said Aunt Flora, "and that's what Jonny and I are going to do."

"Saw wood — I'm not going to saw any wood," I said protestingly. "What's become of the children?"

"Disappeared to one of their Klu Klux Klan meetings," said Aunt Flora bitterly. "I saw that young Battersea bruiser on his way to the field and offered him sixpence to come and saw, but he gave me a mean look and went off to tell Paul I was trying to subvert him by bribery."

"Well, I am not going to saw wood," I said slowly and distinctly. "You can ask the Colonel for one of his hen houses and convert it into a Great Dane stronghold." I made a swift dash towards the door and escaped down the stairs.

I spent a quiet afternoon with Carrie helping her to bottle some red currants. Ivan and Lt. No. 2 appeared at the back door at tea time with a written message from Paul to the effect that stores on the island were exhausted, and the survivors sinking rapidly from lack of nourishment.

"Same tale, I suppose," snorted Carrie. I passed the message across to her and she read it, and looked scornfully at the emissaries. "You can tell them that they can all sink and welcome," she said.

Nos. 1 and 2, who had played this scene many times and knew it by heart, waited for their cue. Ivan gave me a delighted wink, and No. 2 grinned sheepishly.

"Well, what are you waiting for?" demanded Carrie.

"Cap'n's orders, my good woman,"

said Ivan haughtily. advancing into the kitchen and folding his arms with an air of staying permanently. "'Go after the food' was what he said, 'and don't leave till you get it.'"

"Not a bite," said Carrie firmly.

Ivan jerked his head at No. 2, and both Lts. began to search round the kitchen, Carrie watching with a sly smile. Lifting the top of the bread bin, Ivan stooped and lifted out a large parcel, and the search ended. Nos. 1 and 2 marched to the door, saluted, and forgetting dignity made at top speed for their base.

"Mad," said Carrie. "All them kids is mad."

The telephone had rung frequently, but no message had come from George. When nothing had been heard of him at bedtime, Aunt Flora and I went upstairs feeling that the crisis had passed.

"Rude of George," she said, "not to let you know. He's probably busy making more suitable arrangements." She kissed me affectionately. "We'll get a message from the duchess in a day or two."

The next day was so perfect and my spirits felt so light with the threat of

George now removed, that I proposed a day at our beach. Aunt Flora declined, but Phyl and the children were all enthusiastic, and Carrie and I began to pack food for the day. I heard Paul at the telephone telling Ivan of the plan, and was not surprised to hear a shout: "Mother — Ivan wants to join us — may he come?"

"Aren't you parading to-day?" I asked.

"No," said Paul, "we were only going down to the hay-field."

"All right," I said, "he can come — tell him to bring something to drink."

We returned in a heavy shower just before the children's supper time. Aunt Flora was out, and we went upstairs to change into dry clothes. I put Polly and Diana into a warm bath and left them splashing happily, shut the bathroom door and met Carrie coming upstairs with a paper in her hand.

"It's a telephone message," she said. "Came about two."

She put the paper into my nerveless fingers and I read the brief message. "Arrive six-thirty please meet, George." Feeling dazed, I went to Phyl's room.

She read the message and we gazed at each other.

"We can't get into Felling by six-thirty," Phyl said at last. "It's ten past now."

It was true. There was no hope of getting there in time for George's train.

"Duff will be there with the bus," I said after thinking for a moment. "If you're not there George will come back on it and you can meet him in the village."

Phyl shook her head. "No," she said with conviction. "It simply won't occur to him that the Duff outfit is something he's expected to ride in. The realization will come slowly — when Duff has left."

We made an unsuccessful attempt to get through to Felling station with a message for George, and finally Phyl and Paul buttoned their mackintoshes up to the top button and prepared to meet the bus at the Inn.

"If he isn't on it," said Phyl, "we'll simply have to bribe Duff to take us back to Felling."

I went upstairs and told the news

to Polly and Diana, and the landing reverberated with whoops of joy from Polly, who danced out of the bathroom draped in a towel and marched up and down the landing shouting "Blow the bugle, beat the drum, Tell the neighbours George has come."

Diana, unmoved, watched from the bathroom door, tying the belt of her pyjamas and slipping into a dressing-gown.

I went down to the kitchen to see what I could produce in the way of supper for George. There was some hot soup, some cold mutton, and I made up an enormous bowl of what was known in the family as George's salad. I felt better after this hospitable gesture, and called the children down to their supper. I put their trays on a small table in the drawing-room, put a match to the fire, and went out to answer the telephone.

It was George, and my skin crept at the fury in his voice.

"Is that you, Jonny — where the devil is everybody?"

"Oh, hello, George — we — "

"Is anyone meeting me," demanded George.

"Yes," I said, "but we — "

"Did you get my wire?"

"Yes, but we — "

"Well, there isn't a soul on this god-forsaken station," pursued George, "and as far as I can make out, the natives have never heard the word taxi. Does one walk to Rushing?"

"No, of course not," I said. "Phyl and — " I stopped automatically, waiting for the interruption, and there was a moment's silence.

"Phyl and Paul," I continued, "are taking the bus back for you in case you missed it."

"What bus are you talking about?" demanded George. "There hasn't been a sign of a bus — only a — "

There was a horror-laden pause during which George's mind and mine both conjured up the dreadful picture of Duff and his conveyance.

"My God," said George, in a terrible voice — "do you mean to tell me that that — "

Words failed him.

"Yes," I said.

There was another pause, and I was wondering whether he had rung off, when I heard his voice again.

"If there's a train back to Town tonight," it said crisply, "I shall be on it."

With this information, George rang off, but I was unable to feel comforted, as I was aware that there was no London train before nine, and even that had unsatisfactory connections.

I continued to hold the telephone, and spoke into it a few of the witty and sardonic remarks which always occur to me a few moments after the time for saying them has passed.

I put the girls to bed, and hearing Aunt Flora coming in, went down to meet her. I helped her out of her dripping mackintosh and shook the drops off her hat.

"I've had a lovely day," she said. "Have you?"

"Yes," I said, "and it's going to be lovelier — George is here."

Aunt Flora's face was a picture of amazement and horror. "Oh, my poor

Jonny," she cried. "Do you mean actually here?" Her voice dropped. "How's the brute?" she asked anxiously.

"Well, he's stuck on Felling station at the moment," I explained. "He sent a wire, but we didn't get the message until we got home."

"You mean he wired he was coming, and then arrived to find no band and no civic reception?" asked Aunt Flora in squeaky excitement.

"Worse than that," I said. "No taxi and no porter and no Aunt Flora struggling to keep back her tears of joy . . . "

"Has Phyl gone to meet him?" asked Aunt Flora.

"Phyl and Paul," I said.

"My word, Jonny, I wouldn't like to be those two on the way home," said Aunt Flora feelingly. "George'll take it out on someone — not that they'll care a rap. What do we give him to eat?"

"I've got it all ready," I said. "You go up and get a hot bath. Carrie aired his bed and I'm just going to make it."

I went up to the only spare bedroom, a large, square, pleasant room at the end of a short passage leading off the landing. I made the bed and arranged things as comfortably as possible, drew the curtains and switched on the bedside light, and looked round at the cosy picture hoping that George would have cooled off enough to appreciate it. Aunt Flora came in and glanced round.

"It's charming, isn't it?" she said, "but I suppose George won't see it with our eyes. I think I hear their voices — let's get down and get the first shock over."

We went down, to see a wet trio stepping on to the verandah, Paul holding a suit-case and Phyl holding George's arm. As always, when confronted by beauty and perfection in human form, I forgot every sensation but sheer pleasure.

George, even George in a wet mackintosh, his expression set and scowling, was a magnificent spectacle, and I watched with detached appreciation his unwilling, but still attractive, smile as he stooped to kiss Aunt Flora.

"We got Duff to go back," said Paul, "and we picked up a lot of people. It was awfully crowded coming back."

George made no comment on crowded country buses other than a slight lift of one eyebrow. It was very expressive.

"Come and get warm, George," I said, leading the way to the drawing-room, where the fire leapt and roared and the table, which I had laid in here, gleamed in the light from the flames.

"Thanks," said George coolly, moving steadily towards the best chair, and standing politely by it until we had disposed ourselves elsewhere. He sat down and stretched his long legs towards the warmth.

"Phyl's been telling me you wrote trying to put me off. — Pity I didn't get your letter," he added reflectively.

"We weren't exactly putting you off," I protested. "We wanted you to understand that we — well, that we couldn't maintain you in the standard to which you are accustomed."

"I hope it isn't too primitive," remarked George. "I've come down for a rest. Perfect relaxation, was what the doctor said. I didn't realize you lived in quite such back-to-nature circumstances, but one mustn't judge by first impressions."

"Don't start snapping," said Aunt

Flora. "Come and eat a good meal and then go to bed, and you'll wake up in the morning a regular farmer's boy."

George ate well, and appeared to be soothed by the excellent salad. He went back to his chair by the fire and leaned back gazing at the cheerful blaze.

Aunt Flora looked disappointed. She had looked forward to a wordy battle and George sat relaxed and at ease, looking unwarlike and comfortable. She wondered whether perhaps he was more ill than we had supposed.

"What did the doctor say?" she asked him. "You look fairly well, and you ate a good supper."

"Supper," repeated George reflectively. "Don't we dine?"

"We do not," said Aunt Flora. "Now tell us your symptoms."

"The symptoms aren't interesting," said George with a slight frown. "The cure, I'm told, is rest, change and absolutely no theatre."

"Well, that's very simple," said Aunt Flora. "You can rest as much as you like; there's nobody here that moves in the theatre world, and," she ended dryly, "I've no doubt you'll find living here a change."

"Quite," said George, "But I don't think they intended the change to be — well, too drastic. I can't understand," he went on, "what you all see in this complete rusticity."

"We like it," said Phyl unexpectedly, "and if you don't, you can go away."

George looked at her in astonishment, and appeared about to satisfy Aunt Flora's desire for a wordy combat, when I interposed and upheld the suggestion of his retiring early.

"Well, I'll want a bath if there is such a thing," he said.

"You can have a shower," said Aunt Flora with some pride.

"Shower," repeated George in exaggerated surprise. "In such surroundings?"

"In the bathroom," said Aunt Flora coldly.

George wished us all a careless good night and went upstairs, and we were left to discuss the events of the day. We learned from an almost apologetic Aunt Flora that Rex had eaten two books, the handle of her large sun-shade, one of Paul's bedroom slippers and both Aunt Flora's gardening shoes.

I was aghast. "Two books," I counted again, "Paul's bedroom slipper — good heavens — can't you restrain him — or can't you see that he only eats your things?"

"It was only playfulness," said Aunt Flora foolishly. "I shall see that — "

At this moment there was a terrible yell from the bathroom, followed by a loud crash. We rushed upstairs and were in time to see the door of the bathroom open and the face of George, distorted with fury, appear round it.

"What the hell," he shouted, "did you call that thing?" We saw the shower lying on the ground, still emitting jets of apparently boiling water. "It bally near scalded the skin off me," he went on furiously. "Why can't you warn people that they're going to get boiling water all over them?"

"It isn't always boiling," said Aunt Flora indignantly. "How do we know which tap is going to jam?"

"To jam!" repeated George, glaring

at her in fury. "D'you mean it always jams?"

"No, not always — don't be ridiculous," said Aunt Flora.

George drew a towel round his steaming torso, strode to his room and slammed the door violently, and we went into my bedroom feeling a little guilty.

George's door opened presently and we were surprised to hear him wandering up and down the landing. He seemed to be opening doors and banging them again without apparent reason.

Phyl looked worried. "Do you think he's looking for me," she asked.

"Probably is," said Aunt Flora. "Wants to tell you he's leaving first thing in the morning."

At this moment the door of my room burst open and George looked at us with hatred. "Where," he asked bitterly, "is the damned lavatory — or don't you need one in this Elysium?"

There was a slight pause, broken by the hardy Aunt Flora.

"Outside," she said.

"Outside," repeated George, uncomprehendingly. "Outside what?"

"Outside the house," said Aunt Flora. "Down the stairs, out of the front door, turn to your right, keep on — "

"Outside . . . Outside," repeated George in a hollow voice. Then, as the awful truth went home, he advanced threateningly into the room. He opened his mouth, but no words came.

"You keep on," continued Aunt Flora, "and — "

George's powers of speech returned. "I'll keep on," he roared, "I'll keep on and keep on until I'm on the blasted heath and — " He stopped and spoke through clenched teeth. "In the pouring rain, in silk pyjamas and — " he became almost incoherent. Then, making an effort, he pulled himself together and spoke his last word.

"If this doesn't kill me," he said solemnly, "so help me God I'll be on the first train to-morrow."

The door practically came off its hinges as it banged behind him. We stood in silence and presently Aunt Flora kissed us affectionately. She walked to the door and paused, looking back at me with a mischievous smile.

100

"You mark my words, Jonny," she said, "those raspberry canes are going to save us from a number of troublesome visitors. Into the canes one night — out of the house next morning. *Most* satisfactory!"

5

I WAKENED the next morning feeling worried and depressed, and turned the events of the previous evening over in my mind. George, I felt, was as bad as ever, and he was going to make life very uncomfortable for us all. On thinking further, I reflected that the others would not really be affected. Aunt Flora enjoyed her battles with him, Phyl hardly noticed his tempers unless they were directed at me, and the children found him, in any mood, a source of interest and delight. Carrie cared nothing for his shoutings and howlings. Why then, I wondered, did I allow myself to take him so seriously? It was nonsense, and if I had to endure his presence in the house I would behave as usual and do my best to forget he was there. This cheered me considerably, as did the conviction that before the morning was out he would appear among us and demand a Bradshaw and be gone as abruptly as he had arrived. I splashed happily in my bath and went downstairs to join Aunt Flora and the children at breakfast. The children were eager to get to their camp, and rushed across the damp field very soon after we rose from the table. Aunt Flora prepared a tray for George and took it up to him, and when she came downstairs I asked her how he was.

"Can't say," she replied. "He mumbled something that might have been thank you, and might not, and when I asked him how he was, he pretended to be asleep. No wonder you can't stand him, Jonny — he really is unbearable. Don't know where he got that temper — no Manning I knew ever had it. They ran to laziness, like Phyl — and Hugh was very slow to anger."

"I don't mind his temper, or anybody's temper," I said, piling breakfast plates on a tray, "when I've done anything to provoke it, but I don't see why people should be unpleasant to everybody else just because they happen to feel moody or tired or upset. It's a — I can't explain it very well, but I feel it's a sort of social duty to check one's ill-temper just as one does any other kind of outburst. You taught us to curb our feelings," I went on, forgetting the dishes and sitting on a chair with my arms on the table, "but why is it that the same limitations aren't imposed on displays of unprovoked bad temper? Nobody minds being shouted at when they annoy people — Hugh often used to call me a blasted camel and I thought he was perfectly right, but if he had called me a camel just because he'd eaten something that upset him — well, that's a different matter."

"I see what you mean," said Aunt Flora thoughtfully, leaning against the sideboard, "but then in this case George has got a grievance, and it is directed against you. It's your house, and it doesn't come up to what he feels are elementary standards of comfort."

"Well, Burnton wasn't my house, and it came up to any ordinary standards of luxury," I retorted, "and he screamed just the same there — don't you remember?"

Our discussion was cut short by the subject of it, and we went into the hall and looked up at George, in pyjamas, pale with rage, holding an unidentifiable remnant in one hand and shouting at the top of his voice for Aunt Flora.

"Aunt Flora — Aunt Flora — where the devil — oh, *there* you are," he said, looking down with a murderous gaze. "Look at this — just look what your beastly hound has done. And I suppose the local emporiums are full of expensive lines in gents' slippers." He choked. "Show me that dog, and I'll — "

Aunt Flora put on her spectacles and George brought the slipper down a few steps for her closer inspection.

"Your dog," he said. "Can't you control the beast?" Aunt Flora examined the damage. "Tck tck tck," she said in distress. She drew her glasses down on her nose and looked anxiously at George. "You don't suppose the camel-hair will hurt him, do you?" she asked.

"Hurt him? I hope it kills him," said George bitterly.

Aunt Flora frowned. "Don't be childish, George," she said sharply. "You probably left your suit-case open and your things all over the floor."

"Where else should I leave slippers?" asked George.

"Out of a dog's reach until he's trained," said Aunt Flora. "It's putting temptation in his way to strew your things all over the place. You wouldn't blame your valet if he succumbed to the temptation of diamond and pearl studs left carelessly in heaps — you'd blame yourself for putting the temptation in a poor man's way."

"I'll blame myself," retorted George, "if that dog gets in my way again." He turned and marched up the stairs and looked back from the door of his room. "Send him up," he shouted. "Tell him he left half his dinner on his plate."

Aunt Flora went into the garden and was presently heard explaining to Rex that Uncle George had two feet and needed both slippers and he wasn't to be a silly dog and swallow woolly things, because they were bad for a doggie's stomach.

"Let's take him for a run, Jonny," she called to me, "it's a bit drizzly, but nothing much."

We got our bicycles and went slowly

down the road leading to the river, turning off the main road on to a quiet lane where Rex could disport himself without danger. He enjoyed himself immensely, and I compared his wriggling, zig-zag progress with the stately and dignified demeanour of Aunt Flora, sitting bolt upright on her high machine, arms held stiffly before her and knees rising slowly to the rhythm of the pedals. She was an awe-inspiring sight, and when she encountered one of the members of a modern cycling club, crouched low over handle bars and clad in workmanlike shorts and lurid stockings, it was difficult to say which rider looked most amazed.

We stopped at the little bridge over the river, known among the natives as Rushing Water, and got off our bicycles to see whether Rex would like a swim. We walked a little way along the bank and came upon the solitary figure of Miss Stafford, seated, regardless of damp, on a tree stump, chin in hand and looking the picture of misery. Beside her sat her godmother's little dog, a peculiarly repulsive mongrel of doubtful origin.

"Taking the dog for some exercise?" inquired Aunt Flora pleasantly. "You don't look in any danger of overdoing it. And don't look so bored — it reflects on us as permanent residents, and makes us feel we've run short of tourist appeal."

Miss Stafford, apart from glancing sideways at our approach and emitting a small sound of greeting, had not moved. She was not a sight to increase the pleasure of our morning ramble. Her hair, which had been trained to the severe and sophisticated coiffure she affected in London, looked all ends and pieces in its simpler country style. Her clothes, good though they were, sat ill on her full and voluptuous curves, and one thought instinctively of gleaming fabrics, clinging draperies and jewelled bracelets.

"I've got two days more," she said, looking up at us. "Two days, and I don't think I can do it. It's — it's goddam awful," she finished wearily.

"Oh come," said Aunt Flora briskly, "it can't be as bad as that. Old people are trying sometimes to us youngsters, but a week or ten days in the country never killed anybody yet. Can't you look on it as a sort of rest — retreat — recuperation — anything you like?"

"I could if the old girl was human," said Miss Stafford, "but she's not. If I could be by myself in that house for just a few minutes every day I could bear it, but I daren't even buy cigarettes while I'm down here — I'm practically dying for one now, but if I bought them I'd have one in my room and — well, a few hundreds a year would go up in the smoke. I can't go out much — she doesn't like it — and here I am, sitting on a wet plank spitting into the river. Or wanting to."

Aunt Flora made little clicking noises to convey her distress and sympathy. "It sounds depressing," she said, "but couldn't you be like an actress — throw yourself into the part, as it were, and get some fun out of turning yourself into a nice horsey great-outdoors type while you're here?"

"No good," said Miss Stafford, her large dark eyes looking more brooding than ever. "Every time I look at myself in the glass without my make-up I get a fright, and the sight of that mean old woman gets on my mind like an obsession. I suppose" — she eyed Aunt Flora challengingly — "I suppose you think it's a pretty cheap way of getting money, making up to an old lady and hoping she'll pass out as soon as possible — but I know worse ways."

Aunt Flora and I looked round at the lovely, peaceful countryside and pitied the young girl at our feet who could find nothing in the varied beauty about her to take her mind off her rather sordid problem.

"It's strange that so much loveliness can be absolutely lost on anybody," Aunt Flora said, voicing our thoughts, "but I suppose life in a great metropolis changes one's outlook. Even George can't hear any sermons in stones — he's going around looking just as grouchy as you are."

Miss Stafford stiffened and looked up at Aunt Flora with her bold black eyes open to their widest extent.

"Going around — do you mean going around *here*?" she asked, almost with stupefaction. "Is he staying with you?"

"Well, he's with us, but I don't know

whether he's staying," answered Aunt Flora. "He — "

Miss Stafford drew a deep breath, put her hands on the wet grass behind her and leaned backwards looking up at the dull sky.

"Oh Lord, oh Lord, oh Lord," she intoned slowly, "I got salvation."

She rose to her feet, her face transformed, her eyes gleaming. "Well, you're a peculiar-looking angel," she said impertinently to Aunt Flora, "but you did have a message."

"Do you know George?" asked Aunt Flora, rather taken aback at the effect of her mention of his name.

"Not exactly," said Miss Stafford lightly. "I've been at the same parties, but outside the sacred ring, if you follow me. But you don't bother about the formalities when you came across another fellow marooned on your island — What's he doing down here, for God's sake?" she added.

"He's down for a rest," I said.

"Well, he can have it," said Miss Stafford, "when I've gone back to civilization. You won't mind," she went on, "if I exercise this foul animal in your precincts in future? The sight of a man — especially as he's George — is going to save my reason."

We turned and walked back to our bicycles and Miss Stafford watched Aunt Flora mounting with barely-concealed amusement. I wished that I could have administered what Paul would have called a swift punch on the nose, but something else had struck her, and she looked depressed. "I'll come to-morrow," she called after us, "but take it from me, if this news gets around, there'll be a lot of women there before me."

We were out a little longer than we had intended, and came in to hear the familiar roar, this time proceeding from the kitchen. We went in to find George, in a dressing-gown, waving a pair of trousers at the unmoved Carrie. He turned to us furiously. "Isn't there," he demanded, "isn't there one single soul in this godforsaken hole who can take the mud off a fellow's trousers — or do I have to go around in my pants looking for a laundry?"

"Why didn't you ask me before I went

out?" I said. "I would have had them done by this time."

"How in hell was I to know you were going out?" said George. "I didn't know this place ran to coffee houses where women could spend the morning. I think the damned trousers are ruined," he went on, flinging them on to a chair and walking to the door, "but if anyone can do anything about it, for God's sake tell them to do it and hurry."

He went up the stairs and the door of his room crashed behind him.

"He don't change much," said Carrie without emotion, lifting the lid of a saucepan and peering through the steam. "If he don't like it here why don't he go where he's better suited?"

"Did he say anything about trains?" asked Aunt Flora hopefully.

"Not to me he didn't," said Carrie. "He telephoned and couldn't get someone he wanted, and said some nasty swear words. Can't think," she added reflectively "where he picks 'em up."

"I'll do his beastly trousers, Jonny," said Aunt Flora, taking them from me.

Phyl came downstairs, cool and

untroubled and looking lovely in slacks and an attractive sweater.

"George been worrying you?" she asked, slipping her arm through mine.

"Not more than usual," I replied. "You're down late — it's nearly lunch time."

"So it is," said Aunt Flora. "Time I blew the horn. You'd better hold Rex — he doesn't like it."

I went outside and slipped the lead on to Rex and handed it to Phyl, and walked inside and met George in the hall. He was scowling and seemed about to say something when Aunt Flora blew, and he jumped two feet into the air.

"My God," he exclaimed, "what's going on now?"

No answer was possible, as Aunt Flora was blowing again. George strode towards the verandah as though about to stop the turmoil, but paused, his expression turning from rage to incredulity, as he beheld Aunt Flora mounted on her little steps, the horn upturned in a graceful cherubim attitude, waking the echoes. He held his breath, waiting for the next blast, but Aunt Flora came down from her perch and hung the horn on its hook in the hall.

"Great art that," she said cheerfully. "You ought to try it, George. Most people can't get a sound out of it, in spite of blowing their heads off."

"I imagine," said George coldly, "that they prefer blowing their own heads off to having you doing it for them. How often," he went on, "do you summon the cows?"

"Cows — who summons cows?" asked aunt Flora indignantly. "That's to bring the children in — and you see," she added triumphantly, "it does the job."

"Too, too well," murmured George, giving one glance at the children's approaching forms and walking into the drawing-room.

Lunch was a normal meal except for the scowling presence in our midst. The children, after a few unsuccessful attempts to get any response out of George, left him alone. I noticed that he ate a good lunch, and felt a little ashamed of myself as I saw signs of tiredness and strain on his face. Perhaps, I thought, he really was ill and ought to be resting in surroundings more suitable to his temperamant.

After lunch, with these feelings in my mind, I suggested that he should rest in Phyl's long chair on the verandah. There was no sunshine, but the day was warm and the clouds looked like clearing. I fetched a rug and left it at the foot of the chair and put an extra cushion at the back, and went into help Carrie feeling that I had made up for some of my hard feelings.

A little later Aunt Flora came to tell me that Miss Peel had come.

"Did she disturb George?" I asked. "He was just settling down to rest — he'll be frightfully annoyed."

"Well, he doesn't look it at present," said Aunt Flora. "He's pulled out the appropriate stops and Miss Peel looks as though she's listening to heavenly choirs."

I found that this was hardly an exaggeration. Miss Peel was seated on Phyl's chair looking up at George with frank admiration and delight. She struggled to rise when we came out, but George stopped her with a smile and a hand on her shoulder, at which she looked more happy than before.

"It's wonderful," she said, looking at George, "to meet somebody one has seen on the films. I've never seen you in the flesh — that is, I've never seen you act on the stage," she went on hastily, blushing at her slip, "but I would have known you anywhere — and your sister is like you, only of course she's fair."

George, leaning against the back of Aunt Flora's chair and looking like a devoted and dutiful nephew, smiled and listened quietly. His moodiness had vanished, and nobody could have believed that frowns of ill-temper could make furrows on that serene brow. I made a mental note that if he intended staying I must arrange for a constant stream of visitors and thus reduce his outbursts to a minimum.

"It's so odd that your nephew should be here," Miss Peel said to Aunt Flora. "I called to tell you that I'm just on my way to meet a celebrity of my own. My cousin is coming down on the afternoon train." She turned shyly to George. "I wonder whether you've ever met her?"

she asked. "Her real name is Peel, but she writes under the name of Rebecca Rolfe — she felt that would be easy for the children to remember."

George could perhaps be excused for the fact, which he concealed from Miss Peel with a charm and ease pretty to watch, that he had never heard of the celebrated Miss Rolfe. She was a writer of detective stories for children, and entire shelves of her works could be seen in Paul's room and above Polly's bed. Ivan bought every new story the moment it appeared in print, as did thousands of other young enthusiasts throughout the country. Aunt Flora and I had tried to find in the stories some trace of tolerable English or at least a credible plot, but each work was more lurid than the last. No sooner had Miss Rolfe's Arabian hero galloped on his beautiful steed through choking sandstorms, over burnous-draped arrays of foes, past the final chapter and into the libraries of the enthralled young readers, than an Indian or Persian or South American desperado followed in a spine-chilling series of escapades.

I had no wish to meet Miss Rolfe. She was responsible for much of Ivan's genius for booby traps; her tale of the Canadian half-breed happily drowned in the terrible flooding of the river had resulted in floods in thousands of English bathrooms as the scene was reconstructed. We were at present enjoying a lull before the next outbreak, when children carried cardboard daggers and arranged ambushes behind doors, when an ordinary request to pass the marmalade resulted in mysterious signs and passes and the marmalade jar being taken on a journey round the hall and the dining-table, finally appearing at one's side in the hands of a crouching, hissing child. It became very wearing, and mothers had a long account to settle with Rebecca Rolfe.

"She has just finished her twenty-fifth book," Miss Peel told us, "and the doctors have told her that she's to have a complete rest and change."

George frowned a little at this infringement of copyright.

"This is just the place for her, then," said Aunt Flora. "George only came down yesterday and he's feeling the difference already — aren't you, George?" she said, twisting herself round in her chair and looking at him blandly.

George gave her a lazy smile and pinched her ear with what Miss Peel took to be tender affection. Aunt Flora wiped the tears from her eyes and turned back to Miss Peel.

"I hope we shall see a great deal of your cousin," she said. "And I'm afraid you must prepare yourself for frequent visits from the children."

Miss Peel smiled. "Ivan knows she's coming," she said, "I'm rather surprised he didn't ask whether he could come to the station."

Aunt Flora laughed and pointed across the field at the approaching group. "Look," she said. "Ivan and party — are they all going to the station?"

Nothing could have delighted Miss Peel more than the scene which followed. Ivan and Paul, Polly and Diana appeared with eager faces and shining eyes and in spite of my protests, were permitted to accompany her to meet their heroine and help with her luggage.

Soon the happy party departed, all in the highest spirits, and I rearranged the long chair for George's reception.

"You can get a rest now," said Aunt Flora. "You'll need all your strength to keep your end up against the other visiting celebrity."

"Well, no," said George slowly, looking at me rather speculatively. "I've got something I'd like to do first." He paused, and a sense of foreboding came over me. Then: "Jonny," he said abruptly, "that room you put me into is charming, of course, but I'd very much rather be in that corner room of Paul's. I suppose you'd have no objection to my moving?"

I had so many objections that they all seemed to get stuck in my throat in the rush to get out, and I could only say feebly: "Why, George, your room is bigger . . . "

"Yes," said George, "but the other has an extra window, with that really good view of the hills, and it isn't so near the stairs, and it's nearer to the bathroom and I think I could make something of it."

"Make something . . . Well," I

temporised, "would you mind waiting until Paul comes back and we can put it to him."

"Oh, I've done that," said George. "He hasn't the least objection."

I had nothing to say to this, and Aunt Flora attempted a rescue. "Look here, George," she said, "I don't want to hurt your feelings, if you've got any, but you've only been here a day, and you loathe it and you'll drive us all mad if you stay, so why talk of changing rooms as though you'd taken root? Much better stay where you are over the weekend and then pop back to those gilded surroundings of yours." She patted his shoulder in a motherly way. "Now off to your rest and stop teasing Jonny, like a good fellow."

George smiled slowly at her, a delightful, heart-stirring smile, and slipped an arm through hers. He turned to me, gave me a friendly wink and put his other arm round my shoulders.

"Just come upstairs, both of you," he said coaxingly, "just for a couple of minutes, and I'll show you what I mean."

The hall clock said 2.45 as we went up the stairs. Phyl came to the door of her room and raised her eyebrows. "Something happening?" she asked.

"Happened," said Aunt Flora hollowly. "George is staying."

Fifteen minutes later the downstairs clock chimed three, and Carrie came upstairs to announce that Mr. George's luggage was here, and four-and-four to pay. As her head appeared above the landing level she stopped dead and her eyes bulged with wonder and disbelief. George and Aunt Flora, each with an end of Paul's bed, were struggling with it into what, fifteen minutes earlier, had been the guest-room. Two mattresses stood against the landing wall. Bedclothes, folded and piled, lay on chairs and over banisters. Phyl and I were standing with the drawers out of Paul's chest, waiting until the bed had been moved in and the doorway freed.

"Who's movin'?" asked Carrie in a bewildered voice.

Nobody answered her. At that moment the bed was adjusted to the correct angle and Aunt Flora, who was carrying the far end, disappeared backwards into the room, followed by the bed and George, who moved with bent knees in an awkward little run.

"Look out there," roared Aunt Flora. "You'll have me through the window if you're not careful. Round a bit, round a bit — that's it. Now down with it." The bed on the floor, she straightened and looked balefully at George.

"Now look here — you run into the village and get a couple of strong men," she said. "Then you can give them half a crown an afternoon to come and move you from room to room. What's Carrie yelping about?"

"The boy's brought the luggage and there's four-and-four to pay," said Carrie, looking round at the disorder.

"Well, I'll go and pay him and you can get that other bed out with Mr. George," said Aunt Flora, disappearing rapidly downstairs.

Phyl and I settled the drawers and made the bed while the other was moved out. George brought his luggage up, and put it into his new room, which was losing its plainly furnished look and becoming unfamiliar with rugs, chairs and small tables brought in from George's old room.

Aunt Flora, unable to resist seeing how things were going, came upstairs and looked round.

"Well, there you are, George," she said, surveying the new arrangements, "now that's finished and you can settle down. Let me know when you want me to move out of my room."

George made no answer. He was gazing round thoughtfully, and in a moment his brow cleared and he made a rapid re-arrangement of the furniture. He pushed the bed against the far wall, placed the rugs in new positions, and carried a table and a chair on to the landing.

"Great Scotland Yard, you're not moving out again," asked Aunt Flora in a high voice.

George looked at her with an abstracted gaze.

"Now where . . . " he mused. "Ah, I know."

He turned and walked into Phyl's room. A series of thuds followed, and

Phyl hurried across the landing and gave a wail of dismay.

"Oh, George — no! you can't possibly — I've nowhere else to put all those books — "

"Of course you have, Phyl, don't be an ass," replied her brother. "I'll bring Paul's in here in a moment. Out of the way," he continued, butting Aunt Flora with the end of the bookcase and staggering with it into his room.

The bookcase in position, George went back rapidly and reappeared with a lovely little low chair, and placed it in position. He then lifted the model ship off its shelf on the landing and laid it above the corner cupboard in his new room. This done he still, to our horror, looked thoughtful. Aunt Flora moved to her room and stationed herself outside the door, arms folded.

"If you attempt to come in here," she said grimly, "I'll ring up the police."

"Don't talk tommyrot," said George. "I can't see what you're all fussing about — I'm not filching anything. I'm merely borrowing a few bits of things to show you how a room can look if you use a little imagination."

"And a lot of other people's property," put in Phyl coldly.

"All right — borrowed props," said George. "I only want two more things" — our hearts sank — "that fishing fleet picture and that cunning bedside light of Jonny's."

"Sorry, George," I said with finality. "The fishing fleet picture is in Polly's room and she'd die rather than part with it — her father gave it to her — and that cunning bedside light was Hugh's too, and you're not going to have it."

"Not even for a week or two?" asked George incredulously.

"Not for an hour," I said.

George looked puzzled. "What extraordinary women you are," he remarked. "One would think I was going to purloin the blasted things. Now look — forget the picture." He seized me by the arm and hurried me into my room. He went to the bed-table and in a twinkling disconnected the lamp, picked it up and hurried me into his room. He drew the curtains, switched on the little light and struck an attitude like a showman. "There," he exclaimed, "look round and tell me whether you'd ever have achieved a guest room like that."

Nobody wanted to deny that the room looked beautiful. My light, a lantern held aloft by a peering and portly wooden innkeeper, shed a soft radiance on the transformation scene, and George, switching it off and drawing the curtains back, felt that he had won the day. There was silence for a few moments.

"I want my lamp," I said.

"And I want my chair — you can keep the bookcase," said Phyl.

"And you put that ship back on the landing," said Aunt Flora. "It looks nice in here, but it looks nicer out there, and we can all enjoy looking at it."

"Do you really mean to say," said George incredulously, "that you're all so damned wrapped up in your possessions that you can't let them out of your sight for a week? A chair," he went on, his accents gaining in fury. "A rotten chair — a couple of planks knocked up into a bookcase — a ship which nobody's probably looked at for years stuck up on a godforsaken landing." He paused for breath. "I see how it is," he went on bitterly. "A pack of women with in-growing interests — nothing to do but blow horns and work up hysterias about bedside lamps. I could have," he went on with slightly greater accuracy, "the bedside lamps of half the women in England if I asked for them. But not that one." He jabbed a forefinger at the unmoved innkeeper. "I want my lamp," he mimicked. "I want my bookcase, I want my chair. Well, take the bloody things — I don't want them."

He stopped and walked to the window and stood looking out at his new view.

Aunt Flora looked at his back with cold disgust.

"Well, at least," she remarked reflectively, "we didn't have to pay for the performance, as some poor wretches do. Thank you, George," she added, going towards the door, "thank you very much. Please keep all the things — our little tribute, you know."

6

GEORGE astounded us all the next morning by appearing downstairs for breakfast looking cool and comfortable in a pair of flannel trousers and a coloured shirt of open mesh. He appropriated the morning paper and made an excellent breakfast behind it, one hand groping round occasionally for the salt or the sugar. Polly tried to gain his attention by putting a hot spoon in his hand on one of its appearances, and succeeded beyond her expectations.

Aunt Flora, sipping her third cup of coffee, was gazing out of the window looking on to the garden. Suddenly, with a startled exclamation, she put the cup down and pushed back her chair.

"Just look what's here," she said.

We looked and saw Ivan and Lieutenant No. 2 staggering from the shed with a small carpenter's bench on which were balanced two saws. Young Bobbie Wheeler followed with a third saw.

"Is this the sawing gang?" Aunt Flora asked Paul, finishing her coffee hastily and preparing to meet the party.

"Yes, but I said ten o'clock," said Paul.

"Well, they must have had breakfast overnight," remarked Aunt Flora. "What use do you imagine that little Wheeler's going to be?"

"None at all — I didn't ask him," replied Paul.

Ivan's head appeared at the window. "Good morning," he said politely. "Miss Manning, where shall we put the bench?"

"Well, not outside," said Aunt Flora. "The sun'll be shaving our skins off by eleven o'clock. We'll set it up on the shady end of the verandah."

Aunt Flora and the children disappeared in a scramble through the door and George shook the coffee-pot exploringly. "I was going to have a quiet morning on the verandah," he grumbled, pouring the dregs into his cup, "and now they're going to create stink out there all day."

I wanted to ask why he didn't go up and make himself comfortable in his newly-furnished bed sitting-room, but as usual by the time I had framed the sentences in my mind in a suitably withering form, the moment had gone by.

"Where's that monster hound of Aunt Flora's?" asked George. "I've a good mind to take him out for a decent bit of exercise — take his mind off chewing slippers."

"Aunt Flora will be grateful if you do," I said. "And if you can include Polly and Diana it'll get them out of the way of the saws."

"Nothing doing," said George briefly. "I'm down here for my health — not theirs." He drained his cup and put it down. "Slept a bit better last night," he informed me kindly. "I kept waking up the night before in that other room and thinking I was in the Chamber of Horrors."

"I don't know why you're not," I retorted, to my own surprise and pride.

"Not bad, not bad," drawled George, going into the hall. "Little Jonny hits back."

There was a delay while Aunt Flora

explained to Rex that she was unable to join him and the kind gentleman on their walk.

"Give him some decent exercise," she enjoined George. "None of this walking to the first bench and sitting down. Dogs like this need real exercise and" — she surveyed George's six feet of fairly tough manhood — "I don't know that a stroll with a Sealyham wouldn't be more in your line."

"The lead," said George coldly.

"Here," said Aunt Flora, handing the wrong end to George and fixing the other in Rex's mouth. "Now shoo!" she said, patting George's head. "Good dog."

George, his face a picture of disdain at this elementary clowning, went on his way, making a detour to avoid the distressing sounds issuing from the verandah. There was indeed a hideous din proceeding from that quarter. I walked round to look at the boys and found them working vigorously; Ivan was on the bench and Paul on the edge of the verandah; Lieutenant No. 2 was looking at Aunt Flora waiting for orders.

"That's a fine saw you've got, Bobby,"

said Aunt Flora. "Does your mother know you've taken it?"

Bobby appeared to ponder this and then looked up. "Yes, I think probably," he said.

I thought probably not.

"Look out there, young Ivan," said Aunt Flora, as he lifted his hand, still grasping the saw, and wiped the sweat off his brow. "No use getting hot yet — we haven't started. Now, Bobby, you and" — she looked at No. 2 — "by the way, what *is* your name?" she inquired.

There was a series of indistinct sounds from No. 2 and Ivan translated. "It's Stebbing, same as the postman," he said, "but he's called Nobby."

"Nobby," said Aunt Flora musingly. "I've never met a Nobby. It's a nice name to call, I should think — Nobby Nobby, Nobby," she experimented. "Well, come on Nobby, I'll hold this and you can saw — you'll have to have the Wheeler saw and when you've made a bit of a groove Bobby can go on with it."

This appeared to suit Bobby and soon the three saws were squeaking and rasping hideously and shattering the peace of the lovely morning.

"Look at the perspiration!" said Aunt Flora anxiously in an aside to me. "Do you think they'll all run into a pool of tallow like those tigers in that story?"

"I'll bring some drinks out in an hour or so," I promised, and went inside to work.

It was cool working indoors and quite pleasant in the silent intervals between sawings. I went into the big square yard at the back of the house to hang up a row of washed stockings, and heard Aunt Flora's voice calling me.

"Oh there you are," she said, parting two stockings and peering at me. "There's a woman in the drawing-room."

"What woman?" I asked.

"Stranger, name of Lentil or Mental," said Aunt Flora. "Came down on the train with George and would have been on the scent sooner, I think, only the careless fellow put her off by calling it Rushing and not Rushing Farm."

"What does she want?" I inquired.

Aunt Flora gazed at me in wide-eyed wonder, her face framed in stocking.

"Are you being the idiot boy?" she asked angrily "She wants George, of course. And before we know where we are," she continued gloomily, "we'll have swarms of women popping up from nowhere wasting our time."

I hung up the last stocking.

"Hurry up," said Aunt Flora. "It's a curious sight — all bosom and behind."

I blushed at this coarse summing up of the appearance of our unknown visitor, but on entering the drawing-room a few minutes later I was rendered speechless by the aptness of the description and was forced to admit that Aunt Flora had made an admirable precis of Miss Kendal's charms. When I recovered a little, I got an impression of blonde prettiness framed in an enormous hat of plain straw, a linen coat and skirt that even Phyl would not have disdained and shoes with such high heels that I wondered how the poor girl had negotiated our rough drive.

She was, it appeared, the niece of Mr. Kendal, vicar of Felling, and had travelled down with George. She had apparently decided that he was on the verge of a serious breakdown — he might have given her this impression or she might have felt it offered an excuse to call and inquire after his health.

I told her that George had gone for a walk but would be back shortly.

"I would so like to wait, if I may," she said. "I don't often come into Rushing and I felt I couldn't go back without finding out how he was."

It was noisy even inside the drawing-room and Miss Kendal looked as though the sawing put her teeth on edge, so I took her into the garden, and led her to the bench under the beech tree. Here one could see the working party, but their noises were somewhat dissipated in the open. The working party could see also Miss Kendal, and the sight of her ripe charms wrought havoc on the tempo of the sawing. I signalled to Paul and left the visitor in his charge while I went indoors to fetch drinks.

I enjoyed myself for a while with some cider and soda water, some mint and some raspberries and went into the garden with a tray full of glasses and an enormous jug of cider cup. Paul, coming to relieve me of the tray, spoke through the side of his mouth.

"The bench is filling up," he muttered.

I looked in astonishment at the second figure on the bench and with an effort recognized Miss Stafford, no longer depressed and haggard, but assured and made up to the last eyelash. She was in white with effective touches of colour and her dark bold looks were more gypsy-like than ever. I wondered how much more feminine loveliness would be arrayed in the garden before George returned.

Paul and Aunt Flora looked after the sirens while I poured drinks for the children, who sat happily on the front steps, hot and dirty, clutching their glasses and eating a large number of buns.

Rex, bounding in and racing towards Aunt Flora, gave warning of George's approach and to my dismay I saw that to one man and one dog had been added one girl. This, I felt, was really too much and I was still less pleased on recognizing Bobby's eighteen-year-old sister — he had twin sisters so much alike that it was said that even their mother could not tell them apart. I had never had the time or the inclination to solve the puzzle and noticed merely that one of them had worse manners, if possible, than the other.

I looked for help to Aunt Flora and found her with shining eyes and a delighted expression, obviously determined to enjoy every moment of this uncomfortable gathering.

George raised a welcoming hand to Miss Kendal and turned his smile on to Miss Stafford.

"You ought to know me, George," said that lady coolly. "I've been at forty parties with you — but with the party rather than of the party, of course."

After the first searching glance George found the answer.

"I've seen you very often," he said warmly, "with Bill Fletcher — am I right?"

Miss Stafford surveyed him with frank appreciation and delight.

"The royal gift," she said, and continued simply, "I'm all yours, George. The name is Stafford and my pets call me Smoky Joe."

"Why?" inquired the twin Wheeler insolently.

"Why not?" asked Smoky Joe, eyeing Miss Wheeler with contempt.

"You must be hot, George," I interposed. "Will you pour drinks for yourself and" — I looked puzzled — "which of you are you?" I asked.

"I'm Lorna and I want much more cider than that, George," said the damsel without looking in my direction. "Oh, it isn't cider — it's sham," she exclaimed after closer inspection. "Go and lace it," she begged George.

"Lace it!" exclaimed Miss Kendal with coy horror. "You're too young for anything but lemonade."

The young Miss Wheeler made no reply, but regarded Miss Kendal over the top of her glass with so insolent a stare that I found my hand itching.

"I suppose you've come after the saw," said Aunt Flora, who had her own methods of dealing with the erring young.

"The saw?" echoed Lorna in a bored tone.

"The saw," repeated Aunt Flora. "I knew Bobby had filched it. Come with me and identify it," she went on, and to my relief swept the surprised and reluctant miss on to the verandah. Miss Stafford gave an audible sigh of relief and looked at me hopefully as if I could continue this ten-little-nigger-boy system of elimination and leave her in the field with George. I was feeling a little exhausted, however, and felt that George could manage one of each colour very well.

I went indoors for a basket and began to cut flowers for the house. It was not a job I usually did, but I felt it would be impolite to go indoors and leave the visitors — though I was aware they would not notice my absence at all.

I cut sweet-peas and listened to Aunt Flora's dismissal of Lorna by the simple means of telling her that she must go home with Bobby and defend him from the consequences of saw stealing. "It was most useful all the same," she told the departing Bobby. "Come back this afternoon without it — and without your sister," she added under her breath. She turned and came over to me, taking the scissors out of my hand and going on with the cutting while I held the basket.

"That's one gone," she remarked. "I felt sorry for the other two — Smoky Joe could have dealt with her, but not the other one." She paused in her clipping and surveyed the pretty scene under the beech tree. "Striking looking, that Miss Stafford," she observed. "Reminds me of Carmen, somehow."

"I'm rather sorry for George," I said. "Couldn't you get rid of them as you did that frightful little Wheeler?"

"No — George must have his exercise," said Aunt Flora. "He's using his charm and his tact and his brain and when he gets tired of them he's quite equal to extricating himself without the least difficulty."

I looked at the two women.

"Do you think they realize that George is — well not a philanderer?" I asked.

Aunt Flora gazed at me in astonishment. "What on earth do you mean?" she asked.

"Well," I went on hesitatingly, "Miss Stafford speaks of him as a sort of cooling drink in a thirsty desert, and that other follows him on some flimsy pretext, but I feel they're wasting their time — I loathe George in many ways but you can't say he encourages women. I feel I want to go up to them and explain that they're expending all that charm on an absolutely empty house. Then they'd be disappointed and go away."

"They'd be disappointed," agreed Aunt Flora, "but they wouldn't go away."

"It's dreadful," I mused, "to think of any woman being in the state of mind that drives her to pursue young men into other people's gardens."

"I'd hardly call Miss Stafford's a state of mind," commented Aunt Flora. She parted the tall delphiniums in order to get a better view of the little group. "Do you know," she continued, "that other woman is a curious type. Just missed being quite magnificent — a sort of Goddess of Overflow. My word, Jonny, she looks a regular tart — Tartar," she amended hastily as Polly came into view round the delphiniums.

"Hello, Mums," she greeted me. "Miss Peel says please will you ring her up when you have time."

"Of course," I said. "I'll go now."

"I'd better read a bit of her cousin's

latest book," said Aunt Flora. "Go and fetch it, Polly, and bring a deck chair and I'll go and sit near George and his two friends. Here — take the flowers in as you go."

As I finished talking to Miss Peel and put the receiver down, I saw George holding the gate open for Miss Kendal, who had departed without the little formality of saying good-bye to me. I stood on the steps and watched her difficult progress down the drive on those crippling heels and just at that moment Phyl came downstairs — her first appearance — and joined me. Her simple, cool loveliness was infinitely restful after the overdone effects we had witnessed during the morning and I looked at her with pleasure. She sat on the steps and looked with amusement at the boys sawing and planing busily, ankle deep in sawdust and curly wood shavings. Ivan paused and grinned at her.

"Want to do some?" he asked. "It's awful fun."

"Terrific," agreed Phyl. "I wouldn't have you miss it for worlds."

Ivan gave her one of his delightful

mischievous winks and went on with the job, pausing again a few moments later to look thoughtfully at Miss Stafford. They were old enemies and Ivan was no doubt interested in the startling change in her appearance. Miss Stafford stared back at him with loathing and Ivan went back to work on his plank, sawing with an energy and viciousness that made me wonder whether he imagined himself a youthful Maskelyne performing the famous trick of sawing a woman in half.

Miss Stafford lingered to say a word to George. "Goodbye," she said carelessly. "I'll come to-morrow and you can think up something to do in the meantime. Good-bye, Mrs. Manning," she went on. "Sorry you're going to see so much of me in the near future."

Aunt Flora and I made one or two polite murmurs. George watched her departing and put our thoughts into words.

"That girl," he said, "is going to be a nuisance." He then rather belatedly remembered the presence of the children and found that Ivan was regarding him with a puzzled and intent frown.

"Don't you like her?" he asked George with simple directness.

George hesitated for a moment, looking down at the upturned monkey face with a searching gaze.

"That's a pretty rude question," he said finally.

"He's a pretty rude fellow," said Aunt Flora with a smile. She turned to Ivan. "You can't put a question like that to anybody," she told him. "If they say 'No' they're unchivalrous and if they say 'Yes' they're liars. Do you see?"

"Yes," replied Ivan. "I don't like her either."

"Nobody," said Aunt Flora coldly, "is in the least interested in your sentiments. Will you kindly go home to lunch and if you're good you can come back this afternoon and finish the sawing."

Ivan rubbed his aching muscles and looked round at the makings of the enormous erection designed as the habitation of Rex. Finally, he grinned his most wicked grin at Aunt Flora.

"If I'd known you were going to build

146

a kennel for the dog I gave you — " he said, and hesitated.

"Well?" said Aunt Flora.

"I'd have given you a much littler dog," finished Ivan, and went his way.

7

A STORM during the night made the weather cooler and nothing could have been more pleasant than the sunshine and breezes on the following day. I had little time to spend out of doors, being busy with preparations for lunch. I had invited the Colonel and his two sisters to lunch to meet Miss Peel's cousin. I was a little apprehensive about the cousin and wondered what I could find to say to a woman whose mind ran on murder in Afghan passes and buried treasure in Babylonian gardens. I hoped May and Claudia would refrain from bickering — one could feel pity or amusement when they had gone, but it was a strain while it was going on.

George took over the building of the kennel, deciding that Aunt Flora's plans for its erection were too elaborate to be put into execution. The boys worked energetically. George, who was no mean carpenter, insisted on thoroughness and finish and the verandah hummed with activity, the sound of hammering reverberating through the house.

I took drinks to the working party during the morning and invited Ivan and Nobby to stay to lunch with the children. Ivan gave a whoop of acceptance and asked for permission to telephone to his mother for confirmation. Nobby appeared to think that the simple fact of his non-appearance at the postman's table would indicate sufficiently that he was taking lunch elsewhere, but this did not satisfy me, and Polly and Diana, who were getting a little tired of weeding Polly's garden, volunteered to go and inform Mr. Stebbing that his nephew would be out to lunch.

Aunt Flora and I put a table under the beech tree and I instructed Paul to take charge of the junior party and go round to the kitchen to fetch their food when lunch was ready. There was just time for me to slip upstairs and tidy myself when I heard the Colonel's voice.

Phyl and I went down, and May and Claudia greeted Phyl with a pleasantness they never showed to anyone else in

Rushing. They studied George with an air of being determined to resist any appeal he might have, and May let off her first salvo by remarking that she understood he was down here for a rest but she did not think he looked as though he needed one; if he did need one it was odd that he should be doing manual labour on a warm day. She paused for breath and George looked a little shattered at this unlooked for attack. May's eyes swept the company and rested on the form of Nobby, who sat with Ivan and Paul on the floor, his back resting against the verandah railing. She seemed to be loading for another volley, and George with three long easy strides made his way to the railing and sat on it, his long legs crossed in front of him. The Colonel, unable to resist the appeal of the male club, walked across and completed the group.

"I hear you weren't very fit the other day," said Aunt Flora sympathetically to Claudia. "I hope you are all right again?"

"It was one of my dreadful headaches," said Claudia. "They're always worse in summer — it's ridiculous, but the sun seems to knock me over. I never could stand it."

"Shouldn't go about without your topee," said May.

"We get so little summer as a rule," went on Claudia, as if there had been no interruption. "It seems such a shame not to enjoy every minute of it. But I have such a poor little appetite in the heat — some days I can't touch a thing."

"Misses her curry and rice," said May.

George, unaware that this went on all the time between the charming pair, ordered his henchmen to attention and sent them indoors to make themselves clean. He then took the Colonel into the drawing-room, where I had put out the drinks, and the two men were seen no more.

Polly and Diana had not returned and I guessed they had gone to meet Miss Peel. I had been astonished at the way they had both succumbed to the charms of Miss Rolfe, but when they arrived a few minutes later I was surprised no longer. Nothing could have been more charming than the small, neat, smiling and pretty woman who called herself Rebecca Rolfe and who was a plague to parents. She looked like a rosy-cheeked Scandinavian housewife — not that I had ever seen one, but I always imagined the type to be as clean and fresh-looking as Miss Rolfe. Aunt Flora was obviously delighted and astonished at this neat little workshop which turned out such monstrous figures of crime and violence, and voiced her feelings with her usual frankness.

"Upon my word," she said, "I never imagined anything so delightful. Miss Peel should have told us — we were all expecting you to look lurid and terrifying."

Miss Rolfe laughed with infectious heartiness and Miss Peel looked the picture of happiness and pride.

May and Claudia, who knew the type of literature which Miss Rolfe loosed upon the country, were obviously as astonished at the sight of the perpetrator as Aunt Flora had been. May showed a little irritation at Miss Peel's obvious pride in her cousin.

"I love your house," said Miss Rolfe,

looking round with sincere appreciation. "I haven't been in a verandah like this for twenty years or more. I wish they would build one on every house."

"Ah, verandahs!" sighed Claudia with a note of real wistfulness in her voice. "Verandahs with little palms in pots all round them and baskets of orchids hanging in every corner and the beautiful frangipani and that other — I can't recall the name — "

"Forgetting your Hindoo," observed May.

"Hindustani," corrected Claudia frigidly.

"Same thing," said May. "I see you've still got that child here, Mrs. Manning. Don't you ever feel bothered with so many children round you?"

I explained that I didn't and that Diana was good company for Polly, and gave Miss Rolfe a brief summary of the reasons for Diana's visit.

"It's difficult for professional parents to make the best arrangements for their children," she said. "That reminds me — I was promised a great treat — I mean meeting your brother-in-law. He isn't here."

"You shall see him this minute," I said as Carrie sounded the gong and we rose to go indoors. We met George and the Colonel in the hall and George and Miss Rolfe looked delighted with each other.

"What, no cow horn?" said George to Aunt Flora.

"No cow horn to-day," said Aunt Flora. "Unless," she said hopefully, "the children didn't hear the gong properly."

"I'm sure they didn't," said George, looking out solemnly at the party round the table already seated and filling their plates to capacity.

"Well, just one blow," said Aunt Flora, taking the horn from its hook.

It was a devastating moment for some of the listeners who had never had the privilege of hearing the noise before or, like the Colonel and his sisters, had been fortunate enough to live almost out of range of the blast. The Colonel did his best to perform on the instrument but got nothing but grunts out of it, and George did no better.

"I'll get a roof-raising blow out of that," he said, hanging it on its hook and following the company indoors, "before I leave here."

"The day you leave here," Aunt Flora informed him, "it'll blow itself."

Halfway through lunch the party outside showed signs of becoming hilarious and Miss Rolfe laughed at the sounds.

"It's such a treat," she said to me, "to see thoroughly happy children. I stayed with some people recently who seemed to me to have very savage methods of enforcing discipline — of course I'm not really a judge. One of the older girls — a child of thirteen," she went on, "was made to lunch by herself at a small table in the corner all the time I was there. I didn't like to ask what she had done, but whatever it was, a long-drawn-out penance like that seemed to me to be wrong. And besides, it spoilt all my lunches — I couldn't eat anything and I felt that I was being made use of to make the child feel ashamed. Such good lunches," Miss Rolfe finished wistfully.

May looked at me as if hoping I would put this admirable discipline into force at once. The Colonel, however, went over to the enemy side.

"I don't know what Mrs. Manning does to her children," he said, "but it seems to have excellent results." I bowed. "People expect a little too much from children these days, I think," he went on. "They have such grown-up ways that one forgets their extreme youth — that young Ivan can talk like a grandfather and a very wise old grandfather at that. You're just preparing to enter into a really adult conversation with him when one of his booby traps goes off and he has to leave rapidly and flee from justice."

The mention of booby traps was unfortunate and May turned an unbecoming crimson.

"If one could only bring home to that boy," she said darkly, "half the misdeeds he commits, one could have him put under restraint. I believe his parents encourage him."

"He's a pet," said Aunt Flora.

"The Chimp," said George. "How's that for your book, Miss Rolfe? The Chimp, or Ivan the Terrible, the Scourge of Two Villages. It ought to go well."

"I'll get on with it directly after lunch," promised Miss Rolfe. She turned to

Claudia. "Did I hear you mention India?" she asked.

"Oh, yes," said Claudia eagerly. "I was there, you know — oh, years ago — but it was wonderful. I never had a chance of going back."

Miss Rolfe looked at her sympathetically. "But you were fortunate in your visit," she said. "I went out a few years ago hoping to spend two or three months with friends. I was taken ill on the boat and had an appendix operation when we reached Bombay. I didn't do too well and as soon as I was well enough to travel I was shipped back home. It was an expensive journey just to see the landing pier at Bombay."

"That was awful," said Aunt Flora. "So the world missed your first great work, 'The Nabob or the Rajah's Jewel Theft'?"

Miss Rolfe laughed. "It was awful," she agreed ruefully, "to come away without a single glamorous recollection — to have nothing to look back on except an illness which I might just as well have had comfortably at home."

We had coffee on the verandah after

having banished the children into the distance. They had made clay ovens at some time and were now burning what they called touchwood in them, making a great deal of evil-smelling smoke and getting themselves very black.

"How long are you to stay?" the Colonel asked George.

"That," put in Aunt Flora, "depends entirely upon how long we can bear it. But he must finish the kennel first."

"It's going to be a good bit of work," said George, looking admiringly at the beginnings of it. "Aunt Flora was planning something with curious decorations and even more curious proportions. I think it would have turned out like a sentry box in the Chinese manner."

"Rex would have loved it," said Aunt Flora as she took May and Miss Rolfe outside to see the garden. Phyl moved her chair closer to Claudia and listened quietly to her aimless and unprofitable chatter. The men were also chatting easily and I was free to go inside and see how Carrie was getting on. I found the table cleared and Paul and Ivan carrying the last plates into the kitchen.

158

"Thank you, one and all," I said. "Who thought of being useful?"

"I did," said Ivan promptly, his teeth gleaming in his smoke-grimed face.

He followed Paul out to where their ovens lay smoking on the steps and then turned back.

"Oh, I forgot, Mrs. Manning," he said. "That girl what stayed at Mrs. Sayers — "

"*That* stayed at Mrs. Sayers — "

"Yes, that one. She was going away on the bus yesterday evening, and she said I was to say she was sorry not to come and say good-bye."

"Good-bye!" I echoed in astonishment. "Has she gone?"

"Yes," said Ivan, and a curious look of satisfaction spread slowly over his face. It was such a deep, triumphant look that I gazed down into the little black face wondering uneasily what lay behind it. When Ivan assumed an expression of bland innocence my uneasiness turned to suspicion and a vague fear. I opened my mouth to demand an explanation and closed it again, and we stared intently at one another.

"She thought," said Ivan slowly, "that George — that Mr. Manning had gone back to London."

"Oh," I said stupidly, and then pulled myself together. "Well, thank you for the message," I ended feebly. "You'd better run out to your smelly oven."

Ivan smiled happily and vanished, and I sat down and thought over the matter for a few minutes. The more I thought, the more uneasy I became. Finally, I decided that no good could come of investigating any of Ivan's more sinister activities. If Miss Stafford had allowed herself to be misled by a small boy, even so diabolically clever a small boy, it was no affair of mine.

Miss Stafford had left, George would not find her the nuisance he had anticipated, and Aunt Flora and I would not have to make a show of entertaining her in the garden. Another of Ivan's booby traps had sprung successfully. I rose with a rather guilty feeling of relief and went out to join the guests.

160

8

AFTER the rather alarming beginning to George's visit, when the garden had bloomed with questing beauties, we found to our relief that owing to Ivan's magician-like whisking of Miss Stafford from the scene and the mercy of Providence in causing damage to the Wheeler roof sufficiently serious to necessitate the removal of the whole family during the period of repair, we were not likely to be unduly worried by uncomfortable visits. Miss Kendal had never constituted a serious threat — it was not possible for the Vicar's niece to find plausible excuses for too frequent journeys from Felling to our house.

When we had realized these pleasant facts, we settled down to a quiet and peaceful routine, interrupted now and again by George's attempts to bring home to us the astounding tolerance and patience he was showing in the appalling conditions into which circumstances and

Phyl had thrust him. In the intervals between his outbursts, he continued to gain in health and spirits, and organized outings for the children, and had that morning taken the two girls, with Paul and his two lieutenants to a disused mine about two miles away. There had been two showers since their departure, the last one being so heavy that I went out into the garden in fear that some of Aunt Flora's plants might have been beaten to the ground. Everything seemed to be standing up as usual, however, and I turned towards the house and was about to go indoors again when I was stopped by a shout from the gate. Turning, I saw Brian Lorimer approaching with great strides, a delighted grin on his face.

"Good Heavens," I said in astonishment, "how did you get here?"

"Three trains, one bus," replied Brian, tilting my face and giving me a hearty kiss. "Where is she?" he went on, going straight to the point.

As far as Brian was aware, or had been aware for the past ten years, there was only one 'she'. He had loved Phyl almost as long as he had known her, and

162

when she had married Tommy Blair, had remained a steady and faithful friend to them both. We knew that he hoped Phyl would now begin life again with him, but we could guess nothing of her thoughts on the subject.

I answered his question with equal directness.

"Upstairs, I think," I said. "If you yell loudly under that window, you'll probably get some result."

"God bless my soul," said Aunt Flora, appearing on the verandah. "What d'you mean by roaring like that?"

"I wasn't roaring at you, my sweet," said Brian embracing her with fervour. He sometimes complained that he could kiss anybody in the family except Phyl. "Where's that tall fair-haired woman with the divine — oh, there you are," he went on as Phyl appeared. Words seemed to fail him, and he took her hands and wrung them, his plain face alight with love.

"Is this the leave?" asked Phyl, smiling at him warmly.

"This is it," said Brian. "Ten whole days of it — and of you."

"And me," said Aunt Flora.

"And me," I said.

"And George," added Phyl.

"George!" exclaimed Brian. "What on earth is George doing down in this — down here?"

"Down in this what?" demanded Aunt Flora grimly.

"In this charming spot," replied Brian promptly. "Bit rural, I mean to say, for George's taste."

"Yes, it is," said Aunt Flora, "and he shouldn't be here at all, but Phyl went quite mad in London and represented it as a sort of luxurious country hotel, and poor George — "

"Fell for it," finished Brian, sitting on the top step and roaring with mirth.

"Enjoy yourself," said Aunt Flora, looking down at him. "I don't know where Jonny's going to put you — "

"She isn't going to put me," said Brian. "I've put myself — I didn't know whether you had a houseful or not, and I've hired the last room at the local."

"Well, that's a relief," said Aunt Flora. "You'll be comfortable with old Pollitt. Tell him you're a sort of relation of mine and he'll look after you properly."

"You'll be here to lunch," I put in, more as a statement than a question.

"And tea and dinner and to-morrow's breakfast, please," said Brian. "In fact, just leave a plate there all the time."

"Well, come and tell us all your news," said Phyl.

I fetched drinks, and we settled down to listen to Brian's account of himself and his plans. Phyl lay in her long chair and Brian lounged on the end of it, while Aunt Flora and I sat in deck chairs just out of the sun.

"It's grand here," said Brian, lighting his pipe and looking round with appreciation.

We all agreed that it was.

"The journey wasn't exactly easy," continued Brian. "You're rather off the beaten track."

"All the better," I said. "It keeps the crowds away."

"I suppose it does," agreed Brian. "You've got a nice-looking house."

"It wasn't nice looking," said Phyl. "We made it like that. If you'd seen that garden sixteen months ago you would have called it a wilderness."

"And I made it flower," said Aunt Flora with pride. "What you see around you, my dear Brian, is the result of unremitting labour."

"It was fun," I added reminiscently. "Painting and measuring and polishing, and watching it get more and more beautiful."

Brian smiled at my enthusiasm. "Well, it is beautiful," he said. "I suppose Phyl did no end?"

"She did absolutely nothing, of course," said Aunt Flora. "But she did make one or two quite helpful suggestions now and again."

"I know the sort of thing," said Brian. "She sat just like this in this chair, watching you all and occasionally waving a hand and saying: 'A little more that way, I think, Jonny.' Isn't that it?"

The description was not so far from the truth, and we laughed and admitted it.

"It's a wonder she doesn't take root in one spot," said Brian, looking with affection at Phyl. "Do you think," he asked her, "you could manage to walk as far as the Inn and wait while I unpack some holiday clothes?"

Phyl thought she could.

"Perhaps that girl will be there," Brian said hopefully. "There was a perfect beauty in the bus with me — dark red rose sort of thing. She got off and went into the Inn, but by the time I got there she had vanished, and as far as I can make out she isn't in the place."

"Did you go into all the rooms?" inquired Phyl with amusement.

"No," said Brian. "I didn't think of it, but there was no sign of her, and mine was the only name in the little book downstairs."

"Horrid disappointment for you," said Phyl with lazy sympathy. "We'll try and track her down."

Brian looked at her with a heavy frown.

"You're not jealous, I see," he remarked. "But wait until you see her — you'll cling to me like a leech."

"I'd rather be a limpet," murmured Phyl.

"As you like," said Brian, " — as long as you cling."

As they departed I saw George and the children in the distance, and realized with a start that it must be nearly lunch-time. I hurried indoors to make preparations for the meal, and made large quantities of cider cup to assuage the thirst I knew the children would bring back.

We sat down to lunch feeling that the family was growing rather rapidly — first Diana, then George, and finally Brian being added to our circle. Everybody was in the best of spirits, and even George, who regarded Brian as one of the family and therefore privileged to witness all his ill-humours, was good-tempered and very amusing.

Everybody seemed sleepy after lunch. It was showery but very warm. The children got books and lay on a rug on the verandah. Phyl dozed in her chair and Brian put up the rather dilapidated hammock and climbed into it, looking comfortable but precarious.

George decided that after his strenuous morning he deserved a good sleep and went upstairs to have it, and Aunt Flora looked with contempt on the assembly of drones, and went in to do her accounts, which were a source of great trouble to her and indeed to us all, as we were liable to be called upon to unravel the dreadful knots she got into over the various columns.

I walked slowly down through the village to see Ruth Exley. She found it difficult to come and see us when her husband was busy, and I liked to talk to her. The way through the fields was pleasanter but too wet today. I found her in the kitchen preparing to do an afternoon's baking, and for a restful and delightful hour watched her mixing, beating, weighing and rolling out pastry, a snowy overall over her dress, and her sleeves rolled back above the elbow. She was always glad to see me, and we chattered happily about meals and children, our principal preoccupations, with a little village gossip now and again or even a word or two on world affairs, although it was a relief to get back to Ivan's slight cold or Polly's dislike of carrots.

I could not stay long, as Carrie was out and I had to prepare tea. I refused Ruth Exley's invitation to have some with her and made my way towards home.

I walked slowly, and went up the slope

towards the gate admiring the freshness of the green after the rain. When I was half-way up I saw an unfamiliar figure walking ahead of me — a young, slender form with dark hair curling loosely, and pretty ankles. I wondered whether this could be Brian's dark red rose.

The girl hesitated and stopped, and as I came abreast of her and glanced at her face, I knew with certainty that she was.

I stared for a moment into a pair of deep blue eyes under long, thick black lashes and hurried past feeling a little confused and hoping I had not stared too long. As my confusion faded, I found to my annoyance that I had gone past my own gate. I turned back and saw with astonishment that the girl had vanished again. As Brian had explained at lunch to an interested George, "There she was, and there she wasn't!"

As I turned into the gate, however, I found her in front of me again, and she turned and waited for me.

We met and smiled at one another. I hoped fervently that Polly would look like this when she grew up; her hair was as dark though not so soft, and her eyes were as blue.

The girl spoke, and her voice was as charming as her appearance. A frightful thought crossed my mind that this might be another young woman looking for George, but it passed as I looked again at the delicate little face.

"Does Mrs. Manning live here?" she asked.

"I'm Mrs. Manning," I said.

"How do you do," she went on. "I'm Angela Reynolds — I'm afraid the name won't convey anything to you, but I'm Diana's aunt."

I was a little slow at taking this in, being busy fitting the name Angela to the picture and finding that it made a very suitable finish. I wondered who Diana was.

"Diana Kemp's aunt," repeated Miss Reynolds, looking a little puzzled.

I pulled myself together. "Oh — Diana's aunt," I said. "How awfully pleased she'll be to see you. Do come along," I went on, anxious to get my prize inside and exhibit it. "I left the children reading but they may have gone out."

They had; the house was quiet and both Phyl's chair and the hammock were empty. I heard Aunt Flora moving in the drawing-room and took the vision in there.

"Diana's aunt," I announced proudly.

Aunt Flora looked intently at Miss Reynolds for a few moments, and then smiled with complete approval.

"How do you do," she said. "You must be the girl who came down with Brian this morning. He said you were going to the Inn and then you didn't."

"He took the last room," said Miss Reynolds. "The landlord sent me down to someone called Mrs. Trotter — lovely name! — and she took me in."

"I know Mrs. Trotter," said Aunt Flora. "Are you going to stay long?"

The girl smiled at me in a very nice friendly way.

"I ought to have written to you," she said, "but I thought it would be easier to explain. Diana has been on my mind a good deal — I had hoped to have her with me these holidays, as perhaps you heard" — I nodded — "but I couldn't manage it. Then the old lady I work for got ill and is now in a nursing home — and what I really came down for was to take Diana off your hands, and to thank you for being so good as to have her. Miss Crompton told me how kind you were" — she looked at me with an even more friendly look — "and I'm most awfully grateful to you."

The little speech ended, we looked at one another.

"If we had any room," I said, "we would have loved to have you here, but my brother-in-law, George Manning, is with us — "

"I wouldn't have dreamt of it," said Miss Reynolds firmly. "My plan was — if you agreed — to have Diana with me and to be near enough for her to be with your children — her letters have been so happy that I wouldn't like to take her right away."

"You're not going to take her away at all," I said. "If you're not comfortable where you are, we can find you another room somewhere, but Diana must finish the holidays with us."

"I love my room, and it's all very comfortable," said Miss Reynolds, "but

I did want to relieve you of the responsibility of someone else's child in addition to your own."

"I never met a child," said Aunt Flora, "who was less responsibility than Diana. Pity you can't be here with us, but" — she smiled — "let's see as much as possible of you."

There was a shuffling noise upstairs and a door banged, and George's voice was heard at the top of the stairs.

"Where the devil's tea?" he shouted.

Nobody told him, and with a grunt of disgust he started down the stairs. "Car-rie," he roared.

There was no response, Carrie being well on the way into Felling.

"Jon-ny," tried George on a louder note.

"Here," I called from the drawing-room.

"Why the devil don't we have any tea?" asked George irritably. He entered the drawing-room and stood frowning with displeasure. "I'm damned hungry," he said, "and nobody — "

He stopped at the sight of Angela, seated comfortably in a large chair

174

and looking up at him with none of the pleasure usually exhibited by young women at the first sight of George.

"I beg your pardon," he said smoothly, and waited for me to perform an introduction.

Angela smiled and bowed very prettily, but made none of the usual remarks about having seen George before, and they had become such a routine that I thought George was a little at a loss at missing the familiar cue.

"Are you staying long?" he inquired, without betraying too much interest in the matter.

"It depends on how my old lady gets on," smiled Angela, "but I ought to be able to manage the rest of the holidays." She turned to me. "I'm really awfully useful with the young," she said. "If you'll trust yours with me, we'll go on a whole series of expeditions. I've been shut up a bit lately," she ended a little ruefully, "and I'm longing to — to romp."

"I'll do a bit of romping with you," said Aunt Flora. "Sounds attractive. Pity we won't have George with us."

"Are you leaving?" Angela asked him, with merely polite interest.

"I'm down here for a rest," said George, but it didn't sound as good a line as it usually did.

"Well, then, you certainly can't romp," said Angela. "But perhaps I can lure the children away and give you all some well-earned peace."

She was a nice girl, I thought, and seemed to have very sound principles. Not many pretty girls would have spent their holiday amusing a young niece, or taking children out on expeditions.

A noise outside proclaimed the arrival of Brian and Phyl with the children, and Aunt Flora and I awoke to the fact that it was long past tea-time and we had forgotten all about it. Aunt Flora hurried out to the kitchen and I took Angela outside to meet the others.

Brian was delighted with the reappearance of his fellow-traveller, and Diana's greeting, though naturally calm, was warm and happy, and Angela was soon drawn into the fast-widening family circle.

She and Brian made an attempt to

leave after tea, but there was a roar of protest from the children, backed by an announcement from Aunt Flora that they must stay and have supper as it was her night to cook it.

There was a general groan from the family. Aunt Flora's suppers were a weekly feature once again, as they had been in our youth. Every week when Carrie went out, Aunt Flora, who was a capable woman in almost every department of domestic duties but had not the remotest skill with a stove, insisted on cooking the supper. She turned out mysterious and dreadful-looking concoctions, but we had been lusty children with hearty appetites, and the messes disappeared in spite of our grumbles as we dealt with them.

Brian had suffered in the past, and made a noble attempt to save himself and us.

"You sit down and rest," he said, "and I'll produce an astonishing meal. Nothing I can't do in that line. Phyl can be kitchen maid."

"Sit down and rest yourself, my dear fellow," replied Aunt Flora without, gratitude. "If you're good you can do the washing-up."

We assembled at table to find a huge dish full of we knew not what steaming in the centre. Aunt Flora stood, spoon in hand and plates piled before her, waiting for George to say Grace, and proceeded to hand us our portions.

"What is it?" mumbled George, looking at his heap with dislike and suspicion.

"Never you mind what it is," returned Aunt Flora. "Just eat it and stop smelling it in that ill-mannered way."

"It's got a lot of stuff in it," said Polly. "Diana and I helped to make it."

George looked even more disgusted. "If you want to hold cookery classes," he asked Aunt Flora, "why don't you do it when I'm not here?"

"It's not bad," said Paul, who was half-way through his share. "It's rather good, in fact — tastes something like cow cake."

"Probably is cow cake," said George.

Brian, who had been eating with apparent enjoyment, put his fork down and looked suspiciously at Aunt Flora.

"It's awfully good and all that," he

remarked, "but perhaps you'd better confess what's in it."

"Good, solid nutriment," said Aunt Flora. "Nothing but the best ingredients, with every bit of nourishment left in, and nothing thrown down the sink or peeled off or wasted in any way. I wonder you've all got any teeth at all — you hate to have to use them. Not nearly enough coarse food in your diet," she went on warmly, "and a lot too much in the way of messes. Eat it up like a good boy," she ended firmly.

Like all Aunt Flora's dishes, it tasted good enough and there was a good deal of it. Polly and Diana went upstairs soon afterwards, and I felt the first benefit of Angela's good offices when she insisted on my staying downstairs while she put them both into bed. I went up to say good-night later, and found everything in the most perfect order.

Angela and I went downstairs together and found Brian preparing to leave.

"Must get into bed before Aunt Flora's stuff starts taking effect," he said. "I feel a great heaviness in the middle reaches."

"That's only the soya bean flour," said Aunt Flora comfortingly. "It wears off."

"What did you say it was?" asked Brian.

Aunt Flora told him again, and he gaped.

"Do you mean I'm full of soya bean?" he said in a dazed voice.

"We're all full of soya bean," said George. "Every bit of nourishment left in and nothing thrown down the sink."

Brian kissed Aunt Flora solemnly. "If I'm alive in the morning," he said, "it won't be your fault." He rubbed one of Phyl's hands against his cheek. "Good night my sweet-dream of me," he entreated. "Come on, Angela, I'll take you to your Trotter if my soya bean will do the distance."

"It needn't risk it," said George calmly. "I'm taking Angela home."

"You're damn well not," said Brian hotly. "She promised to let me pursue her — didn't you, Angela — and we're going to keep it up until Phyl goes all yellow."

"Green," corrected Phyl lazily.

"All right, green." He waved to

180

George. "You can have all the other women in England," he said generously, "but I'm using this one. Good night, Jonny — thank God I wore my heavy shoes — those what-is-it beans are getting lively. Come on, Angela, my pet."

George watched them out of sight, looking as black as a thunder-cloud, but it might have been the beans.

9

ANGELA'S promised excursions could not take place at once, as I had made an appointment for Polly for the following day with Mr. Crewe, our family dentist in London. Diana begged to be allowed to go with Polly, and Aunt Flora was going up to do some shopping. After some discussion it was agreed that we would take both children and leave Angela to make arrangements with her landlady for the loan or hire of a bicycle belonging to an absent Miss Trotter. This was Aunt Flora's suggestion, and it was a good one, for on bicycles we could be at the sea in a very short time, whereas the bus took a roundabout route through Felling and did not go very near the sea at any point.

"You go with Angela, George," ordered Aunt Flora, "and see that the thing is in riding order."

George, who had not had a close

view of a bicycle since leaving school, promised to make an expert examination before coming to terms.

We gathered on the verandah and looked ourselves over.

"Two children," counted Aunt Flora, "my umbrella, my bag — have you got an extra pocket-handkerchief for the dentist's, Polly?"

Polly had.

"That's a charming hat, Jonny," went on Aunt Flora, looking at me appreciatively.

"It's Phyl's," I said, to the amusement of all present.

"What time will you be back?" asked Phyl.

"I'm not quite sure," answered Aunt Flora, "but we won't be late — the later trains get so crowded." She kissed her as tenderly as though she were going on a voyage of weeks. "Look after her, Brian, and don't keep Carrie's lunch waiting — it makes her so furious."

We proceeded down the drive, Phyl waving from the steps, George and Brian and Paul lounging on the rails and Angela coming as far as the bus to see us off.

We got a little way down the street and heard a shout, and turned to see George running after us waving a sheaf of papers. He caught us up and put them into my hand as we hurried to the waiting bus.

"It struck me you might have time to take these to my agent's office," he said. "There's the address — it isn't half a mile away from old Crewe — just take them in and say I've looked over them and they're all right — and tell him not to give away my hideout," he shouted as the bus began to move. We looked back and saw him standing beside Angela watching the bus disappearing down the street.

"Nice-looking pair," observed Aunt Flora critically.

"Will they get married?" asked Polly without a great deal of interest.

"No," said Diana without hesitation. "Angela hates people what are on the stage. How much money have you got?" she asked, going on to more important matters.

Polly produced a number of silver coins, and Aunt Flora looked at them in astonishment.

"Where in the name of Croesus did

you get all that?" she inquired.

Diana produced a purse stuffed with riches. "I've got ten shillings and fourpence," she announced, after a moment's calculation. "The fourpence was mine before."

"I had ninepence," said Polly. "Two shillings and sixpence from George, two shillings and sixpence from Phyl, that's five shillings and ninepence; two shillings and sixpence from Brian, that's — "

Aunt Flora looked at me with raised eyebrows.

"Did you go round with the hat before leaving," she asked, "or did you forget?"

"It never occurred to me," I said regretfully, and we smiled at one another, remembering the far-distant past when before similar appointments I had made a tour of handy, soft-hearted adults, looking up wistfully and remarking: "I've got to go to that old dentist — oh — thank you *so* much."

I looked at Polly.

"You don't mean to say," I said in horrified tones, "that you actually asked for that money?"

Polly looked back at me calmly.

"Not actually," she said.

Aunt Flora laughed and I opened my bag and arranged George's papers neatly inside.

I left Aunt Flora and the two children at the dentist's door and took a bus to the office of George's agent, whose name, scrawled across the top of the papers in George's handwriting, looked like a child's attempt at a zig-zag. It might, I thought, be Mill, and on inquiring, I was relieved to find that this was correct, and that the gentleman was disengaged.

I was ushered into a beautifully-furnished room with easy chairs and a sofa, rich curtains, some good pictures and a splendid desk in one corner to remind people that they were here on business. My mind made a lightning sketch of the perfect Mr. Mill for this setting — tall and distinguished, with a polished manner. The real Mr. Mill, however, was a great disappointment, being small and rotund, and rather nervous. He bowed me politely to a chair.

"I won't keep you a moment," I assured him, as he was settling himself comfortably in another large chair and looking prepared for a long interview. "I brought these papers from my brother-in-law, George Manning, and he wants you to keep his address secret."

Mr. Mill quite understood the necessity for this. He glanced at the papers and put them aside.

"How is George?" he asked anxiously.

"Very well indeed," I replied, and went on to point out the benefit which George was deriving from the beauty and calm, to say nothing of the comfort and ease of life at Rushing.

"It sounds delightful," said Mr. Mill, with such genuine feeling that I felt proud of my skill as a descriptive artist.

"That lovely stillness;" he went on — "that deep hush — it's healing in itself don't you think?"

I bowed my head in agreement, and wondered if this is what had happened when Phyl described the farm to the tired and jaded George. I began to wish I had sent the papers up by the office-boy, and rose with a feeling that I must get away before Mr. Mill expressed a desire to visit this earthly paradise.

He got to his feet and looked round his domain with a newly-awakened distaste.

"You've made me feel caged — cooped up," he said, smiling at me as he took my hand and shook it warmly. "You've made me think of trees and streams and lovely gardens." He opened the door reluctantly and followed me on to the landing, looking wistful. I reached across him and pressed the lift bell lingeringly, but before it appeared Mr. Mill had made his decision.

"Please tell George," he said, "that I shall come down and see him — no business, you understand — just a visit. It will be a great pleasure," he added warmly, "to see you again."

"That," I thought, "must be Phyl's hat."

"It's unfortunate that my house is full," I began — but he broke in protestingly, as Angela had done.

"Even in your delightful retreat," he said, handing me gallantly into the lift, "there will be an Inn."

Feeling furious with myself for my stupidity, I hurried back to Aunt Flora and the children.

"What upset you?" asked Aunt Flora as we sat later at lunch in our usual restaurant. "The agent fellow didn't make advances to Phyl's hat, surely?"

I reassured her on this point. "But I know now," I went on, "how it was that Phyl lost her head and reeled off pastoral poems to George before he came down to us. I did the same just now" — Aunt Flora looked apprehensive — "at first, I think, out of pride because I wanted him to picture George in a suitable setting, and later because somehow, I found myself growing lyrical about the place. After all," I said defensively, "it is lovely — it has all we claim for it."

"It is, and it has," agreed Aunt Flora, "but people have odd ideas nowadays about what they call essentials. Nature doesn't provide good plumbing and a regular bus service, and yet those who are used to these things regard them as so natural that they can't contemplate being without them."

"But," I pointed out, "it's the people who have the best plumbing and all those things, who sigh most loudly — like Mr.

Mill — for 'trees and streams and lovely gardens'."

"Well, don't worry," said Aunt Flora, gathering up her things. "If he comes down and thinks George isn't being suitably nursed, he'll remove him at once and then we can all have our furniture and pictures back again."

This was indeed looking on the bright side, and I put the matter out of my mind and gave my attention to the children, who were protesting against spending the afternoon in shops.

Aunt Flora agreed with them, although it was pouring in torrents and there was no question of being out of doors.

"You take them to the waxworks or a cinema," she said, "and give them some tea and I'll meet you on the quarter-to-five train." She put up her umbrella and stepped out hardily into the downpour and I remained sheltering in the restaurant entrance with the children.

"Cinema or waxworks?" I asked them.

"Waxworks," they answered unhesitatingly, "but the Chamber of Horrors as well."

We waited until our bus drew up close

by, and I spent a rather exhausting afternoon answering questions and walking slowly from one exhibit to another. I shied at the Horrors, and Polly and Diana, after urging me to be a sport, saw that I was resolved not to be, and went in alone. They had been in several times before — I had arrived too late to stop Polly on the first occasion, and had dreaded her reactions, but she emerged with an unmoved countenance, and afterwards recounted all the details with great relish, ending by observing patronizingly that it would be horrible "if it was real".

We had tea and were on the platform in good time, and presently Aunt Flora appeared looking pleased with herself, carrying several parcels and wearing a new hat, regardless of the rain, which still poured down.

Our train was rather late getting into Felling, but there was no fear that the admiring Duff would not be waiting for Aunt Flora. He relieved her of her parcels and handed her into the seat beside him, holding an umbrella over her while she was in the open, and putting a large mackintosh over her when she was settled in her place.

There was no sign of life when we entered our gate, but inside the drawing-room was a scene of warmth and comfort. A bright fire was burning; Phyl lay on a sofa, her hands clasped behind her head, looking with lazy amusement at Brian and Angela, who sat on the floor with Paul and studied a map of the district. George was in a deep chair with the dogs round him and Rex's head on his knee.

The noisy welcome from the dogs disturbed the quiet scene as we entered, and there was a general move to relieve us of our parcels.

"Did you get wet?" asked Angela anxiously.

"I don't think so," said Aunt Flora, "but the children had better have hot baths before their supper. Has it rained all day here?"

"Poured," said Brian. "Didn't you notice how your kennel had grown?"

"Rex's kennel," corrected Aunt Flora. "No, I didn't see it, but I shall be delighted if you've got on with it."

"We did heaps," said Paul. "What did you bring me?"

"Everything that your mother put on the list," replied Aunt Flora, settling herself in a deep chair and holding her feet to the fire. "Vests, house-shoes — "

"Oh — those!" said Paul with disgust. "School stuff. What did you bring *me*?"

"Wait and see," said Aunt Flora. "Go along to the kitchen and tell Carrie we're all starved and need an early supper."

"Carrie isn't there," said Paul, "she went up to her room early, but she left supper ready."

"Up to her room!" exclaimed Aunt Flora in astonishment. "Why?"

"You forgot," said Phyl, "that this is one of her listening evenings."

Carrie had a wireless set in her room, and kept a weekly chart on which she marked the days and times of the performances of her favourite comedians. She ordered her work to fit in with these times, and retired to her room to listen and laugh. Her reappearances were a little trying, for she recounted each joke with roars of laughter and assured us between them that if that man got any funnier she would be fit to kill herself.

Angela went upstairs with the children and Aunt Flora's eye roamed the drawing-room in search of volunteers or pressmen.

"George, you and Paul go and get the supper," she commanded. "And bring in some more coal," she added, looking at the coal scuttle, which required replenishing.

George settled himself more comfortably in his chair.

"I'm here for a rest," he reminded her. "Brian and Paul can do it."

"I can't do it," said Brian, "I'm a visitor, dammit."

"So'm I," said George.

Phyl got to her feet, stretched luxuriously, and slipped her arm into Paul's.

"We'll do it," she said, which meant, as Paul understood perfectly, "You'll do it and I'll watch."

"Good girl," said Brian approvingly, stretching himself comfortably on the sofa she had vacated. "I like to see a nice, homey, domestic type of woman like you. Hurry with the food, my sweet," he urged. "The stomachs of the men are totally empty."

Aunt Flora snorted, and swept upstairs to tidy herself, and I followed, hearing shouts of laughter from the bathroom as I passed it on my way to my room.

We all felt better after a hot, substantial supper, and gathered in the drawing-room for the evening, while the rain beat on the windows.

"Let's play bridge," suggested George, looking at everybody but Aunt Flora.

"What a good idea," she said. "Get the card-table and we'll cut to see who'll be the first four."

George looked gloomy. "You'll be tired after your long day," he said with unusual consideration. "Sit by the fire and take it easy."

"Nonsense," said Aunt Flora. "Get out those nice new cards with the pretty ladies on the back and deal me a nice grand slam."

George put the table up without enthusiasm, and Brian, who had had some experience of Aunt Flora's bridge, looked apprehensive.

Angela, it was discovered, did not

know how to play bridge, and preferred to sit on the hearthrug playing simpler card games with the children.

I wanted to mark Paul's new clothes, and to the great relief of everybody, Aunt Flora remembered that she had to do her accounts after her shopping.

"Bother the things," she said irritably. "But if I don't put down the items while I remember them, I shall get at sixes-and-sevens."

"Jonny, you'll have to play," said Brian. "I'll mark the clothes for you some other time. Come on and cut for partners."

George gave the pack an experienced fling and drew out a card. Phyl and I drew, and Brian with great care selected a card and turned it over, disclosing an ace.

"Jonny and Phyl," he announced, looking at the upturned cards. "Oh, damn, the men can't play together. Jonny and I will take on the family. Phyl, you can choose seats."

"I want the one near the fire," said Phyl.

"Well, you can't have it," said George,

"that means I have to sit on that beastly low one."

This created an impasse until it was discovered that Aunt Flora could sit comfortably on the low one by the fire and exchange hers with George. This done, the two groups settled down to their games, and Aunt Flora knitted her brows and concentrated on the dreadful business of settling her accounts.

"I can't remember," Phyl complained, "what the answer is when your partner calls that forcing bid and you haven't got anything."

"You're not playing those silly conventions again, are you?" inquired Aunt Flora, looking at us over her reading-glasses.

We informed her that we were, and she fidgeted angrily. "Why can't you play real bridge?" she asked fretfully.

"Because it went out in eighteen-ninety-six, my dear Aunt Flora," George told her. "It's your turn to call, Jonny, and in case you've forgotten, I said one heart and Brian one spade, but I don't know what he's calling on because I've got all his honours."

"Has he, Brian?" I inquired anxiously.

"He's lying," Brian reassured me. "You just put me up to game and we'll romp home."

"Quiet please," said Aunt Flora. "I can't think properly when you're chattering. What a dreadful hand you've got, Phyl," she continued, leaning forward and looking commiseratingly at the cards in question. "Regular what-is-it — I never can remember the name when you've only got the twos and threes of everything."

"Well, that helps a bit," said Brian. "George can't go up to four with the ten of spades and a Yarborough."

"Stop peeking," said Phyl severely to Aunt Flora, "and go on with your adding-up."

"I can't," complained Aunt Flora. "George will have to do it when he's dummy." She went back to her columns and Brian surveyed my satisfactory dummy and proceeded to deal swiftly and competently with the game.

"Four spades," he announced presently with satisfaction. "Not that they were really there, but that's where skill comes in. Whose deal is it?"

"Well, the cards are on my right," said George, "but I think Phyl was playing with them. It's her deal."

"It isn't," I said, "George dealt last and it's Brian's, but I don't really mind."

"Well, we'd better stick to the rules," said George, cutting the cards for Brian.

"You've got to be dummy this time, George," said Aunt Flora firmly. "I can't make head or tail of this mix-up."

"I'll do your additions for you," offered Polly, who with Diana was preparing to go to bed.

"Well, you can try," said Aunt Flora. "That's the column, but it's a bit difficult for you."

"No, it isn't a bit," said Polly.

Brian, having put me up on a shocking hand in order, as he explained when putting it down, to be dummy and get a rest, watched my struggles with admiration.

"Keep it up," he urged, "and we shan't be more than three down."

"Having no more diamonds, partner?" inquired George automatically.

"Well, now you come to mention it," said Phyl, "I've got two, but they

199

can't claim a revoke because we said it first."

This caused a major fracas, and Aunt Flora called us to order.

"What's eighty-nine pence?" inquired Polly.

"Bless me, how do I know?" said Aunt Flora. "You're supposed to be telling me."

"It's seven shillings and five pence," said Angela.

"Then I put the five in the pence column and carry seven, don't I?" asked Polly.

"Yes," said Angela.

"Well, I can't," complained Polly, "because Aunt Flora's got a nine in the pence column."

"I wouldn't worry with it to-night, my pet," said Aunt Flora, taking back the book. "Thank you for helping. George can do it now he's dummy." She handed the book to George and he pored over it with a frown.

"What an incredible mix-up!" he exclaimed.

"That's what I told you," said Aunt Flora. "There" — she pointed — "is what I spent to-day, and that's what I took out of the bank and that's what I've got left."

"But that's more than you took out," said George.

"Yes — isn't it puzzling?" said Aunt Flora.

George pushed his chair back from the table and bent his head over the figures. "What's S.F.J. written across this figure for?" he inquired.

"That's Spent for Jonny," explained Aunt Flora.

"Well, what's that doing down at all?" inquired George.

"Well, I spent it and she has to give it back, but I haven't told her what it is yet."

"But why put it down at all?" asked George reasonably. "Make a separate account for her and don't enter it in here."

"Don't be silly," said Aunt Flora. "of course I must enter it. I spent it, didn't I?"

"No, you didn't," said George, keeping his temper. "Jonny did."

"You don't listen," complained Aunt

Flora. "I've told you she doesn't even know about it."

"But you spent it for her."

"Yes, with *my* money, and so it's got to go into *my* accounts," said Aunt Flora with finality.

George gave her a cold look and turned his gaze once more on to the book.

"What's G.K.?" he asked.

"Well, there are so many things I don't remember to put down at once," said Aunt Flora in excuse. "I can't carry them about for long in my head and sometimes I know I've spent it but it's impossible to — "

"Well, what's G.K.?" repeated George impatiently.

"I'm telling you, my dear boy. God Knows — "

George handed back the book.

"My dear Aunt Flora," he said, "if I were you I would put a large G.K. right across the page."

"Thank you, George," said Aunt Flora with genuine gratitude. "I'll do it at once."

10

THERE was no rain during the night, and the next morning at breakfast there were signs of a heat mist. By the time Brian appeared, which he usually did before breakfast was over, the mist had cleared and the sun shone warmly.

"Some coffee, Brian?" I inquired.

"Thanks," he said, pulling up a chair between Polly and Phyl, who for the period of Brian's visit brightened the breakfast table with her presence.

"Where's George?" he inquired. "Shall I go and turn him out?"

George's appearance at this moment saved him the trouble, and I saw for the first time the benefit that the change, whether of air, scene or company, had wrought in him. He no longer looked tired, his face had filled out, and his expression, absent and serious as he stood at the sideboard weighing the respective merits of porridge or stewed fruit, had lost its strain.

Aunt Flora looked at him with satisfaction and passed him his coffee and the morning paper.

"It's going to be a fine day," she remarked. "You children ought to ask Angela to take you for a swim."

"Not us," said Paul. "The girls can go. We're meeting at the Camp to-day."

Polly and Diana thought that a swim would be a very good idea, and departed in the direction of Mrs. Trotter's to discover what Angela thought about it.

"You two men," went on Aunt Flora, "could just about finish the kennel if you set about it."

This raised very little enthusiasm, and Brian, who was in very good spirits and had an air of being very pleased with life, announced that he would give up his day to doing whatever Phyl commanded.

"Kennel," said Phyl instantly, to Aunt Flora's delight.

I heard hammering as I made beds upstairs and came down later in the morning to find George and Brian working busily while Phyl lay in her chair and read the paper. Angela and the girls had gone seawards with bicycles and bathing suits.

"Where's Aunt Flora?" I inquired.

"She's taken all the dogs for a walk," said Phyl. "The boys are at their meeting."

This was apparent from the sounds proceeding from the distant field and the figures of late-comers hurrying across our orchard on their way to the gathering.

"What do all those kids do?" asked Brian, resting from his labours and looking across at the fields. "I say, George," he went on, without waiting for an answer, "I think a game of cricket wouldn't be a bad thing — the grass has dried a good bit."

George looked at him with approval of this scheme gradually dawning in his eyes.

"You're right," he said at last. "Let's go. Have they got the things out there?"

I told him they had, and Rex, bounding on to the verandah twenty seconds later, was disgusted to find that those builder fellows who had been getting on so well with his house had vanished again. Only the difficulty he had with the language prevented him from saying what he thought of them. Aunt Flora, who did not labour under this disadvantage, expressed his feelings for him in a very thorough way.

I went to the kitchen and returned with a large basket of peas and a basin and settled myself in a deck-chair to shell them.

"I'll come and help you," said Aunt Flora, and, bringing the second chair, settled herself beside me. She shelled busily, but her mind was not on the work and she popped the pods with absent-minded energy, causing showers of peas to scatter themselves on the ground round our feet. I drew her attention to this fact, but she went recklessly on, her sharp pops alternating with the louder report of the cricket ball being hit. I felt it would be wise to retrieve some of the peas, and crawled round picking up the fallen ones.

"I've got a wonderful idea, Jonny," she said presently. "It came to me while I was out with" — she turned towards my chair and found that I was missing. "God bless my soul," she exclaimed, looking round and discovering me on the ground some distance away, "what on earth are you grovelling about on the ground for?"

"I'm getting the peas into the basin," I replied a little tartly. "It's a somewhat roundabout route — but I think most of them will get in in the end."

"Well, stop playing marbles and listen to me for a few minutes," said Aunt Flora.

I re-seated myself and gave her my attention.

"It's about George," she said, "George and the neighbours. He's looking fit now and I think we ought to do something in the way of entertaining — people have been very delicate, but I do think they'd like to come and talk to him, God knows why. What do you think of asking everybody to tea one day — out of doors?"

"What do you mean by 'everybody'?" I enquired.

"Well, I don't mean everybody," elucidated Aunt Flora. "I mean all our friends, like the Colonel and those two poor girls, May and Whoisit, and the Exleys, and of course Miss Peel, and

Angela will want Mrs. Trotter to come, and Brian can ask Pollitt, and Nobby will want the Stebbings. The Wheelers are away, thank God — I couldn't have borne those two dreadful girls, although I shall miss young Bobby."

As there was nobody on this list but those whom Aunt Flora considered People Like Ourselves, there was no point in suggesting that such assorted ingredients might have the effect of producing a heavy mixture. Rushing was well used to Aunt Flora's overlooking of the orthodox social layers.

"When you've got them all here, what will you do with them?" I inquired.

"Well, if we could only choose a fine day," said Aunt Flora, "I thought we'd put tables in the garden and have a sort of mild garden party — games, perhaps."

"We haven't a tennis-court," I pointed out, "and I can't see May and Claudia sending up the score in rounders."

Aunt Flora looked disapprovingly at me.

"My dear Jonny," she said mildly, "I do think that sort of destructive criticism is useless and a little foolish, and I've always discouraged it in you children" — Aunt Flora had gone back thirty years — "if you think the idea impracticable, say so at once, and if you approve of it, try and improve on it."

I murmured an apology, and popped peas with genuine contrition.

"We'll put it to the vote at lunch time," said Aunt Flora, rising and causing a cascade of peas which had gathered on her lap. "I'm going in now, if you can manage the rest yourself."

I thought I could, and proceeded with the task.

Aunt Flora went out shortly to lunch with May and Claudia. Our own lunch was a noisy affair, and a fierce argument developed as to whether the cricketers were to spend the afternoon at the sea with the ladies, or return with the gentlemen to the field. Polly and Diana, themselves no mean performers in the water, had been astounded at the form shown by Angela. Phyl, languid and passive on land, became a creature of speed and power in the water, and Angela was the first woman in Polly's experience who came anywhere near Phyl as a swimmer.

"I bet she can beat you, Phyl — I bet you," she said excitedly, leaning forward and addressing Phyl across the intervening forms of Brian and Angela.

Phyl smiled lazily at Angela.

"Of course Angela can beat her," said Brian. "She's twenty years younger."

"Twenty years?" echoed Polly, aghast.

"Twenty years," repeated Brian firmly, "and Phyl hasn't swum for ages and she'd probably sink at once if she tried now. I'll put my half-crown on Angela."

"I wouldn't," said Paul. "I haven't seen Angela, but Phyl left me miles behind the day George came down, and that isn't long ago."

"You surprise me," said George. "It feels like a lifetime. Personally," he continued, eyeing Angela speculatively, "I'm backing Phyl. After all, I taught her — "

"You didn't," said Phyl. "I was miles better than you until you were nearly sixteen."

"Well, let's go and see," said the practical Diana. "I'll bet on Angela but I

210

don't want to risk a whole half-crown."

"A what?" inquired Paul.

"A whole half — oh you know what I mean," said Diana in disgust.

"Don't go this afternoon," begged Paul, looking across at George. "Let the girls go and they can tell us who won and we can go back and finish our game. After all," he added, "all those other fellows will want to go on."

"True, quite true," said Brian, "and what's more, your dear uncle and I have no bicycles, and nothing would induce me to enter that bus on a day like this."

"And if you wait until to-morrow," went on Paul, "I'll get Ivan to borrow his father's bike for George, and you can get one from old Pollitt and then we can all go."

"And it'll be pouring with rain," said Polly furiously, recognizing that the decision had gone against the swimmers. "You and your beastly cricket."

"You can join in if you like," said Paul, with a victor's generosity.

Polly opened her mouth to tell him what she thought of this proposal, but Diana spoke first.

"Angela," she said without emotion, "is a demon bowler."

Brian whistled and all eyes were turned on Angela, who in a voice as calm as her niece's, said: "Yes, I am."

"You mean," said George, "that you can get all the little fellows out with ease."

"I mean," said Angela, "that I can get all the big fellows out with ease."

Brian was busy emptying all the half-crowns out of his pocket and counting them anxiously.

"My dear Angela," said George, leaning his arms on the table and addressing her in his low, quiet, beautiful voice, "I don't want to lower your prestige before our respective nieces, but I can almost claim to be a demon batsman."

"In your day, no doubt," began Angela with a smile.

"Twenty years ago," yelled Polly.

"Order, order," said Brian, knocking on the table. He rose and prepared to address the gathering.

"I have stood in this market-place," prompted Paul.

" — for twenty years," continued

Brian, amid laughter. "I hereby challenge the cockahoop Angela Reynolds to join our game and knock out the aforesaid George — "

"He wasn't aforesaid," pointed out Paul.

"Well, the undermentioned — "

"All right, darling, we get the idea," said Phyl kindly. "What does Angela get if she does it?"

"The awards," said Brian, "will be numerous. My half-crown, and George's and Diana's — how much is it?" he asked her.

Diana looked at George as speculatively as he had looked at her aunt a few minutes before.

"All my money," she said firmly, and the room rang with applause.

"Will that be enough in the way of awards, Miss Reynolds?" inquired Brian. "If you do this foul deed, of course George will never speak to you again."

"Add that to the list of awards," said Angela carelessly.

George bowed, and the two looked at each other. George, I think, saw her for the first time.

213

A delicious peace descended on the house a little later, and when Carrie departed on a visit to Felling shortly after lunch, I was left alone in the house, and the unusual silence so soothed me that I found myself nodding over my clothes-marking, and decided to give myself the luxury of ten minutes' sleep. I made myself comfortable on the sofa in my bedroom, and before I had time to feel guilty, fell fast asleep.

I awoke to find Phyl standing in the doorway, one hand on the door-knob.

"I'm afraid I woke you," she said apologetically. "I didn't dream you'd be asleep."

"It was lovely," I said, with a satisfying yawn. "What happened?"

"She did it," said Phyl. "It really is true — she's an amazing bowler — sends them with a terrifying screw. Brian, of course, just fooled — he yelled when the ball came at him, and ran in terror and the stumps went down with a lovely crash. I wonder the yells didn't wake you."

"And George?" I asked.

"He did his best," replied Phyl, "but

there's something awfully cool about Angela. I don't know whether you've noticed. George can rather put people off their stroke, as you know, when he turns on all the batteries, but this girl doesn't seem to be at all affected. Of course George didn't mind being bowled, but I think he was a bit baffled by this serenity — this calm assumption that he is, after all, just another fellow."

"Isn't he?" I asked.

"No — not quite," said Phyl. "I don't want to overlook his faults, but it's ridiculous to deny that he has more than his share of good looks and charm. I sometimes wonder if Angela is putting up a screen to hide the real effect he has on her."

"No," I said at once. "I think she really has a strong prejudice against actors, and you forget that she has seen plenty of George in his home-circle moods."

"That's true," admitted Phyl, "and she's such a lovely creature that she must be used to pursuit. She's probably in love with someone and has no room in her heart, as the singers put it, for George."

She paused and looked thoughtful, one hand playing with the fringe of the rug I had thrown over my feet.

"That reminds me, Jonny," she said, "I came up here to talk to you about something — "

She stopped for so long that I realized she had forgotten the beginning of her sentence. I wriggled my feet under the rug to recall her wandering attention, and she looked up with a start.

"You came up here," I said, "to ask me about something. I know what the something is, but you'd better tell it in your own words."

Phyl stared at me. "Do you really know?" she asked slowly.

"I'm only making a guess," I said. "Isn't it about Brian?"

"Yes, it's about Brian," said Phyl. "Is it so obvious?"

"I don't know what you mean by obvious," I said. "You come down and eat breakfast for the first time for years, and you go out with him without coming to me and asking me why he can't find a nice suitable young girl and leave you alone, and he hasn't once come to me to tell me that he has loved you hopelessly for ten years and it's driving him mad and won't I do something about it."

Phyl smiled in a rather troubled way.

"It's odd, Jonny," she said, "that at those times in your life when you really need a clear head everything goes hazy and muddled — at least that's my experience. I could reason quite clearly about Brian a month ago — and now — " Her voice trailed into silence.

"Did this happen when you met him in London last time?" I asked.

"No," said Phyl. "That was the usual meeting with the usual arguments and the usual awful business of feeling he was miserable and not being able to help him. When he came here I felt happier, and went on feeling happier." She broke off. "I'm sorry if I'm drivelling," she said. "I'm such an awful fool, Jonny. I've made up my mind that I love him, but I'm awfully frightened about — about starting again. Tell me — if a Brian turned up for you, would you marry him and begin all over again?"

"I don't think so," I replied honestly, "but the cases are hardly parallel. There isn't much between us in age, but there's a lot in appearance and temperament. I'm a made-by-the-million, ordinary, pleasant, domesticated type absorbed in bringing up two children. Perhaps I ought to make less of them and more of myself, but I enjoy working for them and I'm happy — I thought I never could be without Hugh, but I find that I am. I suppose people who lose a leg or an arm or their sight, find the same thing after a time — there's always something missing, but life goes on. You're different," I said after a while. "Women who look like you, are made for — other things," I ended lamely. "I look just right at Rushing with Aunt Flora and Carrie and the children, but it isn't your setting — you should be where people can see you — you look out of place at a sink. I think you and Brian could be very happy."

"So do I," said Phyl, "but I feel sorry somehow that Brian is losing something — sorry that he isn't going to marry someone younger — someone fresh and — oh, you know what I mean," she said helplessly. "It's all so different from the first time, and I'm afraid I'm

218

cheating Brian out of something almost enchanted."

"I wouldn't worry about that, Phyl," I said gently. "Brian wants to marry the present-day you, not the person you were five or ten years ago. He's asking for something that you can give him in full — and although mine is perhaps a biased view, I think he's getting an awful lot."

Phyl smiled mistily. After a while she looked at me earnestly.

"Do you ever feel — lonely?" she asked.

I smiled. "Not in the way you mean," I said. "When I see happy women with their husbands, I get a rather dreadful sensation — a sort of jealousy, I suppose — and in a childish way; I hate being without a male escort on those few occasions on which I do make public appearances. I loathe poking my head into box offices — I feel that's purely a man's department."

"I know what you mean," interrupted Phyl smilingly. "You stand, perfectly gowned, in the foyer, the focus of all eyes — "

"Exactly," I said. "While in the

background a privileged male fumbles in his pocket and bends down and pokes his head into that little hole and gets the best seats and, taking me gently by the arm, leads me into my stall."

We laughed.

"I like the picture," I said, "but I should hate the reality. Nothing could sound more humdrum than living at Rushing, sewing and mending and helping Carrie, and yet I don't want anything else and I'm quite happy."

"Do you believe all those things people say about repression?" asked Phyl.

"Of course I do," I said. "I think you've been as happy as I have here, but I'm certain that if you hadn't known that at any time you were free to go away and marry Brian, you would have suffered from whole layers of repression. You would have come out in spots," I ended with relish.

"I don't believe it," she answered. "But, joking aside, won't you ever want anything else?"

"No," I said with conviction. "One can burn up a good deal of emotional fuel in twelve years. If I feel any spots coming when I'm sailing into those roaring forties," I promised, "I'll send you an urgent summons."

We were silent for a long time, busy with our own thoughts, and finally I shook off the rug and my dreamy mood, and recalled Phyl to the present.

"Carrie's out until six," I told her, "and I've got to make tea. What a good thing Brian hasn't any illusions about your capacities in the domestic sphere. He won't expect any comfort in the home."

"But sailors don't care, do they?" asked Phyl.

"Uncle Edward was once a sailor," I reminded her, "and Aunt Flora says he would never have become the man he did if only his wife had made him happier at home."

"Perhaps she hadn't my allure," suggested Phyl, following me downstairs. "You will say some nice things to Brian when you see him, won't you, Jonny?" she added anxiously — "about my virtues and how fortunate he is, and so on."

"When are you going to tell Aunt Flora?" I asked.

"Brian's going to do it in the good old formal way," replied Phyl. "Is she going to be home to tea?"

I didn't know, as she very often stayed to tea before returning from the Colonel's, and an unexpected and sharp shower had fallen a little earlier and might have delayed her; but a quarter of an hour later there was a dreadful medley of loud sounds, dogs barking, children returning and the village departing homewards. I had laid tea on the verandah, and took out two plates piled high with bread and butter, and saw Aunt Flora coming up the drive and hungry forms approaching from the field. Aunt Flora was wearing an old mackintosh of the Colonel's and the dogs leaped and barked in welcome round her. The cricketers made a concerted rush to wash their hands, and I helped Aunt Flora off with the mackintosh.

"Was it nice?" I asked, "or was there too much scrapping?"

"There wasn't a single fight," replied Aunt Flora. "Claudia had been ill all night and looked wretched, and May was being positively affectionate. Oh, Jonny," she exclaimed suddenly in accents of distress, "look at this appalling rent in the Colonel's mac. Oh, Rex, you bad, bad dog," she went on, "look what you've done." She shook the damaged part angrily at Rex, and Rex looked at it in an interested way. Aunt Flora's distress was very great, and tea was held up while we examined the damage.

"He won't mind," said Polly, "it's an awfully old mac . . . "

Aunt Flora looked at her with severity.

"It may be an old mac," she said, "but it was serviceable, and people do not borrow things and return them in damaged condition."

Polly wilted.

"I'll mend it after tea," I promised. "Come and eat something."

Aunt Flora came to the table, but refused my offer of mending. "I'll do it this evening," she said glumly. She sewed beautifully, but hated mending and patching, and preferred to use her skill on lovely colours and beautiful fabrics. Tea over, she settled herself in a corner of the verandah surrounded by dogs and work-baskets. She was fond of the Colonel; she knew that his budget did not include

223

many items of clothing, and was grieved to feel that she had damaged a part of his scant and shabby wardrobe.

"When I've finished this," she said, "nobody will be able to tell where the place was."

I went over and looked at the work. "It's a beastly place, darling," I said commiseratingly. "Tell me when you're tired, and I'll finish it."

"I'm tired of it now," she answered, "but I'm going to finish it myself."

The evening wore on and Aunt Flora sat over her mending, her temper becoming more frayed than the cloth she was repairing.

"Shall I read to you while you're working?" asked Polly.

Aunt Flora looked at her over the end of her spectacles.

"No, thank you," she replied. "I shouldn't be able to enjoy listening until this is done."

"You're doing it too thoroughly," said George, looking over her shoulder at the neat stitches. "A mend in an old mac can surely be allowed to show a little."

"This mend isn't going to show," she

said grimly, "and I'd like you all to go away and leave me in peace."

Nobody went away, however, and by supper-time, Aunt Flora, exhausted and triumphant, announced the completion of the great work, and we all gathered round to examine it. It was certainly a good repair, and almost invisible.

"Well, now we can eat," said Brian with relief. "Come on," he went on, holding out his hand and leading Aunt Flora with ceremony into the dining-room. "The old boy would have preferred nice big stitches which he could have shown people and told them that his friend, Miss Manning, did them for him, but you're a mulish old lady and must have it all your own way." He pushed in her chair for her and leaned down to whisper in her ear. "After supper," he hissed, "I would like an audience in the privacy of your boudoir."

Aunt Flora waved a hand and brushed him away as though he had been a troublesome fly.

"She's yours, my dear boy," she said calmly. "Best thing she could do."

She looked from Phyl, who was staring

at her, to George, who was staring at Brian.

"I never realized before," she said, "how much alike you two are. You look like twin codfish. Will someone," she ended irritably, "kindly sit down and pass the salad?"

11

THE next day was Sunday, and it was, moreover, our Sunday; that is to say, it was the Sunday on which the Vicar of Felling came over and conducted an eleven o'clock service in Rushing Church.

Phyl and the children came down in their church clothes and a little later Aunt Flora appeared looking cool and elegant in a grey suit. She sat down and looked round the table, her eyes coming to rest in disapproval on George's sports shirt.

"You don't propose," she asked, "to come to church in those clothes?"

"No," said George, buttering his toast.

There was a pause.

"Do you propose," asked Aunt Flora, "to come to church at all?"

"No," said George.

The children looked expectant. There was the answer, plain and bold as they had always longed to give it. It was Aunt Flora's turn, and they waited tensely.

227

Aunt Flora frowned across the table and waited for George to look at her. He finished his toast and looked round for a second piece, but as the toast rack was at Aunt Flora's elbow he was obliged to ask her for it.

"Will you please pass the toast?" he asked, looking at her calmly.

"No, I won't," said Aunt Flora. "I don't mind in the least what kind of heathen Chinee life you lead in London, but when you're with me I would like you to conform to the habits in which you were brought up."

"Please pass the toast," replied George. "I'm not going to church. I'm down here for a rest — "

"And a change," put in Aunt Flora neatly.

" — And I'm not going to line up in the family crocodile and file into the family pew."

"Every villager," said Aunt Flora, "knows that you're here, and if you're not at church they'll think that I failed to bring you up as a good Christian."

"Every villager," answered George, getting up and getting the toast, "already knows that every actor leads a life of riotous evil-doing, and I'm not going to shatter the illusion by kneeling in their godly midst."

The children's heads had moved in exact timing from side to side during this exchange, as though they were spectators at a tennis match.

"Do you really mean," asked Aunt Flora slowly, "that you're not coming with us?"

George pushed back his chair. "For God's sake," he said irritably, "can't we talk about something besides church-going — "

There was a welcoming outcry from the dogs, and a moment later a vision appeared in the doorway and hovered there uncertainly, feeling the tension of a family dispute. The children sprang up and Aunt Flora smiled in welcome and admiration.

"Angela! What an enchanting toilette," she said.

It was. She was in a simple, short-sleeved white dress with scarlet buttons; she wore little scarlet gloves and on her dark curls was perched a saucy little hat of scarlet straw. The outfit suited her dark beauty to perfection. She was amused at her little success, and smiled at us happily over the bobbing head of Polly.

"Mrs. Trotter tells me that this is Our Sunday," she said. "Will you let me sit in your pew?"

"It'll be a pleasure," said Aunt Flora. "We're right in front — there's a dreadful draught from behind when the hymn-singing goes on, but we'd love to have you."

Angela laughed. "It's years since I've been into a village church," she said. "I'm looking forward to it."

"It's years since George went into a church of any kind," said Aunt Flora. "I was just trying to work on his feelings."

Angela looked at George, eyebrows slightly raised.

"Don't you give Sunday performances?" she inquired innocently.

George went rather white.

"Not as a rule," he said steadily, "but I make exceptions in good causes, and I think Aunt Flora can be termed a good cause."

"Very handsome of you," said Aunt Flora. "In plain English, do you stay at home or do you come with us?"

"I go with you," said George, looking at Angela.

This little problem settled, nothing remained but to see that the children did not indulge in any romps before church time, as on more than one occasion it had been necessary to effect last-minute changes of attire owing to their having dirtied or damaged their clothes. Nothing of the sort occurred this morning, however, and we sorted ourselves into small groups and set out at intervals, thus giving the congregation time, as Brian expressed it, to adjust themselves between one sensation and the next and so avoid general panic.

Aunt Flora went first with an unwilling George. He wanted very much to go with Angela, and employed great skill in order to bring this about, but as Aunt Flora wished to have him with her, and Angela did not, he found the situation a little beyond his control. He looked extremely displeased as he opened the gate and stood aside for Aunt Flora.

"You're next, Angela," said Brian, "you and your two attendant angels. Off you go, and Phyl and I will count fifty and come after you." He watched the pretty trio departing, and looked at me with a grin. "I think," he said, "that George is soon going on a nice little goose chase, poor devil."

"Won't he catch the goose?" asked Phyl anxiously.

"I'm not betting, my sweet," said Brian, taking her arm and starting off down the drive, "but I'd say not. She hasn't ruffled a feather so far. You're next, Jonny," he called back to me.

I called to Paul and he put down his book reluctantly and joined me. "We the last?" he asked.

"We are," I said.

"I hope," he said gloomily, "they aren't going to have any hymns that Polly knows. She does show off so when she's singing."

This was true. If Polly knew the hymn she found the page eagerly, cleared her throat, took a deep breath and piped for the express benefit of those within earshot. She admired her singing very much. The other children acknowledged that it was good, but were shocked at her unashamed pride in her performances, and considered that singing so loud in church that people in the next rows could hear was a slur on the family.

We reached the church, and in the little porch I saw Miss Peel, and looked surprised, as she was our organist and usually piped a melancholy little tune — it always sounded like the same bars over and over again — for about ten minutes before the Service began.

"Why aren't you playing?" I asked. "Has the organ gone wrong again?"

Miss Peel shook her head, and I saw to my surprise and distress that she was near to tears.

"That woman — that dreadful niece," she began incoherently, and paused to collect herself. "Mr. Kendal's niece walked in just as I was opening the instrument and calmly told me that she was going to play for the service. She didn't even ask if I minded, and now she's sitting there looking so dreadfully — well, showy — and I don't like to speak ill of anybody, but it looks to me as though she's just showing off in front of your brother-in-law. I had to come out for a few moments to recover myself. To be swept off the music stool in that way — "

Miss Peel wiped away a tear. "I'm awfully silly," she apologized. "But I always love being at the organ — my father gave it to the village, you know."

"Come and sit next to us," I invited. "She won't get much satisfaction out of sitting staring at George — he's an expert stare-dodger and she won't get a mite of satisfaction."

"I don't really mind," said Miss Peel, who had pulled herself together, "but it was a little humiliating in front of the two boys."

"Which two boys?" I asked.

"The two who pump for me," said Miss Peel. "Ivan and the other boy — Stebbing. She was very rude to them."

"If she was rude to Ivan," I said, "you needn't give her another thought. Her number is absolutely Up."

With this cheerful and Christian thought we passed into the church and took our places near the assembled family.

Looking at the organist, I was glad that Miss Peel had told me of her presence. What effect she must have had on the unprepared congregation I was unable to judge, but Mr. Kendal's entrance passed almost unnoticed, and his injunction to his flock to kneel and pray was followed with obvious reluctance. Miss Kendal swayed gracefully at the organ when playing was required, and sat back and gazed soulfully at George when it was not. The simple inhabitants of Rushing had never seen anything more startling in their lives than this heavily-made-up charmer, and there was noticeably less coughing and shuffling than usual.

The service proceeded in the normal way until the singing of the first hymn, when the notes of the organ died away and were heard no more. The congregation faltered and then proceeded with the hymn unaccompanied, but it was not a success, and presently the back rows and the front rows were singing different lines simultaneously, and Mr. Kendal, who was a good musician, was looking as though he felt rather ill. Miss Kendal vanished behind the screen in order to look into the causes of the disaster, but I knew my Ivan and trusted him to stand up to the situation like the good fellow he was.

The organ recovered its breath during the prayers that followed, and the first verse of the following hymn was literally a roaring success, but with verse two came another complete breakdown on the part of the instrument, and we struggled to the end to sounds that rendered poor Mr. Kendal white with anguish. His niece was by this time equally white with fury, and some of the sounds resulting from her second disappearance behind the screen were audible even above the wails of the congregation.

Hymn number three, which preceded the sermon, was sung to an accompaniment which came and went in a wheezy and asthmatic manner, very much in the way a breathless person manages to bring out a few gasping words at intervals. We became breathless ourselves before the end, and were relieved to sit down and settle ourselves for the restful period of the sermon. Mr. Kendal unfolded his notes and read them in quiet, level and infinitely soothing tomes. It was a perfect undertone to one's dreaming or scheming, to the old men's dozing and to the children's quiet fidgeting. Miss Kendal no longer stared at George, but brooded in her corner and no doubt meditated murder in her heart against the monkey-faced boy who had made her ridiculous before the assembled company.

I looked from the tall, thin Vicar in the pulpit to his small thin wife in her pew and wondered how they bore the visits of the plump and luscious niece. She was probably, I reflected charitably, one of those unfortunate people with misleading exteriors. Hugh could have told me — men were sometimes better able to judge these things than other women. I remembered the times I had invited quiet, mild-looking women for weekends in the past, and had found Hugh getting behind me for protection. I took another look at the brooding Miss Kendal and decided she could not be the pure and demure miss I was trying to make her. Her garments were designed and made on definitely provocative lines, and sophistication was written on them. I found that my eyes, once focussed on the generous contours, had so much actual acreage to cover that it was some time before I could force them to turn again in the direction of the pulpit, and still longer before my mind caught the drift of Mr. Kendal's sober speech.

We filed out of church without the usual piping of the organ, but heard instead the furious sounds of strife behind the screen. I joined Ruth Exley in the porch and told her Miss Peel's little story.

"So that's it!" she exclaimed. "Stay with me and wait for the pieces," she begged.

As she spoke, her son, quite whole and entirely at ease, emerged from the church and joined us.

"'Morning, Mrs. Manning," he said with his engaging smile. "Are we goin' home with you the same as usual?"

I said that we would be delighted to welcome him, and he turned happily to the group which contained George and which was now breaking up into small parts and moving towards our gate for the usual after-church party on the verandah. He swung into line beside George and Paul, and the latter looked at him sternly and suspiciously.

"What happened to the organ?" he inquired.

"Wouldn't work," replied Ivan carelessly. "Miss What's it," he went on, looking at George, and trying not to appear unduly puffed-up, "said I was a child of Satan."

"Quite so," said George, and Ivan looked as though his cup of happiness was full. It literally ran over a few minutes later, when George took the trouble to pour out some of my home-made ginger beer and hand it to him. George raised his own glass and the two faces vanished in fizz and foam respectively.

May and Claudia were not present, and we learned that Claudia was still unwell and May attending her. Miss Peel, radiant and bright-eyed, her cousin, the Colonel and Mr. and Mrs. Kendal and Mrs. Exley sat or stood talking to the various members of the family, and I was kept busy supplying Brian and Paul with drinks for the company. Miss Kendal, we learned later had refused Aunt Flora's kind invitation to come to the house and had departed Felling-wards in a towering fury. Nobody missed her, and we broke up into groups of varying size and noisiness until Aunt Flora, glass of cider-cup in hand, called us all to attention.

"I think we should drink a toast this morning," she said. "Perhaps you'll propose it, George."

There was a great deal of confusion after this. The Colonel, reading the news in Brian and Phyl's faces, fell to slapping Brian on the back in delighted congratulation. Miss Peel kissed Phyl, Miss Rolfe shook both her hands, the Kendals went from Brian to Phyl and back to Brian in eager questioning and friendly shoulder patting. The children refilled their glasses in noisy merriment, the dogs sensed the excitement and barked noisily. Brian made his way to Phyl and stood with an arm across her shoulders, and finally George, with practised ease, made a slight movement to indicate that he was about to speak.

There was an instant hush.

"Brian and Phyl — long life and happiness," he said simply, and we drank, a dreadful clamour breaking out immediately afterwards from the children, who wanted Brian to respond with a speech. This he declined to do but recognizing that the children were in need of an outlet for their spirits, he led them on a chase through the garden and into the field. They streamed after him, their cries getting fainter, and the visitors prepared to leave.

The Colonel was the last to go, and was halfway down the drive, accompanied by the children, who were back from their run, when Aunt Flora suddenly remembered her labours of the previous evening and called him back.

"Your mackintosh," she explained. "You lent it to me yesterday — go and get it out of the hall, Polly."

Polly returned with the mackintosh and Aunt Flora groped about its folds to locate the repair.

"I ought to tell you," she began "about this — "

"Oh, the tear," said the Colonel,

taking the coat from her and throwing it carelessly over his arm.

"Yes, the tear," said Aunt Flora slowly, looking a him in bewilderment. "How did you — "

"Oh, that's been there years and years," said the Colonel breezily. "Tore it getting through the wire at the back of one of our fields. Not worth mending, I told May, and she entirely agreed with me."

He waved a genial farewell to us all and started on his way once more, leaving behind him a stunned silence. Polly opened her mouth to speak, and after one glance at Aunt Flora's face, shut it again.

There was a strained pause for a few moments, and then Brian, who was behind Aunt Flora, sank quietly into the chair she had occupied while mending the mackintosh. He bent his head and stitched busily at an imaginary tear, his face screwed into an expression of appalling ferocity. The sight was too much for Paul and Polly, who struggled in vain to control their countenances. Aunt Flora, coming out of her stunned silence and looking round, saw with astonishment and alarm that Polly was about to go into an apoplectic fit, and looked to see what was causing it. She watched the unconscious Brian for some moments — he was quite lost in his part, and was biting threads and guiding them through the needle with grim earnestness. Catching Aunt Flora's eye at last, he looked extremely sheepish and ceased his labours, but the tension was broken, and the Colonel must have heard the roars of laughter as the episode of his torn mackintosh passed into the family annals.

12

PHYL and Brian went up to London by an early train the next day and George, who seemed to have spent the night working out new tactics, had an early breakfast and announced to the infuriated Diana and Polly, who were only half-way through their cereal, that he was going to call for Angela. He vanished before the two young ladies could finish their mouthfuls and give vent to their feelings, and they were left gazing speechlessly at one another. Angry frowns were on both faces, but Diana's brow cleared slowly and after a few moments she picked up her spoon and went calmly on with her meal. Polly looked at her.

"Will she go out with George and leave us?" she asked anxiously.

Diana finished a large mouthful and scooped up another spoonful.

"No," she said briefly and calmly and with such complete conviction that

Polly's fears were instantly laid to rest. I glanced at Aunt Flora and saw that she, like myself, would have loved to question the child in order to find out on what grounds her knowledge or conviction was based, but we refrained, and on thinking it over I realized that if George's interest in Angela continued, he would soon be asking the questions on his own behalf.

I said as much to Aunt Flora when the children had finished breakfast and departed Trotter-wards. She considered the matter as we cleared the table, and looked a little depressed.

"It would be troublesome," she said, "to have George falling in love down here."

"I suppose you mean," I amended, "that it would be troublesome if he fell in love with Angela and she spurned his advances?"

"Yes," said Aunt Flora. "He's so appalling when he's out of spirits. Here he was, just beginning to be quite well-behaved and looking in such splendid condition — it would be dreadful to have him on our hands as a rejected suitor — and it would upset Angela."

"Brian and I," I said, "are of the opinion that nothing in the situation will upset Angela, and that George is going to get all the upsetting."

Aunt Flora put the last pile of plates on to the wagon and paused before wheeling it into the kitchen.

"And Phyl, of course," she said with a smile, "thinks that George is irresistible and that the impact will knock any girl off her feet."

"Quite," I said.

"Well, I'm not sure that I don't incline to that view myself," admitted Aunt Flora. "And speaking from an entirely material point of view, it would be a very good match for her. Most girls would at least consider that side of it. And another thing — wouldn't the feminine heart rejoice at the thought of being the centre of a brilliant, glittering — glamorous they call it nowadays — circle?"

"I suppose so," I replied, "if it could be sure of being the centre, but there's only one centre per circle, and wouldn't it have to be George?"

Aunt Flora considered this gloomily

for awhile, and then grasped the wagon impatiently.

"Well, I don't know anything about it," she said irritably. "For all we know, George may have spent the last ten years falling in and out of love — although I doubt it," she went on thoughtfully. "I never heard his name connected with any woman's, and if anybody he cared for had ever turned him down, you may be sure he would have seen to it that we all shared his misery — he always believed in working it off on the family."

She disappeared through the doorway and called back to me.

"Don't go away, Jonny — I've a lot of things to discuss with you."

The things related solely to her coming party, and the discussion began in the dining-room and continued at intervals in whichever part of the house I happened to be working when Aunt Flora wanted to talk to me. Each time she thought of a new idea, she sought me out and told me about it.

"The guests — " She began to count them. "The Colonel and May and Claudia if she's better, three,

247

Miss Peel and her cousin, five — "
Aunt Flora's voice died away and
she continued her calculations mentally.
"About fifteen besides ourselves, I make
it," she announced finally. "That's a good
number, and we can manage very well.
I'm going to see how many small tables
we can muster."

I went upstairs and began bed-making,
and Aunt Flora reappeared after an
interval and sat on the sofa in my
room studying her plan of tables for the
garden if fine and the verandah if wet.
Carrie appeared with a duster to clean
the windows and studied the paper over
the back of the sofa.

"Five tables," she counted. "Where's
five teapots comin' from?"

"From nowhere," said Aunt Flora.
"I'm using the urn."

"How will you stop them dogs pulling
off the tablecloths?" inquired Carrie.
"And that Rex," she continued, folding
her arms and leaning against my bedrail,
"he'll eat all the stuff as quick as you put
it out."

Aunt Flora pondered this. "The dogs,"
she said at last, "will have to be fastened

up. Rex's kennel will be finished and he'll look beautiful inside it."

"If I know 'im," said Carrie, "he'll go round the garden dragging it after 'im."

"Nonsense — it's far too heavy," said Aunt Flora.

"'Ave it yer own way," said Carrie with a resigned air. "An' what about them as brings their own dogs?"

"Well — they'll have to look after them," said Aunt Flora impatiently. "God bless my soul, the garden's large enough for a dozen tables and two dozen dogs."

Carrie pushed up the window, perched herself on the window-sill and began to rub the outside. "We'll all need another 'oliday when this one's over," she remarked. "Mr. George and 'is tantrums and a party and a weddin' and Mrs. Hugh with two trunks to pack, and — "

I missed the rest as I had moved into Paul's room. I had got as far as the bathroom before Aunt Flora reappeared. She settled herself on the rubber-seated chair and watched me cleaning and rearranging the medicine cupboard.

"Do you remember what we decided to do with everybody?" she asked.

"We didn't," I replied. "If I were you I'd leave it until lunch-time and get ideas from the children." I sat on the edge of the bath and raised the subject I had been thinking over as I worked.

"Has Phyl said anything to you about when they're being married?" I asked, "and oughtn't we to be sorting her silver and china and things, and separating them?"

"No," said Aunt Flora. "They're both in a rather bemused state at present, but I gathered from Brian that they're being married here quietly on the last day of his leave, and they both want her room left for them to occupy on future leaves. Brian's going to put it to you as soon as he gets back from London, but neither of them wants to start a home elsewhere at present. I thought you would agree."

"Of course." There was a pause. "It'll be funny without Phyl, won't it?" I said.

"For a time," agreed Aunt Flora. "But it's so much the best thing for her that one can only feel happy. Such a dear

250

fellow," she went on dreamily — "so patient all these years." We both fell silent, thinking of Phyl and her future, and in a little while Aunt Flora rose briskly. "She's a lucky woman," she said. She went out of the door and then turned back. "That's why I'm taking such trouble over this party," she said, "a sort of rehearsal for the wedding."

"Why don't you combine the two events?" I asked.

"Oh no!" she exclaimed in horror. "The party is pure Rushing — just ourselves and our friends. The wedding will be much more general — so many outsiders."

"Do you mean relations?" I asked.

Aunt Flora looked surprised. "Well, I suppose I do," she said. "I do rather feel they're outside our circle, somehow. I must be getting as bad as you over this place. I feel I'm settled here until my time comes to move into the next world."

"I'm glad," I said, feeling the familiar choking sensation rising in my throat. "I love it here more and more."

"You're a foolish woman," said Aunt

Flora affectionately, on her way out.

The telephone bell rang as I was on my way downstairs, and I picked up the receiver and heard George's voice.

"Hullo, Jonny — do you mind if I keep the children out to lunch? We've bicycled as far as a place called Smallfish and we've found a pub and they've promised us some lunch."

"All right, George," I said. "Thanks for ringing up. Don't tire the children."

"Don't be an ass," replied my brother-in-law. "I'd be dead with exhaustion before either of them turned a hair. They're outside with Angela drinking cider on empty stomachs — they're all practically reeling."

With this reassuring piece of information he rang off and I went into the garden to look for Aunt Flora and relay the news. I found her in the tomato house picking large, red, ripe specimens for lunch.

"Don't bother to tell Carrie," she said, when I had finished and was getting my teeth into a peculiarly luscious tomato.

"I'd like to have Ivan and young Stebbing to lunch and we can plan games for the party. I'll ring Ivan's

252

mother and you can take the dogs down and let the Stebbings know."

Thus the table at lunch had an unfamiliar look but was not noticeably quieter than usual. By the time the three boys had finished a third helping of apple charlotte and cream, the plans were in an advanced stage, and as far as I could gather from the rapid interchange of suggestions, acclamations, vetoes, improvements and irrelevant conversation, young Stebbing was going to conduct clock golf at one end of the lawn while Paul superintended croquet at the other end and Ivan had a throw-the-cricket-ball competition somewhere in the middle.

I was interested to find that by the end of lunch Aunt Flora and I were able to understand Nobby's utterances without the aid of Paul's automatic translations. He was entirely at his ease with all the children, and was a familiar figure in our midst, but he seemed to have difficulty in enunciating when answering questions put by grown-ups. He had several valuable suggestions to make, and communicated them to Aunt Flora

by way of Paul or Ivan. He seemed
to be trying to attract their attention
now, but they were having a heated
argument of their own, so Nobby turned
his attention to his biscuits and cheese.
Having put away a large amount of
both, he tried once more to get a word
in between the bickering of the other
two.

"What is it, Nobby," I asked. "Have
you got another good idea?"

Nobby turned to me, lowering his head
in characteristic fashion and looking up
rather like a bull about to charge.

"I fink the dogs," he began in his low,
hoarse tones, "I fink the dogs — all the
dogs what they all come wiv — they
oughter make 'em rice."

"Make them?" I questioned.

"Yus," said Nobby.

"Make them what?" I repeated.

"You know — rice," said Nobby more
urgently, and Aunt Flora gazed across at
him with an ecstatic look.

"Oh, Nobby," she said. "What an
awfully — what an amazingly good
idea! For goodness' sake, you two"
— she turned impatiently to Paul and

Ivan — "will you stop arguing and listen to Nobby's idea."

"Well — what is it?" asked Paul.

I, too, was anxious to have the situation cleared up.

"He says," said Aunt Flora, "that we ought to get all our own dogs and all the visitors' dogs and have dog races."

There was a second's pause while this went home, and then a chorus of acclamation, through which Nobby sat with flaming cheeks and downcast eyes.

"Gosh, oh gosh," said Ivan, jumping up and leaning over to give the author of the suggestion a back-breaking thump by way of congratulation. "Simply super. Terrific. Shatt'ring." Enthusiasm mounted as the numbers and names of the animals flowed into our memories.

"Three of the Colonel's," said Aunt Flora.

"Three of mine," yelled Ivan.

"Rex, and Bruno," counted Paul, "and Vixen and Rover."

"Rex and Bruno," I suggested, "against Trit and Trot."

There was a roar of laughter, Trit

and Trot being Mr. Pollitt's tiny little terriers, about eight inches in their white-stockinged feet. The joke was so good that it lasted until we had all cleared the table and the boys had gone into the kitchen to help Carrie with the washing-up.

"It will be good fun," said Aunt Flora, "and we'll get Brian and George to arrange the races. We might make a book," she went on, warming to the idea. "I think people ought to enjoy it."

The boys were so full of the idea when they appeared after their work that they decided to take our dogs over to Ivan's house and hold preliminary trials forthwith. Aunt Flora had a good deal to do in the garden, and I was anxious to do something towards packing Paul and Diana's trunks. There would not be very much time — we were getting near the end of the holidays, and the days would be full with parties and weddings. I thought of the bustle and noise of the summer and contrasted it with the peace to come, when Aunt Flora and Carrie and Polly and I would be alone and the only bustle would be the departure of Polly to school each day. Each picture had its attractions, and I loved life here whether it was quiet or gay, sunny or snowing.

The cyclists came home very late, and if cider had made the children reel earlier, fatigue was having the same effect now. Polly was so excited at their total of thirty miles for the day that she could hardly be persuaded to finish her supper. Diana, also tired but as calm as ever, gave me an account of the route and a careful and detailed list of what they had eaten for lunch. Angela was fresh and hoped I would not think the children had done too much, and George did not care if I did. I made Angela sit and rest while I put the children into bed, and when I came down I saw that George, who appeared to have a good deal of energy in hand, was putting the finishing touches to the kennel.

"What colour do you want it painted?" he asked Aunt Flora.

"A nice dark sort of green," she replied.

"I'll do the painting," offered Angela.

"You can and welcome," said George. "Paint smells upset Jonny so I presume that the painting will be done in a damp and remote shed."

"It will," I corroborated. "I'm sorry, Angela, but a paint smell does practically kill me and if it can be done in the big shed I shall be awfully grateful."

"I'll buy the paint to-morrow," said George. "Angela can come and see that I choose the correct shade of green, and I'll show her how to apply it in the proper manner."

Angela showed her gratitude in a half-apologetic and very tired yawn.

"You're sleepy — go home and go straight to bed," ordered Aunt Flora.

Angela got up obediently and George, who had borrowed Mr. Pollitt's bicycle, went with her, he told us carefully, to return it.

We watched their departure, and admired George's successful attempt to open the gate without getting off his bicycle.

"I've been thinking," said Aunt Flora slowly, "that George has two great disadvantages to overcome with Angela. First her prejudice against actors, if we can believe Diana, and I think we can, and second the fact that Angela has seen him at his worst."

"Well, isn't that the real George?" I asked.

"I don't think so," said Aunt Flora, turning and walking back slowly towards the house. "The term 'party manners' indicates that we turn our most pleasant face to society. It isn't a pose — it's a duty, and when the duty is done we can go home and rest, take off our party clothes and party smiles and get into old slippers and let our face muscles relax. The extent to which George relaxes at home is merely the measure of the extra duty he has towards society." She paused at the verandah steps and looked at me with an absorbed frown. "Just think, Jonny," she continued, "what self-control it must demand — you and I get tired and irritable after having had to be pleasant to strangers or bores for an hour, and George has to do it practically all the time."

It was a dreadful idea when one

thought of it in that way, and for a moment I felt tenderness and pity for George.

"But," I asked after a few moments, "do you call it relaxing when he shouts his head off and swears and insults the members of his family and steals their furniture and — and so on," I ended lamely.

"Well, I may be wrong," said Aunt Flora, "but I think we ought to take a kinder view of it. All the same," she went on soberly, "it's a lot for a girl to swallow."

We went into the house and were shortly followed by Brian and Phyl, and I found that getting supper ready was a more urgent problem than the state of George's affections.

I knew that Aunt Flora would have liked Brian to give her some account of what arrangements they had made during their day in London, but Phyl looked a little tired, and she decided to leave the matter until the next day. George returned in a bad humour and made no effort at conversation, and we were all relieved when he decided to go straight to bed at the end of the meal. Brian watched him go and turned to Phyl with a mischievous smile.

"If I behaved like that, my sweet," he asked, "would you be feeling tremulous with excitement — dizzy with anticipation — racked with impatience at the thought of our impending union?"

Phyl leaned her tired head on his shoulder and yawned luxuriously.

"Don't be rude to George," she murmured sleepily. "You're jealous because he's so handsome and because you haven't got his — his — "

"Gift of supper-time conversation," finished Brian. He looked across at me. "Has the pursuit continued today?" he inquired with interest.

"Probably," I told him, "but as it took place on bicycles some miles from home, I can't give you a firsthand account of it."

"If his spirits are anything to go by," said Brian gloomily, "he's lost a lot of ground. I hope there won't be a crisis before I get my nuptials over and done with." He squinted down at Phyl, who appeared to be sleeping peacefully.

"You don't think," he asked Aunt Flora anxiously, "that she'll grow like George when she's older?"

"I don't think so," Aunt Flora reassured him. "George wouldn't like it."

13

AUNT FLORA rose the next day resolved to wring from Brian and Phyl some definite statement regarding the arrangements for their wedding. Brian arrived early on the Pollitt bicycle, a pair of bathing trunks under his arm and a towel flung over his shoulder.

"Who's going to swim?" he shouted through the window to the breakfasting family.

The children shouted in an assenting chorus, and Brian lifted himself through the window and dropped in our midst.

"Let's go," he urged, "mother hen and all," he added, cradling Aunt Flora's chin in his palm and shaking her head gently from side to side.

"Stop that at once," she said indignantly, "before you give me indigestion. You're not going swimming. You're going to stay here until I've got some idea of your plans for your wedding."

"Wedding!" repeated Brian in astonishment. "We're not being married to-day."

"Quite so," replied Aunt Flora, "but I presume there are some preliminaries to be discussed, and if you and Phyl can keep sane for a few moments, Jonny and I might be able to glean some information. It's no use arriving in a towel and shirt like this on the day and announcing that you intend to be married the same afternoon."

"But I told you," said Brian in an injured tone, "I said we're being married on the last day of my leave, and the bridegroom will then return at once to his naval duties and his bride will turn her attention to the household work and management for which she is so justly famed."

Having delivered this sentence in one breath he paused for a fresh supply of oxygen.

"Have you finished?" inquired Aunt Flora.

"Absolutely," said Brian, "and now we can all go and get into the water."

"May I ask," continued Aunt Flora,

"where you propose to be married?"

Brian leaned both hands on the table and looked down at her in surprise.

"My dear Aunt Flora," he said. "How you do go on!" He turned to Angela, who entered at that moment, and stretched out an appealing hand. "Come and help me," he begged. "Aunt Flora won't let me go swimming until I've been properly married — she's dogging me like the reporters dog George, and screwing intimate details out of me. It isn't decent — don't you agree?"

Aunt Flora looked at George.

"Perhaps you speak his language," she said hopefully. "Could you find out where he proposes to marry your sister?"

"Why don't you ask me?" said Phyl. "He hasn't really told me anything, but I can do some guessing."

"Thank you," said Aunt Flora. "Now we may get somewhere. First, who is to marry you?"

"Why — Brian, of course," said Phyl in astonishment.

There was a roar of laughter and Aunt Flora threw up her hands in despair. "Guess again, darling," invited Brian.

"Oh," said Phyl, realizing her mistake. "You mean who is going to marry us."

"If you prefer it," said Aunt Flora patiently. "Who is going to marry us, and where are us going to be married?"

"One, Mr. Kendal, two Rushing Church," said Brian. "That makes me the top boy. Any more questions?" he asked of the assembled party.

"Yes," I said. "Have you sent invitations to any of your relations?"

"Good God, no!" exclaimed Brian in genuine horror. "How can you ask such a thing, Jonny? You ought to know I haven't one relation I'd allow within miles of my wedding."

"What about your Uncle Lionel?" asked Aunt Flora.

"Old Lion!" said Brian aghast. "He hasn't spoken a word to me since I tied him up in his whiskers all those years ago. I doubt if they ever got him out; anyway, I never hear anything of him now."

"Your Uncle Bernard?" inquired Aunt Flora.

"Which one is he?" asked Brian. "Oh, you mean the something-in-the-City fellow. Didn't you ever hear what happened to the old boy? Why, he went from bad to worse and at last — " Brian indicated by a series of exaggerated nods, winks and shakes of the head that Uncle Bernard's fate was not a suitable topic of discussion before the children.

"Your Aunt Clara?" pursued Aunt Flora.

"Dead," said Brian in a hushed tone, covering his face reverently with the towel.

Aunt Flora rose with dignity.

"I give it up," she announced. "If someone will kindly ring up the nearest Mental Home and ask them to send out an interpreter, we shall no doubt make some progress."

Brian uncovered one eye and looked at her suspiciously.

"No more questions?" he asked.

"Not one," she replied. "Just let me know how the wedding goes, please."

Brian unveiled the rest of his countenance and put his arms round Aunt Flora.

"Come along," he said gently. "We're all going to swim. Where are those saucy long frilly bloomers with the all-concealing blouses you used to wear when old Boney was expected to land on the beach with a lot of handsome Frenchies? I'm sorry," he went on, "but I shan't be able to talk sanely for quite a time. I got a special licence yesterday and it's had a peculiar and very exciting effect on me. I swear that if you come and sit quietly on the beach while I swim to America and back I'll give you all the details you need, all in perfect sequence. Let's all go on one last terrific expedition."

We went, and it was certainly an expedition. George divided us into fatigue parties. Phyl collected swimming suits and towels while Carrie, Angela and I cut sandwiches and filled them with tomatoes, cucumber and lettuce cut by Aunt Flora and brought in and prepared by Polly and Diana. George and Brian lined up nine bicycles and set to work pumping and oiling, while Paul vanished to fetch Ivan and the Stebbing, who were so much a part of our family that no outing could be considered complete without them. By shortly after half-past ten, Carrie stood on the top step of the verandah watching us parade.

"You'd better go first with Phyl," George told Brian. "Keep ahead of the children, otherwise they'll drown themselves before anybody gets there. You three boys next, and then Polly and Diana. Jonny, will you stay with Aunt Flora and see she doesn't exceed the speed limit?"

I promised I would.

"You've forgotten me," said Angela.

George looked almost genuinely surprised.

"So I have," he said. "Well, that rather leaves you with me. I hope you don't mind?"

"Charmed, I'm sure," said Angela.

"We're off," said Brian, mounting his machine and making off at a good pace.

Aunt Flora and I enjoyed our leisurely ride. There was a light cool breeze blowing, and as we got to the top of each gentle slope we could see the other members of the party strung out ahead.

"I'm not going as far as the beach," said Aunt Flora. "It's going to get too hot there later on. I'll find a nice shady tree in a field and get lunch ready, and you can all come up when you're tired of swimming."

The others waited for us at the top of the last hill before the drop to the coast, and George promised to find a suitable field not too far from the beach. We caught the party up again sitting round the gate of a pleasant meadow with large shady trees and some cows grazing peacefully.

"I'm not going in there," said Aunt Flora. "I'm not going to get lunch all ready and then have a bull attacking me."

"Those are all perfectly harmless cows," said George, "and you can rest here without any qualms. The animals won't even notice you."

Aunt Flora looked doubtful, and the young Stebbing, who shared her dislike of the larger type of domestic animal, looked with distaste at the nearest cow, which was sitting ruminating a little distance away from her sisters.

"Well, if you think it's all right," she said finally. "You can leave all the lunch packages here and I'll read my book until you come up for lunch."

We settled her comfortably not too far from the gate, and when I went back after a pleasant swim she looked rested and contented.

"You look hot," she said. "Come and get cool, and then we'll put out the food."

Polly and Diana came up soon afterwards, followed by Nobby, his wet hair standing straight up on his head and a flaming sunburn rash dyeing his skin. He looked with a happy grin at the good things spread beneath the tree, and glanced anxiously at the cow, whose curiosity seemed to be awakened, as it had moved considerably nearer and was watching us with great interest.

"If that animal comes any nearer, I'm going on the other side of the gate," said Aunt Flora nervously.

"Me too," growled Nobby hoarsely.

I collected our wet bathing things and moved towards the gate.

"Come and hang your things over the bars," I said to Polly and Diana, and we arranged the dripping garments neatly, leaving room for those still to come. I had hardly straightened the last suit when a bloodcurdling scream from Aunt Flora froze the blood in my veins, and swinging round, I saw the cow, head down, bounding straight towards the pair under the tree.

Aunt Flora seemed rooted to the spot, and Nobby, his face grey in spite of the sunburn, turned in panic towards the gate. As I lunged forward, he stopped dead and turned back again, and stumbling between Aunt Flora and the approaching cow, screamed in a high, nasal, terrified voice.

"Scram!" he yelled.

The cow stopped dead. The word was unfamiliar, but the tone unmistakeable. Nobby took two more shaky steps and reverted to his native tongue.

"Gert-cher," he shouted. "Gwan. Be orf. 'Op it."

The cow, a hurt look in its eyes, turned sorrowfully away, and as I ran towards the pale and trembling Aunt Flora I heard Brian and George behind me. They got over the gate with more haste than skill, both of them pale with apprehension.

"My God, what's happened," said

George, his breath coming fast.

Aunt Flora pointed a shaky finger. "The bull," she said. "I told you — it charged — it came right at us." She stopped and looked at the sick-looking countenance of Nobby Stebbing.

"Nobby," she said solemnly, "you're a hero. You saved my life."

Nobby was sitting on the grass looking an extraordinary mixture of colours, and George produced a mug and some water, and looked round in bewilderment at the peacefully-grazing cows.

"What bull?" he inquired.

"That near one," said Aunt Flora, who had recovered from her fright and was steadying the mug for Nobby.

"That's a cow," said George. "Cows don't charge."

"When I was young," said Aunt Flora with rising anger, "an animal that put its head down and charged across fields was a bull. Nobby stepped in front of it and stopped it — isn't that so, Jonny?"

I said that it was indeed so, and that the boy had shown a remarkable degree of courage.

Angela, Phyl and Paul, who were the

last to arrive, and who had been too far away to hear Aunt Flora's scream, looked with interest at the young hero, and Polly and Diana sat on the grass in front of him and regarded him with awe and respect.

"What made the — what made it charge?" asked Brian.

"I can't tell you," replied Aunt Flora. "We were sitting here quietly, and when I turned round it was snorting a few paces away, and still approaching. Animals like that ought to be under some kind of restraint."

Brian opened his mouth with the intention, I thought, of repeating his assertion regarding the sex of the aggressor, but changed his mind.

"Are you all right?" he asked anxiously, studying Aunt Flora for any signs of shock or damage.

"I'm perfectly all right, thank you," she replied, "and if you don't believe Nobby saved my life, you must at least be grateful to him for saving the lunch."

On this point there was no cleavage of opinion, and we gathered a little later round the happily intact feast, and after eating an excellent meal, drank a toast to young Mr. Stebbing. The effects of the meal and the toast combined to render the party immobile during the afternoon, and we lay in the shade resting and discussing what we would do later in the afternoon if our lethargy wore off. George read his letters, which he had been unable to finish before leaving home in the morning, and Brian, true to his promise, presented himself before Aunt Flora to give her details of his plans.

"As far as I can see," she remarked, after listening to his account, "you haven't done anything but talk about it so far."

"I got the licence," he said defensively.

"Have you asked Mr. Kendal about marrying you at Rushing?"

"No," said Brian. "I thought you'd do that."

"It's nothing whatever to do with me," said Aunt Flora, "but as he'd better hear about it before the actual time set for the ceremony, I'll go and see him this evening. What about your dress, and flowers?" she asked Phyl.

"There's a dress coming," said Phyl,

"a sort of ice-blue which I think you'll approve of, and I'd like a huge mixed bouquet from the garden."

"Wedding cake?" inquired Aunt Flora.

"No," said Phyl and Brian together. "No wedding cake," went on Phyl. "We want to have a wedding without the effects."

"Don't be an ass," said George. "What do the guests come for?"

"Well, if they come for cake," said Brian, "they're going empty away. No cake, no confetti, no slippers, no reception, no bridesmaids, no ushers, no reporters, and of course, no honeymoon."

This recital threw a gloom over the whole party except George, who had lost interest and returned to his letters.

"No bridesmaids?" asked Polly in a stricken voice.

"No, my pet," said Brian in contrition, "but if Phyl has no objection you can walk down the aisle on the other side of me."

"I don't want to walk down the aisle so much," said Polly, "but I wanted a bridesmaid's frock like those long ones with frills."

276

"It's a swindle," said Phyl, "but honestly, Polly, it can't be done."

"What time do you want the wedding?" asked Aunt Flora.

"Early please, darling," said Brian. "We've got to catch the two-thirty-five from King's Cross, and you see that doesn't give us a fat amount of time. If Jonny would see that Phyl is packed before the wedding, we have a faint hope of leaving in time."

"Well, an eleven-o'clock wedding in Rushing church, followed by a sort of breakfast-lunch," said Aunt Flora. "How will that be?"

"Perfect," said Phyl.

"And invitations," concluded Aunt Flora. "Do you really mean you're going to be married in a sort of hole-and-corner way, or will you give some of your relations a chance of being present?"

"I leave it to Phyl," said Brian. "There's nobody really near, as you know — near in relationship, I mean, and as you also know, all my expectations have already been realized."

"All?" said Phyl in mock disappointment.

"Not one weeny millionaire uncle or aunt?"

"Not one," deplored Brian.

"Well, I think we can get along now," said Aunt Flora in relief. "You will turn up at the ceremony, won't you?" she ended anxiously, looking at Brian.

He held up one hand solemnly in promise.

George looked up from his letters and I found his eyes fixed on me with a suspicious look.

"What," he asked, "have you been saying to old Mill?"

"Old Mill?" I inquired in a puzzled voice, purely for temporizing purposes.

"My agent, Robert Mill," repeated George. "He's either potty or you've been stringing off that pack of lies that you and Phyl seem to have by heart. What did you say?"

"I told him you were better," I said guardedly.

George gave an unbelieving grunt and went on with the letter, and I turned to Phyl and Brian.

"I would like to make a suggestion about the wedding," I said.

Brian invited me to go ahead.

"Well," I went on, "I think you ought to ask Miss Peel to play the organ."

The faces of Phyl and Brian registered horror and dismay, and Aunt Flora looked at me with an appreciative smile.

"That, my dear Jonny," she said, "is an extremely mean suggestion."

"Why mean?" inquired Paul, who was lying on his back with his hands clasped behind his head listening lazily to the conversation.

"It's mean," explained Aunt Flora, "as your mother well knows, because she knew Brian and Phyl would loathe the idea, but would have to agree to it because although they wouldn't have thought of it themselves, they now realize how hurt Miss Peel would be if they didn't ask her."

Paul had to raise himself on one elbow to digest this rather complicated piece of psychology.

"You mean," he asked, "that the bridegroom and all will hate it if Miss Peel plays and she'll hate it if she doesn't, and her feelings are more important than theirs?"

"Something of the sort," agreed Aunt Flora. "Well, does she play?" she asked the bride and groom.

"I don't see why," argued Brian. "I said no cake, no slippers, no reception, no — "

"Yes, yes, darling," said Phyl hastily, "we heard you the first time."

"Very well," said Brian. "If we can disappoint Polly about her frock with the frills, we can disappoint Miss Peel about her celebrated rendering of the Wedding March."

"Well, personally," said Aunt Flora, "I like a little quiet music at a wedding. No hymns of course — just a sort of pleasant undertone."

"I hate it," said Phyl. "It sounds as though someone's wailing in the distance."

"No organ," said George, without looking up from his letter.

"Thanks, George," said Brian with genuine gratitude. "I'm surprised at you, Jonny," he went on indignantly, "for pulling out a suggestion like that — can't you use a little imagination?"

"Can't she . . . yes, she can use more

than a little imagination," said George, sitting up and waving his letter in our direction. Just listen to this:

'I don't think there is any more I can tell you now, but I cannot conclude without saying how much I envy you in your charming surroundings. You are fortunate in being in a lovely home in a peaceful and restful setting; to have in addition care and affection is, I feel, almost too much! I hope you will give my kind regards to your sister-in-law and tell her how much I enjoyed her visit. If I can get anywhere near Rushing, you may be sure I shall look in and see you!'"

He folded the letter and looked at me severely. "Can you," he asked, "explain the coincidence of Manning and Mill both labouring under the same delusion regarding the same house and the same surroundings?"

I had some difficulty, as usual, in trying to choose a suitable retort from the many that flowered in my mind, and after watching my earnest frown for a moment or two, Aunt Flora came to my aid.

"Don't you agree with everything Jonny said — that is, if she said anything?" she asked.

George's eyes strayed slowly round the peaceful circle. He saw Paul, still gazing up at the lovely blue sky, and Nobby, curled up half asleep beside Aunt Flora and no doubt dreaming of a future full of heroic rescues of ladies who might be as nice as Aunt Flora and perhaps even younger and more beautiful. Polly and Diana lay flat on their faces, cheeks resting on the grass, legs waving in the air. Phyl and Brian, their backs against the tree, Aunt Flora perched comfortably on a pile of coats, all looked relaxed and happy. His eyes came to rest on Angela, whose hair, wrists and pretty ankles were decorated with daisy chains made and presented by Polly and Diana, and he spoke at last in a slow, rather grudging way.

"I hope old Robert does look in," he said. "His ideas of the normal standard of living are on an even higher plane than mine are reported to be. If he says:

'George, my boy, you've been done,' I shall know that I have sunk into a state of apathy and — "

"Degradation," suggested Brian.

"A little strong," smiled George, "but you get the general idea."

"You're not trying to tell us, are you," asked Phyl, "that you've got used to pigging it with us?"

George ignored this, and it is doubtful whether he heard it. He was gazing at Angela thoughtfully.

"Do you remember," he asked her, "that house we saw at Smallfish?"

"Yes," said Angela.

"Wouldn't you like to live in it?" pursued George.

"Wouldn't suit my old lady," replied Angela without the slightest hesitation. "That hall draught would kill her."

The dreams fled from George's eyes, and he met her level glance coldly.

"A good thing," he growled.

Aunt Flora waited hopefully for a continuation of these interesting hostilities, but George had pulled himself together, and with a disappointed air she began to rouse the party. There was a split-up into groups of those who decided to swim, those who wished to return home, and those, like Brian and Phyl, who wished to stay with the cows.

I was about to get on my bicycle and follow Aunt Flora homewards when I saw George leaning on the gate staring moodily in the direction of the beach, where Angela and all the children had gone.

"Won't the four of them be a little too much for her?" I asked doubtfully, wondering whether I ought to stay.

"Oh, my God," groaned George, "now I'm nursemaid. Running about after four brats and a girl who wears daisy chains and is too anæmic to work up a small holiday flirtation."

He glared at me and waited for me to deny the accusation against Angela's corpuscles, but I was feeling rather sorry for him, and said nothing.

"I do wish," he continued, working a little more of his bitterness off on the person at hand, "that you could sometimes have an answer ready. Why don't you buy a book and learn the ordinary responses?"

"I think," I retorted, stung at last, "that it isn't really my lack of response you're worried about. Why don't you buy the book yourself — and give it to Angela?"

I mounted my bicycle and rode furiously in the wake of Aunt Flora.

14

ANYONE who has ever planned an outdoor function during an English summer will have no need to be told that the day of our party was neither wet nor dry, but a maddening succession of downpours followed by bright, sunny, warm intervals full of promise. When George, Brian and the boys had taken the tables out at noon, brought them in before lunch, put them out again immediately afterwards and rushed them indoors in a heavy shower just before two o'clock, there was a general strike, and Aunt Flora announced that the party would take place on the verandah and the dining-room would be cleared for games. If the dogs were disposed to race, they must do it by themselves. The children were bitterly disappointed, having spent much time arranging a race-course with stakes and string, and drawing up a card of events, but there was no help for it, and the racing must be postponed.

Hardly had this pill been swallowed than the rain ceased, the sun shone and the sky became as clear and blue as though rain clouds had never marred its loveliness. We had been the sport of the weather long enough, however, and turning our backs resolutely on the entrancing scene, set about arranging tables according to Aunt Flora's verandah plan. It became warmer and warmer and finally, it was evident even to our embittered and suspicious minds that the weather had settled and we were going to have a fine afternoon. With weary groans the table-bearers toiled down the steps and set their burdens down according to Aunt Flora's outdoor plan, and there was a general rush to get into suitable attire before the guests appeared. The brilliance and warmth of the day allowed us to wear our lightest and brightest dresses, and I wriggled with a feeling of pleasure and comfort into a cool muslin of the type known as dotted, and which I thought ruefully I would soon have to discard as unbecoming to my age, and cut up for Polly. I walked into Phyl's room for her inspection, and she told me I looked charming.

"Thank you," I said modestly, "but I think it wants a droopy hat and I'm out of droopy hats."

Phyl received this in the spirit in which it was meant, and produced a charming specimen of droop.

"There you are," I said, studying the effect in her long glass, with great satisfaction. "What did I tell you? — the perfect finish. You don't look so bad yourself," I added generously, looking at her.

We looked a gay party as we stood assembled on the lawn, waiting for the first guests to arrive. George gave a very smart South-American finish to the group in his beautifully-tailored linen suit, and Brian asked with envy if he had another one he could lend out for the afternoon. Angela arrived looking almost child-like in a white linen dress with a sailor collar, and Phyl, after one glance, went upstairs and reappeared with a saucy little white sailor straw with an upturned brim which she perched at exactly the right angle at the back of Angela's curls, making an adorable picture.

"Thank you," said Angela, when the chorus of admiration had died down. "If I'd known what a social whirl I was coming to, I would have brought a few more dozen dresses and hats, and my pearls and tiaras and so on. Stupid of me to come prepared only for rude country sports."

"With rude country louts," said Brian. "Do you look as ravishing as Angela does in that hat?" he asked Phyl, who assured him that she did.

"By the way," he continued, "whose party is this? Is it George's day, or are they coming to see the happy pair, or has it degenerated into a dog meeting?"

"They're coming to see my flowers," said Aunt Flora, looking round with justifiable pride at the colour and beauty she had worked so hard to produce. "There's nothing to prevent them from looking at you and George when they're surfeited with loveliness."

The gentlemen bowed.

"That does me out of a job," commented Brian. "I was going to do a bit of ushering." He stepped mincingly up to an imaginary visitor. "How d'you do. So nice of you to come. May I show you the flowers? No? We have a nice line in celebrities — stage and screen variety — No? How about the World's Laziest Woman, shortly to become my completely unhelpful helpmeet? — No? Then what — !" He uttered a realistic yelp of agony, and hopping on one foot, clasped an imaginary dog-bite. "Ah-dogs. This way, please — straight through to the field."

The children enjoyed this performance immensely, and Aunt Flora smiled indulgently.

"I don't know what the children will do without you," she said. "I can't rise to George's performing fees."

"And George couldn't rise to my heights," declared Brian. "Come on, fellow," he challenged. "See if you can improve on my his — my histri — my acting."

George smiled but ignored the challenge, and the clamour made by the children as they tried to force him out of the chair on which he was lounging stilled as our first visitors made their appearance. Our doubts as to whether we were perhaps a little overdressed for a simple village gathering fled as we beheld Mrs. Trotter's magnificent flowered silk dress and daisy-bedecked hat. Two small Trotters accompanied her, and Mr. Trotter was promised for a later hour.

"There were two pigs to kill," she explained, "but they won't be long now. I had a job to get these two away," she added, looking at the forms of the two boys, now playing happily with the rest of the children.

We all felt gratified at the knowledge that our guests were leaving the pigs in order to give us the pleasure of their society, and I went forward to greet the Colonel and two very elegant misses. Claudia looked pale and much thinner and I led her to a comfortable seat under the beech tree and sent Phyl to look after her, handing May over to a rather startled Brian. The Stebbings came over with Miss Peel and her cousin, and I had to look twice before I recognized the scrubbed, tidy figure with them as our friend Nobby. The garden filled rapidly, and I looked with pleasure at the gay colours moving in the sunshine. A few visitors strolled in the orchard and the children could be heard in the field trying to keep the numerous dogs from breaking down the stakes put up with so much labour.

The first part of the afternoon was undoubtedly George's. It would have been difficult for anyone to withstand the combined appeal of his good looks and charm, good humour and good tailoring. He was at his best; the day was perfect, the setting delightful, and he could forget the treacherous taps, the danger of walking into the raspberry canes and the general unpleasantness of life in an imperfect house with his nearest relations. I wondered what Angela thought of him. She had never seen him in this role, and it suited him to perfection. Even I found it difficult to believe as I watched him and listened to his low, attractive laughter, that he could be surly and selfish, moody and malicious. I saw their two figures together frequently, but was too busy to judge whether Angela's gaiety and sweetness sprang from any other cause than delight in the day and the company.

It was too warm for the grown-ups to exert themselves very much before tea, but Ivan and Paul managed to get through their throw-the-cricket-ball competition, which they had divided into two heats, one for the children and one for the older competitors. The delightfully-named Tommy Trotter won the first heat with ease, and there were three more grown-ups to be urged into the field before the second heat could be decided. Mr. Trotter, newly arrived from the pig-killing, was persuaded to have first turn, and Mr. Stebbing followed him and did very well, almost beating the record made by Brian. Only May remained, and was clearly of the opinion that all this was very silly and to be got through as speedily as possible.

"What do I do?" she snapped, glaring suspiciously at her old enemy, Ivan.

"You stand there," he said, indicating the spot. "That's the place for the girls 'cos they get a bit more chance than the men — "

"I shall stand here," said May, planting herself firmly on the spot lately occupied by Mr. Stebbing. "What do I do?"

"You get three tries," explained Ivan, "you just throw it anywhere — no, not exactly that way," he added hastily, as May prepared to launch her first shot into the thickly-populated orchard. "Across the field, hard's you can."

May threw the ball in the direction indicated, and watched with disgust as it made a short journey through the air and landed just beyond the race track.

"Not bad," said Ivan encouragingly, running forward to catch the ball thrown back by Paul, and handing it to May for her second shot. "If you bend your arm back like this," he said, "and then fling the ball up from that position — weight on that foot — "

"I know all about it," said May ungraciously, having watched his instructions with close attention.

Her second shot was decidedly better than the first, and the ball, describing a most satisfying arc, landed with a thud an inch away from Mr. Trotter's sheep dog. May looked grim as Ivan caught the ball and handed it to her for her third try.

"Out of my way!" she said, so threateningly that the group of interested spectators instinctively moved back two paces. She performed one or two preliminary jerks and then let fly with the ball. There was a second's pause and then a roar of applause as all eyes followed the path of the ball and saw it fall a foot beyond the farthermost mark.

"Oh, gosh," said Ivan breathlessly, his eyes fixed in incredulous admiration on the blushing and gratified May. "You've done it."

May straightened her hat and brushed her hands together nonchalantly.

"Nothing in it," she declared, stalking through the little gate.

I congratulated her on her performance, and led her to a shady table, but she caught sight of two respectable old gentlemen seated at a small table near the verandah steps, and stopped.

"Isn't that old Hayne?" she inquired, "over there talking to Pollitt?"

Mr. Hayne was a retired nurseryman, and had in his day been an authority on tomato plants. May's eyes brightened — he was a difficult man to get hold of, and gave away very little information to anybody in Rushing but Aunt Flora, and May anticipated good results from an half-hour's tête-à-tête and the effects of a good tea. I took her over to the two men, who looked at me without gratitude, and I turned to find George approaching.

He took me by the arm in a delightfully affectionate way, and smiled at me, but his tone was far from friendly.

"That girl," he said, "proposes to sit with the children at their table, and you've got to stop her."

I agreed instantly. "Of course she can't," I said. "We want her with us."

George released me and I went to the long trestle table set for the children as far away from the smaller tables as possible. Here there was a quarrel in progress as to who should sit next to Angela. I interrupted firmly.

"I'm sorry," I said, "Angela's coming with me."

Angela looked surprised.

"Really and truly?" she asked. "I promised them I'd sit here."

"Not to-day," I said, smiling at the hot, flushed, merry face under the sailor hat, and ignoring the indignant groans of the children. I led her away and found George, by a remarkable coincidence, standing close by in conversation with Miss Peel.

"I've got to go and see to tea," I said, handing Angela over to him. "Will you please look after Angela — she was proposing to join the children's party."

George looked surprised.

"Surely not to-day?" he said, smiling at her in gentle reproof.

I thought Angela looked at me with a tinge of suspicion in her glance, but I hurried away to the spot where Carrie, at a serving table, was filling teacups from the large urn and putting them on to the wagon to be wheeled from table to table. Everyone looked in good spirits, and Aunt Flora moved about seeing that wants were attended to, and empty plates refilled.

Paul and Ivan made a hasty but no doubt adequate tea, and went round distributing race cards. They were remarkably well drawn up and caused a good deal of amusement, and the dog owners were entreated to finish their tea quickly and repair to the course. Soon we were assembled at the grandstand, which became grander as more and more chairs were brought from the lawn and placed in position.

Miss Peel and her cousin, Mr. Hayne and Mrs. Trotter, none of whom owned dogs, were appointed dog-holders at one end of the track, and the owners stood at the winning-post calling their animals and urging them with whistles, cries and any other encouragement that occurred to them. The first race was the Home Stakes and the runners were our own Rex, Vixen, Bruno and Rover. There was a little confusion as Rex rolled ecstatically over the string separating his lane from Bruno's, and Rover ran off the course to greet his dear friend Mr. Pollitt, who was standing at the side of the course shouting encouragement. Vixen ran a straight and swift course into Paul's arms and was declared the winner, and Brian, on a box beside the grandstand, pronounced the career of bookmaker to be a ruinous one. Vixen, the oldest and most sensible of our dogs, had been the favourite, and Brian declared himself no longer in a position to support Phyl adequately.

There were six races on the card, and as the third was run I stood back to look at the spectators, painting a picture that was to stay in my mind and bring a reminiscent smile to my lips for many years to come. Mr. Hayne and Mr. Pollitt had joined Brian as assistants, but the shouts from their stand announcing the odds were almost lost in the clamour of dogs barking, children shouting and spectators arguing. Miss Peel, tears of laughter streaming down her cheeks, watched the efforts of Trit and Trot to hurdle over the string, under the impression that they were taking part in a steeplechase. Dogs which had not been entered in the race took part without warning or notice and won easily.

George and Angela acted as Starters, while the Colonel was Judge, and the effect of the combined noises was quite indescribable. Carrie stood on a kitchen chair brought out specially for the purpose and I feared she would fall off with laughing so much, and hurt herself. Aunt Flora was making a good deal of money off Brian, and made notes on her programme like a true race goer. Old Barnes was doing yeoman service repairing string and hammering in stakes, and enjoying himself immensely.

I smiled to myself at the success of the party, and started across the field to join Ruth Exley, who was laughing helplessly at Ivan's efforts to control his dogs. As I moved I sensed rather than heard someone behind me, and turned to find a vaguely-familiar figure hesitating at the little gate. I went forward wondering who the late-comer could be, and whether he was a friend of Aunt Flora's from Rushing or Felling. I held out my hand, and finding it impossible to make a speech of welcome in the midst of the din, invited him by a gesture to join the meeting. He hesitated and I thought he must be a little shy, so I put a finger on his sleeve and urged him forward. He placed his hat on one of the chairs in the grandstand, and I led him to the bookmakers, where Brian, encouraged by the sight of a prosperous-looking stranger, flourished his board and yelled names and odds hoarsely.

The races came to an end amid applause and laughter, and there was a swift and simultaneous movement towards the long table on the lawn, where cool drinks were now laid out. A small group lingered to watch May and the small Trotter play off the final of their competition and Aunt Flora, who seemed to have the stranger under her wing, was among those watching. I went out after handing drinks, in time to see Tommy win by a very small margin. The stranger was swept on to the lawn and I had a moment to ask Aunt Flora about him.

"Who's that?" I asked. "He came awfully late — should I offer him tea?"

"I don't think so," replied Aunt Flora. "And I haven't the faintest notion who he is."

I stared at her. "You don't know?" I said stupidly.

"No," she repeated. "I don't. Perhaps he's one of Pollitt's guests and was attracted by the screaming. That reminds me — my throat is like a nutmeg grater. Come and pour me out something to drink."

I was uneasy, and decided to look more closely at the stranger, whose face was faintly familiar but whom I was quite unable to place. However, he would soon go with the rest of the party and the mystery would be cleared up by Brian or the children.

The stranger, however, made no move to go. One by one the visitors, with warm thanks, departed. George and Angela had long since left to accompany Claudia home as she was tired and wished to slip away and rest without disturbing May and the Colonel. Our numbers thinned and soon there remained only the family and the stranger. I was too busy with farewells to worry seriously, but as I walked to the gate with the Exleys, who were the last to go, I was beginning to feel uneasy. I saw George and Angela returning, and waited at the gate.

"That the last?" inquired George. "Jolly good party."

"There's one left," I said. "He came late and he seems to want to stay late.

Nobody has the slightest idea who he is, but I've seen him before somewhere."

We stepped on to the lawn and the man turned and faced us. George stopped in complete astonishment, staring in unbelief, and then stepped forward with out-stretched hand.

"Good Lord, it's Robert Mill," he exclaimed. "How in the world did you get here?"

Mr. Mill took George's hand and shook it absently.

"Hello, George," he said, without looking in his direction. He was looking past him and gazing at me and I sought desperately for some words to make my apology. Mr. Mill, however, came straight towards me and put out a hand for the second time that evening.

"Mrs. Manning," he said in gentle reproof, "you didn't remember me — but I remembered you very well indeed."

Having expressed this kindly sentiment, his eyes fell on Phyl's hat, and words appeared to fail him. The general opinion, freely expressed later in the family circle, was that I would have continued to stand and stare at him in hopeless embarrassment for the remainder of the evening if George had not taken pity on me and, putting a hand on Mr. Mill's shoulder, swung him round to present him to the others. He led him forward into the centre of the lawn.

"This," he said formally, "is my dear Aunt Flora."

15

BRIAN discovered to his surprise that there was a good deal in connection with his forthcoming marriage which could neither be ignored nor passed on for the attention of others, and we saw little of Phyl or of him in the days that followed. Aunt Flora worked in the garden with additional energy to make up for the hours she had wasted on picnics and parties, and Paul, Ivan and Nobby, who had all been struck by the pallor and limpness of Claudia, decided to put themselves at her disposal and help her and May in every way possible. The outcome of this was an urgent telephone call from May two mornings later telling me that the Colonel proposed to take the three boys out for the whole day to the sea. Although she did not say so, I gathered that he was expected to push them all over the cliffs at some convenient spot.

George, after two brief talks with

Mr. Mill, entirely confined to business matters, returned to his normal routine and disappeared every morning after breakfast in the direction of Mrs. Trotter's, closely followed by Polly and Diana, whose suspicions were now definitely aroused and who had no intention of being given the slip by any uncle, present or to come.

I had the ordinary work of the house to see to, and in addition at this time I usually began the sorting of winter clothes for the children, in order to be ready for the beginning of the school terms. The absence of all the members of the family offered a splendid chance of working without interruption, but unfortunately Mr. Mill showed no sign of leaving Rushing. He appeared with regularity during the middle of the morning, and seriously impeded my progress. It was impossible to avoid offering him a cool drink and a seat on the verandah, and I had to maintain a calm and hospitable exterior while I fretted at this waste of time. It was just like George, I thought furiously, to vanish on his selfish pursuits and leave somebody else to look after his friends. I tried to lead the visitor into the garden and graft him on to Aunt Flora, but she seemed to sense this intention, and went on resolutely with her weeding. It is impossible to carry on a cultured conversation with the back of a woman crouching over a flower bed, and I was forced to return to the verandah and meet the growing admiration in Mr. Mill's eyes.

I am quite used to male attentions, having for years been pursued by scores of earnest and smitten young men who all besought me to use my influence to make Phyl return their passion. I acquired an extraordinary degree of skill in weeding out starters from non-starters and despatching the latter with a maximum of speed and a minimum of sorrow. The lapse of years had perhaps robbed me of some of this technique, for I could not shake Mr. Mill off without resorting to more direct methods, and this I did not care to do.

I asked Aunt Flora to abandon her garden and take the Mill off my hands, but she refused.

"I must catch up, or the garden will

be a wilderness — and you're perfectly capable of getting rid of the man if you want to," she said irritatingly.

"How?" I asked wrathfully. "I've done everything but tell him to go — a man with his *savoir-faire* — "

"Ought to know when it's *comme il faut* to take his *congé*," finished Aunt Flora in disgust. "I do wish you would avoid foreign interpolations. You know," she continued, "I've always made it a practice not to interfere in matters of this sort. He's a very pleasant fellow and I'm not disposed to come and rescue you."

"You'd interfere soon enough," I said indignantly, "if I gave him any encouragement."

Aunt Flora pulled out a particularly obstinate weed and looked up at me with a wide smile.

"You haven't had any masculine society to yourself for a long time," she said. "Don't you appreciate it?"

"Not in the least," I replied. "I'm dying to get on with all those thousands of jobs."

"Well, can't you move about in a busy way and make him feel he's hindering you?" suggested Aunt Flora.

"I've tried that," I said hopelessly. "I came in clasping a pile of Paul's most intimate and uninteresting underwear, and he gazed at me as though I were holding a sheaf of lilies."

Aunt Flora laughed heartlessly.

"Poor Jonny," she said finally. "It's hard on you and perhaps you'll have to end by being a little firm, but there's no point in our both wasting time, is there?"

"I didn't say there was," I pointed out. "All I'm asking is that you should waste time instead of me."

"Oh, is that all?" said Aunt Flora. "Are you suggesting that if I sat on the verandah with Mr. Mill he would get bored and go away?"

"You put it so bluntly," I said.

"But that," persisted Aunt Flora, "was the general idea?"

"Well, yes," I admitted.

"Well, I feel overpowered by the compliment," she said, "but I'm not going to abandon my garden, so you'll have to dispose of your admirers by yourself."

George was even less helpful. I took the dogs for a run after supper and met him in the hall as I returned. He was on his way to bed, and I stopped him on the bottom step and asked him if he would kindly entertain his own friends.

"You don't mean Robert?" he asked in surprise. "My dear Jonny, my business with him took exactly ten minutes and was concluded days ago."

"He came down to see how you were getting on," I pointed out, "and you haven't even seen him for the last two days. And I want to get on with a lot of work and I can't. If you don't want him here, why don't you get rid of him?"

George leaned on the banisters and looked at me with amusement. "Why should I spoil the budding romance?" he asked. "The fellow obviously adores you" — he seemed about to add "God knows why", but rather to my surprise the words remained unspoken — "and you ought to be flattered. Think of all the lovely actresses who've made unsuccessful efforts to get him all these years."

"They can have him," I said. "And

you've got to stop bicycling around the country for a day and see what you can do about getting rid of him."

George continued his interrupted journey up the stairs. "It's your show," he said briefly over his shoulder. He paused at the top and leaned over the rail, wagging a forefinger at me.

"Pause before you let him go," he said. "Remember, he might be the last train home — "

I prayed earnestly that he would overbalance and break his neck, but nothing so gratifying occurred, and I was left to wonder how soon the joys of the country would pall on Mr. Mill and cause him to return to wherever he had come from.

The morning brought relief, however, as there was such a downpour that it seemed impossible for anybody to leave the house. George agreed with this view, and then put on his mackintosh and went out hatless into the rain, bound as usual for the Trotter residence. He returned some time later accompanied by Angela and looking less satisfied with life than when he had left, from which I concluded that he had tried to persuade her to go out without the children, and she had refused. The rain persisted, and it was decided that it would be a good thing to paint the kennel while waiting for the weather to clear. There was no green paint of the shade Aunt Flora preferred, but there were a good many tins of various colours in the shed which had some paint left in them. The children disappeared with George and Angela to the shed at the far end of the garden, and I hoped that Mr. Mill, if he came, would hear their voices and join them. I worked upstairs all the morning, and enjoyed myself more than I had done for the past three days.

Carrie appeared as I put aside the last of the garments I judged Paul had outgrown and stood at the door of his room watching me for a moment.

"Do you want me, Carrie?" I asked.

"If you're doin' nothin'," she said, "you could give me a hand with the kitchen sink."

"Is it stopped up again?" I asked.

Carrie said that it was, and I said I would come and see what I could do.

"Put somethin' round your head," she advised. "I've been goin' round the walls, and there's a lot o' dust about."

I draped Paul's scout scarf hastily round my head and descended with Carrie. I succeeded in unstopping the sink after a while, and prepared to return to work upstairs. I got as far as the door which led into the hall, and stopped in horror at the sight of Mr. Mill, sitting on the verandah and patiently turning the pages of a magazine. The thought of yet another morning wasted in unprofitable chatter was intolerable, and my one idea was to escape if possible. I slipped past the open doorway, and once past, it was impossible that he could see me, except in the unlikely event of his coming into the hall. He had certainly not been there when I came downstairs, and he could not have heard my labours in the kitchen. If I could get up the stairs unheard I was safe.

I tiptoed cautiously and ungracefully to the bottom of the stairs, and began a stealthy creeping movement up them. One by one they were safely and silently negotiated, and at last I reached the topmost one and glanced back at the dangerous territory I had put behind me, only to see the figure of Ivan, rigid with surprise and curiosity in the hall below. His mouth was open, and the wonder in his eyes was mixed with a fear that I had taken leave of my senses. I sent up a prayer of thankfulness that it was Ivan and not Paul or Polly who had observed my strange ascent. Polly would have shouted "What on earth are you creeping upstairs for, Mummy?" and Paul would have rushed after me and said "Caught you!" and in both cases the plan would have failed. Ivan was well accustomed to observing and weighing up the movements of his elders, and I blessed his steadiness and silence.

I put my finger up to my lips in a brief warning gesture, and turned the corner of the landing, feeling extremely foolish and raging against Mr. Mill, the innocent cause of my having made a fool of myself before one of the children.

However, I was free to go on with my work, and I unwound the scarf from my head and turned towards the door of Paul's room. Ivan's voice made me pause, and I heard his invitation to Mr. Mill to join the painters in the shed.

"It's fun," he said, "and perhaps they'll let you do a bit."

"Thank you very much," came Mr. Mill's reply, "but I don't think I would care about it just now."

"But you've got nobody to talk to," protested Ivan, who could see no sense in anybody's sitting alone on the verandah.

"As a matter of fact," said Mr. Mill, "I am waiting for Mrs. Manning."

"Oh, she's upstairs," said Ivan airily, "and she can't come down."

Mr. Mill coughed in a rather embarrassed way, no doubt anxious to hear the reason for this statement, but prevented by delicacy from probing further.

"She's got her hair all done up in curls or something — it's all tied up," went on Ivan, "so you'd better come and do the kennel."

Mr. Mill apparently decided that if I was definitely not on view it was no use taking up his stand on the verandah, and I heard them, to my relief, on their way to the shed. There was, I thought, no fear of his being asked to stay to lunch — Aunt Flora was lunching with Miss Peel, and George would prefer to give all his attention to Angela throughout the meal without the necessity of addressing occasional remarks to Mr. Mill.

The children came in shortly before lunch in a quite dreadful state. The kennel itself, I thought, could hardly have more paint on it than Polly had on various parts of her person and dress. My protests were drowned in a chorus of vociferous descriptions of the success of the painting, and as soon as lunch was over I made my way, urged by the eager children, to inspect the work of art.

It was an astonishing sight, and I was informed that everybody had had a hand in the work. Angela was responsible for the dog-biscuit decoration, and George had executed a cross-bone design above the door. Mr. Mill had painted a neat imitation of a brass plate on one side, bearing the inscription Manning Rex. Altogether, I was able to say with sincerity that I had never seen anything like it.

"What does Aunt Flora think of it?" I asked with some amusement.

"She likes it," they told me, "but she's going to wait and see what Rex thinks of it. It's not dry enough for him to come near it yet."

It was a dreary afternoon, but the rain kept off and I suggested walking to Felling to meet Phyl and Brian and return with them in the bus. The children liked the idea very much, and I turned bravely to George.

"Why don't you ring Mr. Mill up and ask him to tea?" I suggested. "I'll give the children tea in Felling before the train gets in, and I do think you ought to make some sort of gesture while he's down here."

"I won't do it alone," answered George promptly. "If Angela'll stay and act as hostess I'll do it."

I looked appealingly at Angela, and Angela looked speculatively at George, while George looked calmly out of the window.

"I'd very much enjoy Mr. Mill's company," she said at last.

"You shall have it," said George, and went to the telephone.

When I could speak to Angela alone,

I besought her to find some means of inducing the visitor to leave before we returned. "That is, if you can," I added. "He's difficult to move."

Angela gave me a delightful and understanding smile.

"Poor Mr. Mill," she said. "Can't I give him the smallest ray of hope?"

"No," I replied, "you can't."

"Don't you like anything about him?" asked Angela.

I thought for a moment. "Yes," I said finally, "I think he's got remarkable eyes — they're exactly like black shoe buttons, and I'm fascinated by the way he says 'Quite-quite' to every remark one makes. How's that?"

"Definitely no romance," decided Angela with a disappointed shake of her head.

I could not resist one small probe as I went upstairs to get ready. "You're not romantic either, are you?" I asked.

We looked at each other steadily for a little while. I thought how much I liked her, and I saw affection in the eyes looking into mine. I was swept by a disloyal conviction that she was far and away too good for George, and wondered how we could hope that she would bestow her sweetness, sincerity and goodness on our wilful and temperamental candidate.

"I don't think I am — very," she replied at last. "I'm proof against certain forms of it, anyhow. I like the stodgy and the humdrum. The more showy qualities are definitely and absolutely out."

I went up the stairs, and my heart sank in the most contradictory way. I was afraid that George was definitely and absolutely out, and to my surprise I felt extremely depressed about the whole thing.

I got myself groomed and tidy, but my thoughts remained in a loose and untidy state. From feeling low-spirited about George's chances I became cheered by the thought of what Angela would avoid in the way of matrimonial jars, and then I wondered how she could throw aside a chance of marrying so fine a specimen of manhood. It was all rather confusing, and with a sense of infinite relief I suddenly realized that it was purely George and Angela's affair and had nothing whatsoever to do with me.

16

PHYL and Brian were in very good spirits on their return, although Brian sobered a little when they reviewed their activities of the past day or two and realized that he had thrown out wedding invitations to several relatives whom he had not in the least intended should grace the function. Aunt Flora tried to get some idea of names and numbers, but Brian was unable to remember more than the bare fact of having told several people — or the same person several times — how charmed he would be to welcome them at the nuptials, as he preferred to call the ceremony.

"Well, how many people did you visit?" asked Aunt Flora, "and can you remember how many affirmative responses you got?"

"Affir — ? Oh, you mean how many yeses," said Brian. "I have a general recollection of a chorus of quite definite yeses. I didn't mean to invite anybody," he added hastily at sight of Aunt Flora's grim countenance. "I only did it to be pleasant — I shouldn't think anyone took it in the least seriously. You can't come to a wedding," he argued, "until you've had one of those dreadful little white things with silver lettering to show at the door, and as those who do come, if any do, will be unable to produce the required pass, you can make that the excuse for throwing them out. 'No invitation? Out!' you can say," he ended, hurling an imaginary body through the door and dusting his hands.

This speech over, he considered the matter at an end, and Aunt Flora looked at me hopelessly. "We'll cater for a limit of thirty," she said, "and after that, 'No invitation? Out!'" With this she returned to the garden, where old Barnes awaited her, and I obeyed a summons from Phyl, who had been calling loudly for me from upstairs.

Her room looked like the packing-room of a fashionable dress shop, and frocks, on hangers and off, hung or lay wherever there was room for them.

Angela sat on a small vacant space on the bed, and Polly and Diana, cross legged on the floor, goggled with delight and appeared to be giving Phyl the benefit of their wide experience in correct dressing.

"The problem," Phyl told me, "is to decide what I shall travel in. It has to be strong — Brian says I may have to stay in it until my luggage catches up with us. Polly says that one." She pointed to a tweed suit in a delightful mixture of soft shades.

"Why not?" I inquired.

"Too hot," complained Phyl.

"How do you know?" I asked. "You're going North and we're not going to have many more really boily days. That and some of your lightest blouses — what does Brian call those diaphanous ones?"

"Blow-me-downs," said Phyl. "You don't think I look too country-town in that?"

"You're only going to be in the great metropolis for an hour or so, and then only on stations," I pointed out.

Polly was delighted with this sealing of her choice, and departed with Diana to more juvenile pursuits. I cleared a space on the bed and sat down by Angela, and Phyl sat on the corner of an open trunk.

"All girls together," she smiled. "Is it true, Jonny, that Mr. Mill is trying to extract a nice domesticated wife from our midst?"

"I wouldn't go so far as that," I said cautiously. "He certainly has given me a lot of encouragement. Aunt Flora says he's mashing me."

"And would it be delicate to inquire into your feelings?" inquired Phyl.

"Not very," I replied, "but as you missed the first act I shall tell you in strict confidence that the show is going to be withdrawn and everybody's money returned."

"He isn't a bad sort of fellow," Phyl commented without much enthusiasm. "Brian's looking forward to a nice cosy chat when they meet at the pub to-night."

"I hope he enjoys it," I remarked. "He ought to be interested in listening to a summary of Mr. Mill's impressions of someone Brian has known intimately for — how many years is it?" I asked.

There was a pause while we counted.

"I make it about fifteen years," I said finally.

"Good heavens," exclaimed Phyl in dismay, "it makes me feel like Methuselah! Why, Angela can hardly have been born — were you, Angela," she asked, turning to her.

"Oh yes, I was well launched," said Angela. "I'm twenty-three," she added obligingly, in the hopeful pause which followed.

We looked at her with frank interest and affection and I noticed for the first time that she seemed a little quiet and subdued. I was on the point of asking her whether she felt unwell, but remembered that I had just happily succeeded in banishing the George-Angela problem from my mind as requiring no co-operation on my part, and was in any case prevented from putting the question, owing to Brian's arrival from below. He stood at the door and surveyed the array of garments with growing horror.

"Are those all yours?" he asked, leaning

against the door weakly and looking at Phyl.

"Uh-hu," said Phyl.

Brian looked appealingly at me, and I spoke soothingly, and reassuringly. "I'll get them all packed and sent off," I promised, "all except the one she's wearing, of course."

"Thanks, Jonny," said Brian gratefully. "Lord knows when she's ever going to use them all. Where's the wedding-dress?"

"Not arrived yet," said Phyl. "And you won't see it when it does, but I'm sure I shall be a credit to you."

"What are you all doing?" inquired Brian, his eyes taking in the scene. "Cosy girlish confidences?"

We made no reply to this, as there was a loud shout from below, and everyone within a radius of two miles was made aware that Mr. Manning was calling Miss Reynolds. There was a silence in the room and we all looked at Angela, but to our amazement she made no move whatsoever.

"Angela," came a second and even more earsplitting yell. Angela took no notice at all, and Brian looked at her.

"Excuse me," he said with playful exaggeration, "Romeo is shouting for you."

"Let him," replied Miss Reynolds briefly.

Apparently sensing this permission, George gave another blast, and Brian looked worried.

"You can't let a fellow burst his lungs without doing something about it," he protested. "Couldn't you lean out of the window and throw him a word or two?"

"Please tell him," requested Angela, "that I can't come."

Brian hesitated, and Phyl, getting up slowly, walked to the window and looked out.

"She can't come," she said.

"Why not?" demanded George. "She's supposed to be coming into Felling with me — and the children," he added bitterly. "What are you all doing up there?"

"Chatting," said Phyl. "Go away."

She turned from the window, and her expression was the one she had worn all her life when anybody treated George in a manner to which he was unaccustomed. She looked steadily at Angela, puzzlement and uneasiness warring with the affection in her glance.

"If you find George a nuisance," she said evenly, "why don't you tell him so?"

To the utter horror of the three watchers, two tears appeared on Angela's cheeks and rolled slowly downwards. We stared at them as though they were a completely new and unheard-of phenomenon and Phyl's face whitened. Angela returned her gaze steadily, and got slowly off the bed.

"I do and I will," she replied, and leaving us, walked into the bathroom and locked herself in.

Brian took three steps and sat weakly on the place she had vacated, and after a few moments of thought, looked up at Phyl, who was still staring at the bathroom door opposite.

"You seem to have, so to speak, precipitated a crisis, my darling," he said gently. "Perhaps it would have been as well to let George have all the innings."

Phyl turned and moved towards him

with so obvious an intention of leaning on his shoulder and having a good cry that I hastily vacated my place by his side to make room for her. I was feeling a little unsteady myself. I left the weeping Phyl to Brian, hesitated outside the bathroom door, wondering whether I ought to do anything about the weeping Angela, and then went on into my own room. I shut the door and repeated to myself the now familiar formula that the affair was absolutely no business of mine, and having convinced myself of this, opened the door again and went downstairs to find Aunt Flora and pour the whole tale into her experienced ears.

She was, to my relief, in the tomato house, which I felt was a perfect place for pouring out a confidential report of the recent proceedings, and I turned my steps eagerly towards it.

I went by way of the verandah, and my passage was barred by the form of George, who sat in what could almost have been termed a disconsolate attitude, gazing into space. He turned round at my approach and shifted slightly to allow me to get past him.

"When does Angela propose to come down?" he asked in surly tones.

"I don't know," I said vaguely, hurrying past him. I hesitated, however, when I had gone a few paces, and turned back. I looked at George, and he, sensing my struggle to put something into words, looked intently back at me. "Well?" he prompted.

"I don't often give advice," I said slowly, "and I loathe doing it now, but if I were you, I'd go out with the children and leave Angela alone for a bit."

George's brows came together in a terrible frown.

"What the devil are you talking about?" he asked with cold fury.

"I don't really know," I said, feeling suddenly exasperated with him and his affairs. "But I do know that a man can sometimes get on a woman's nerves, and you appear to have succeeded in getting on Angela's." I was appalled, the next moment, at the pain and humiliation in his eyes. "Don't take it too seriously," I added hastily, "but if you can bring yourself to follow my advice, you'll keep away from her for a while."

I turned and fled, feeling that I must reach Aunt Flora before things became entirely out of control. I burst open the door of the tomato house and entered at top speed, closing the door behind me and meeting the amazed glance of Aunt Flora.

"It's George and Angela," I panted.

"Dear me," said Aunt Flora, adding a fat tomato to the row. "Have they attacked you?"

"Attacked me?" I asked. "What do you mean?"

"Well, my dear Jonny," she said, standing back and looking appraisingly at the beautiful fruit. "You came in here as though someone were pursuing you, and you mentioned George and Angela."

"You're being flippant," I protested, "and this is serious."

"You're being very calm and making the situation as clear as possible," said Aunt Flora. "I know there hasn't been an accident because you never lose your head over real trouble."

"I think this is real trouble," I said, "and I'm sorry I behaved like a fool, but I'm not the only one — Phyl's crying and so is Angela, and I told George he had got on her nerves and he looked like a dog when you kick it."

Aunt Flora frowned thoughtfully as she tried to sort out this lucid account of what had occurred.

"Why are Phyl and Angela crying?" she inquired finally, giving it up.

I opened my mouth eagerly to pour forth a vivid account of the proceedings.

"George called Angela and she wouldn't come," I began, and stopped, realizing with astonishment that the tale was told.

Aunt Flora waited patiently. "Well?" she asked after a while.

I opened my mouth again, feeling sure there was a story somewhere if only I could think of it.

"That's all," I said.

Aunt Flora supported herself on the strongest-looking tomato plant. "George called Angela," she said. "I knew that already — thought it would shatter the glass here."

"Well, she was upstairs with us," I said. "And she wouldn't go."

"Does she have to attend immediately whenever George bellows for her?"

in-quired Aunt Flora.

"No," I said, "but she could have said something out of the window and she wouldn't, so Phyl told him to go away and she asked Angela why she didn't get rid of George if he got on her nerves and Angela said she would and she's shut in the bathroom now, crying."

"Did you say Phyl was crying too?" inquired Aunt Flora.

"Yes — she's crying on Brian, so she's all right," I said, "but you've got to do something about Angela and George."

"Is he crying too?" asked Aunt Flora.

"No, of course he isn't," I said impatiently, "but he's hurt — I had to say something or he would have gone up and then I don't suppose she would ever have spoken to him again."

Aunt Flora looked at me. "I wish," she said irritably "you'd decide which side of the fence you're on. If my memory isn't at fault, when we last discussed this subject you considered that George was a totally unsuitable husband for her."

"Well, I think I still think so," I said, "but it isn't a thing one should interfere in, and so I decided not to worry over it any more."

"That's an excellent idea," said Aunt Flora, "and fits in with my view exactly."

I stared at her.

"Aunt Flora," I said earnestly, "you've got to do something. I meant that *I* couldn't interfere — it isn't my job — but you can't let them make a hash of things. I honestly don't care whether they marry or whether they don't — at least I don't think I care — but the thing must have a fair chance. I don't know what George has done, but it couldn't have been anything unpleasant — he isn't at all like that — and all I want you to do is . . . well, just do something," I ended feebly.

"George is thirty-two," she pointed out, "and a man of the world. Angela is about twenty-two and has been her own mistress for many years. If the two of them can't find their own solution to a problem which countless millions of other couples have solved without any help from anybody, I don't think they deserve to be happy. I am not," she concluded firmly, "going to conduct

George's wooing for him."

We looked at each other.

"Aren't you going to do anything at all?" I asked in dismay.

"Certainly," replied Aunt Flora. "I am going to get Angela out of the bathroom."

We left the tomato house and went indoors. There was no necessity for Aunt Flora to remove Angela from the bathroom, however, for we met her at the head of the stairs, and she greeted us with a collected air and a welcoming smile.

"I was coming to look for you," she told Aunt Flora. "Please could I have a talk with you somewhere?"

"Certainly," replied Aunt Flora. "My room, I think, is about the only stronghold in the house. Even George," she said, leading the way, "knocks before he comes in."

I opened the door for her and ushered her and Angela in, closing it again firmly. I was turning towards the stairs once more when the door opened and Angela clutched my dress and, to my unspeakable relief, pulled me inside and closed the door behind us.

17

"IF it's about George," began Aunt Flora, "It's sure to be a long session, so we might as well be comfortable. You can sit on the window seat, Angela, and Jonny and I can sit on the sofa."

"It's only a little about George," said Angela. "I'm afraid most of it will be about me." She sat on the window seat with one leg curled under her, and looked at me a little wearily.

"I'm sorry I made such a fool of myself in Phyl's room," she said, "I've been longing to talk to someone all day, but it's impossible to talk to Phyl about anything connected with George — she's very pro-George — quite rightly, of course," she added, and Aunt Flora nodded in agreement.

"I'm going away," went on Angela, slowly turning and gazing out at the hills, "but I love you all so much that I must try and tell you how things have gone wrong."

"Is your old lady worse?" inquired Aunt Flora.

Angela turned back and shook her head.

"No," she said. "But I was looking forward to staying at Rushing until Diana went back to school. I loved being with you all — I only came down to do what I could for Diana. I knew Miss Crompton wouldn't let her come to anybody who wasn't absolutely reliable" — she gave me a little smile that begged forgiveness — "but I felt I might be of use in some way. Diana has never been so happy, and nor have I, and the reason is that we've never been in a real home before. I shall never forget being here." Her voice became a little unsteady, and she stopped.

"That was surely not meant as a hail and farewell speech, I hope?" asked Aunt Flora gently. "There's a flaw in it somewhere, if it was. You came, you loved us, and when, please is the next train to London. Is George so great a nuisance?"

"No," said Angela, "although perhaps I oughtn't to have let him be a nuisance at all. I thought his attentions," she said after a little hesitation, "were the filling-in-time variety. He hadn't much to think of down here, and as long as Polly and Diana were with me it didn't seem important whether George made one of the party or not. Men can be extremely pleasant to a girl without having the slightest intention of — engaging her affections. And I took George's pleasantries in the spirit I thought they were meant. Nobody in the world could have said I encouraged him — and I hadn't the remotest idea until last night, when we walked back with Mr. Mill and left him at the inn door, that George was doing anything else but — "

"Philandering," finished Aunt Flora. "Well, any of us could have put you right. George is several kinds of villain, but not that kind. And are you going back to London because he has fallen in love with you?"

"No," said Angela. "I'm going away because I think he's constitutionally incapable of taking 'No' for an answer — he thinks it's merely a matter of

337

applying a little more of the most appealing brand of charm, and he'll go on with the applications and I shall go mad."

"I think you're wrong on that point too," said Aunt Flora after a pause, "but it isn't a matter on which I would take the responsibility of advising anybody. Isn't there anybody of your own family you could talk to? It may seem a little sordid to bring up the purely mercenary side of the matter, but George is — well — extremely eligible."

"If he had — how did Mrs. Bennett put it — 'a house in Town — everything that is charming — ten thousand a year,'" said Angela, "I'd still be of the same mind. He's an actor, and I will-not-marry-an-actor."

There was a silence, and Angela left her window seat and came over to Aunt Flora, slipping into a sitting posture at her feet and resting her hands on Aunt Flora's knees.

"I'm awfully sorry," she said, "but perhaps I can try and explain — You see," she went on after a little while, "my father was an actor — not a very successful one, but he was a charming man, and very well liked by everyone who met him. He never made very much money, although we were always very happy and weren't, I think, ever in what they call distressed circumstances. My mother had just finished her training as a dancer when they met and she never appeared professionally, but she taught my sister and me and we appeared several times together until I was about eleven, when I refused to dance or sing or perform any more. My parents didn't press me at all — I begged to be allowed to go to a boarding school and I went. My sister loved all the things I loathed — the travelling, the change, the succession of boarding-houses and landladies and theatrical fellow-boarders. She went on dancing and eventually married Malcolm Kemp and they became a dance team — they're very happy, but Diana's like me — she loathes the life and wants nothing in the world so much as a settled home and steady people round her. All my life," went on Angela, grasping one of Aunt Flora's hands to give emphasis to her words, "I've met charming people. People whose business it was to be pleasant, people who lived from day to day and moved from one town to the next, one show to the next, enjoying the changes and the reunions and the excitements and the glitter of the lights — and those who want the life can have it. I don't. I want a steady diet of plain people, with a secure and unchanging setting, a place where you can bring your children up and give them their own rooms filled with their treasures instead of a suitcase covered with labels — and a garden and pets and a place they can bring their friends to stay during holidays — friends whose own parents are dancing all over the country and can't give their own children a home." Angela seized Aunt Flora's free hand and held it. "You see?" she asked urgently. "I don't want George. I don't want a circle of brilliant and charming people revolving round me and filling my house or my flat — I want a house like this, in the country, and I want to be like Mrs. Manning and think of nothing but meals and the children's health and mending. My most cherished ambition," she said, with almost desperate earnestness, "is to live in one house with my husband and children and dogs and never leave it until I die."

She stopped and released Aunt Flora's hands, and Aunt Flora rubbed them back to life slowly and thoughtfully.

"Are your parents dead?" she asked.

"Yes," answered Angela. "My mother died after an operation when I was twelve, and my father was trapped in a theatre which caught fire, and died — that was when I was seventeen, and I did one or two office jobs, living in a furnished room in London, and then got this secretary-companion to my old lady. She's a pet, but it's another succession of hotels and more hotels. I've got a — I suppose you'd call it a phobia now. Nothing that George can offer has the slightest attraction, you see. Charm — my own family had oceans of it — glitter — definitely no — money — it's necessary, but in his case it merely means moving up to the luxury hotel standard." She looked up at Aunt Flora. "You see now, don't you?" she asked.

Aunt Flora was still kneading her fingers, and did not reply immediately. I thought she was waiting for the last tank to get into position before moving off to do battle for her nephew.

"No, I don't quite see," she said gently, "I understand a great deal, but nothing you have said seems to be at all connected with George."

Angela frowned in astonishment, and opened her mouth to make her points clearer, but Aunt Flora held up her hand. "No," she said, "I heard it all, and it all registered perfectly, but the connection is still obscure. One: You dislike moving about — "

Angela nodded.

"But George doesn't move about," pointed out Aunt Flora. "He has been in London — except for visits, of course, which I take it even you would have to make — for the last ten years and more. When his plays opened in the provinces his man kept his flat open and his treasures in good order. He only did one film in America and I forget how long he was away, but his flat was chosen and furnished by me just after his first big success, and he has never changed it. He has been asking me for years to keep house for him, but I had my brother on my hands for a long while — his wife was like you in her passionate resolve to stay in one place all the time, once his service at sea was ended, and it gave the poor man D.T.s in the end, and after her death I took over his remains and so I couldn't come to George. When Uncle Eddie died I did think of it, but we came down here and Jonny talked me into living here, so George is still without a mistress for his home, but the home itself, I assure you, my dear Angela, has been entirely in one place all the time."

Angela drew a breath and opened her mouth.

"Two," pursued Aunt Flora, "you don't want to live with someone who has what is called charm. The word occurred so much in George's early notices that I took the trouble to look it up in the dictionary, and it said 'the power to please and delight'. Well, if you don't want to be pleased and delighted in the home I can recommend George as the very thing for you. I would have thought your glimpses of him with his nearest and dearest would have qualified him for your purposes."

"But — " began Angela.

"Three," said Aunt Flora, as though a bee had buzzed, "you want a home and children. Although I'm not in a position to say so definitely, I would guess that George, in proposing to you, also had the thought of a home and children at the back of his mind."

"He's an actor," said Angela stubbornly. "Reporters flock round him and publish rubbish about his private life. They invade his home and want to know what goes on. He's a public person and only a fraction of his personality remains available for his wife and family."

"What job," asked Aunt Flora, "would you like your husband to do? — or does he have to stay in one place, like you and the children and the house and the dogs?"

"He can do a nice stuffy office job," said Angela. "Out at eight-thirty and back by six-thirty, Saturdays and Sundays free."

"And he must be stodgy and entirely devoid of charm?" added Aunt Flora.

"Yes," said Angela.

"God forbid," said Aunt Flora, "that I should ever visit you. You said you were fond of us," she went on. "Have you any idea why?"

"I have," said Angela affectionately, "but wouldn't it embarrass you if I told you?"

"Not at all," said Aunt Flora. "Do go on."

"Well," began Angela eagerly, "you're a darling, and so is Mrs. Manning — she's my ideal of perfect domesticity — and Phyl is lovely and the children are pets and Carrie's a friend, and you're all so united and happy that it makes me happy to be with you, and I had a dream when I met you that perhaps I could come and live with you as a sort of nurse-companion when you got old and feeble — " Again her voice wobbled dangerously and she stopped.

"You aren't calling us a stodgy, stuffy set, are you?" asked Aunt Flora.

"No," smiled Angela, "but you don't use your charm for a living, like the people I'm talking about. It seasons your more solid qualities — it isn't all charm and nothing firm and dependable underneath."

"I always heard," said Aunt Flora, "that theatrical people were the most loyal and dependable in the world."

"Among themselves, yes," said Angela, "but they're not a settled race, and I want to leave the nomad tribe and settle in Canaan. If it hadn't been for George," she added, "I could have stayed here — "

"We've been longing to get rid of George for quite a long time," said Aunt Flora. "I don't see why you shouldn't stay and let him do the moving. If you go and leave him, he'll make life quite frightful for us all and probably wreck the wedding because its associations would be too much for his sensibilities."

"He can't be as bad as all that," said Angela with a smile.

"Nobody knows how bad he can be," replied Aunt Flora, "because nobody has ever seen him in love before."

Angela put an appealing hand on Aunt Flora's knee. "I'm awfully sorry about it all," she said. "Can you forgive me? — but I promise you with all my heart that I didn't dream he could be serious. I would have gone away at once if I'd had the slightest idea — "

Aunt Flora patted the small brown hand rather absently.

"You mustn't worry," she said. "I didn't think myself he'd fall in love with you — I didn't think he'd have the sense." She paused and looked down at Angela. "You must make your own decisions," she said. "I might have tried to give you advice as you haven't parents of your own, but, of course, in this case I must be a little prejudiced — although God knows," she went on, "George will be a difficult problem for any woman who has the courage to marry him — but one thing I must say, and that is, that you must be under no delusion as to George's real character. George," she said firmly, "is a very fine fellow indeed. You may rule him out on the grounds of unsuitable profession, excess of charm (except in the home) or anything else you please, but you must remember that he is honest, well brought up, and not much more selfish than the average man. Don't imagine that your stolid husband is going to have better or more sterling qualities than George — the contents may turn out to be exactly the same, whether they're wrapped in silver paper or the more homely brown." She stopped and smiled. "That's the end of the lecture, my dear, dear Angela," she said. "We all love you very much, and if ever you do change your mind about George, I shall be almost as happy as he will."

There was a long, rather unhappy silence, and Aunt Flora broke it finally.

"I think you'll find that once you get away from George — and from us all — your mind will become clearer and you'll realize that your problem isn't really such a tangled one. Go away as soon as you can," she said, "and don't tie yourself up in arguments. Forget Rushing and forget George, if you can. If you can't, and if you feel you can meet him and give him a fair chance, come down to Phyl's wedding and have a talk with him. You'll find that even a few hours right away from here will do miracles in the way of clearing up the position — "

She rose and walked to the window and stood looking out for some time, and when she turned, her face looked a little drawn.

"Stay up here for a little while," she said. "George is just back and I'm going down to talk to him."

She went to the door and Angela opened it for her and held up her face, tears falling fast down her cheeks. Aunt Flora kissed her and patted the damp face.

"I hope we shall see you at the wedding," she said gently, and went out.

Nobody ever knew what she said to George, but he went out immediately afterwards, nobody knew where, and when he returned, late that night, Angela was on her way back to London.

18

RUTH EXLEY came over on hearing that Angela was no longer with us, and proved her sterling worth by inviting our three children over for all meals until the day of the wedding.

"Do let me have them," she begged. "Ivan has practically lived here and it would be kind to let me attempt to make some sort of return. It'll get them out of your way."

I was only too glad to accept the kind offer, and our preparations proceeded without the usual noise and interruptions.

We had been right in our supposition that George's rejection would make us as miserable as he himself was, but we were wrong in thinking he would cause storms and upheavals in the house. Rages and scenes, we now learned, were for the minor troubles of life, such as unsuitably furnished guest rooms or water temperatures. George was now in real trouble, and we saw nothing of him. He presumably ate somewhere, but he was not present at meals at home. He came home to sleep, but I heard him walking about his room at night, and from Aunt Flora's pale and tired appearance at breakfast, I knew she too was losing sleep. I felt sorry for her, sorry for George, and sorry for Phyl and Brian, this being a poor prelude to the nuptials.

Brian had a hard task to persuade Phyl that she was not, as she imagined, the cause of all the trouble.

"If I hadn't spoken then, like a fool," she said sorrowfully, "nothing would have happened, and George would have been happy."

"If you hadn't spoken," Brian assured her, "and if Angela hadn't wept, and if Jonny hadn't run for Aunt Flora, there would have been a colossal showdown with George behaving his pretty awful worst, and that would have blasted his future completely. As it is he stands a fifty-fifty chance. The girl will go back and pine for his handsome presence, and by the time he's walked the worst of it off in the hills, poor devil, he'll be able to appear before her with Christian resignation."

"That doesn't sound very sympathetic," said Phyl reproachfully.

"Doesn't it, my sweet?" said Brian. "Well, remember I've been through it — " and Phyl said no more.

So George walked on the hills all day and on his bedroom floor most of the night, and we proceeded with the preparations for the wedding, now only two days distant. I had a little uneasy feeling of having forgotten something, and on coming back from the Colonel's after paying a brief call to leave some fruit for Claudia, I met Mr. Mill on his way to our verandah, and realized with a shock that the recent storms had entirely submerged my little struggling romance, driving it from everyone's mind — including my own. I was glad to see Mr. Mill — he had not been well treated, I thought, and deserved more consideration, and he should have it now that Phyl and Brian were available to entertain him. He joined me with a smile and we walked on together, the dogs sniffing a little suspiciously at him before they fell into line behind us.

"Won't you come back to lunch?" I invited.

He accepted with frank pleasure, and I tried to make a little apology for our not having made his stay in Rushing more pleasant.

"I'm afraid you came at an abnormal time," I explained. "The wedding is going to be a rather hurried one, and Brian, of course, imagines it's merely a matter of walking into church and saying: 'I will'."

Mr. Mill smiled.

"Well, I'm rather inclined to agree with him," he said. "The rest is surely more for the gratification of the guests. I've never been married, but I don't think the cake and the confetti would penetrate my consciousness at such a time."

I tried to make a reply concerning the penetrating qualities of confetti, of which I had had experience, but before I could frame it in a satisfyingly witty form, Mr. Mill put a hand on my arm and indicated the little path on our left, which led through two or three fields to our small orchard and which we called the long way round.

"That leads to the house eventually, doesn't it?" he asked, "let's go that way if you're not in a hurry."

I hesitated a little.

"Please do," he begged.

"Very well," I said, "if you promise I can be back in time to get the things from Aunt Flora and make the salad."

He promised, and we went on, presently coming to rest on a comfortable stile between the fields. It was a pleasant day, and Mr. Mill looked appreciatively round at the lovely scene.

"I'm afraid I made a great many overstatements when I called at your office," I said. "George was appalled at my misleading picture of life in the country. You know his idea of the simple life."

"Quite, quite," said Mr. Mill. "But perhaps it is really the simple life — if you want water, you turn a tap; if you want milk you open the front door and there it is. If you want fish, rows and rows of it, suitably prepared for edible purposes, lie on slabs round the corner. What could be simpler?"

I had to confess that nothing could. "I shall not talk about the simple life any more," I said, "unless I'm living it under those circumstances — but I hope I never do," I added.

Mr. Mill studied me in silence for a time, and then spoke gently.

"You like life at Rushing, don't you?" he said.

I admitted that I liked it very much, and added that I considered my modest earthly requirements were pretty well catered for in most ways — in almost every way but one, I added to myself, and that was a want which Mr. Mill could do nothing to alleviate.

"I don't know exactly what makes me so happy here," I said haltingly. "It's just a large, rather uncomfortable house in nice surroundings — I know all the things I like about it, but I can't put them into words. I'm not very — " I searched for a word and Mr. Mill kindly supplied one.

"Articulate?" he suggested.

"That would do," I said. "It sounds dreadfully inhospitable, but I don't even mind the fact that we're so remote and un-getatable, since it saves us from that dreadful succession of — "

"Casual visitors?"

"People who say they've just dropped in," I said firmly. "There's a monotony and peacefulness about our life — except, of course, during holidays, that I find very — "

"Satisfying," supplied Mr. Mill. He studied me with almost brotherly affection for a few moments.

"You're a very peaceful person," he said. "You do your appointed tasks quietly and steadily and you don't make the mistake so many women do of getting involved in more than they can manage. They make their lives a — " he hesitated.

"Hotch potch," I offered, in return for services rendered.

Mr. Mill tried it over and rejected it, but it had in some way served to remind me of lunch. I rose hastily and Mr. Mill got reluctantly to his feet. He handed me over the stile with old-world gallantry, and had such serious difficulty in getting himself over after me that I could scarcely prevent myself from holding up my arms to lift him over as I did Polly. Instead I walked on slowly, and in a few moments found him by my side, a little breathless and dusty. We walked on together, and presently he looked at me with his pleasant smile.

"I think we're both old enough, Mrs. Manning," he said, "to be able to speak frankly. I've spent a good deal of time on your verandah, and I suppose you know why. I don't know why I ever imagined there was anything I could offer which could make you think of leaving all this." He waved a hand in a half circle. I found myself entirely unable to reply to this, and gazed at him with what I hoped was a suitable sisterly expression. He pulled Rover's ears absent-mindedly for a few moments, and then went on half to himself.

"I'll never forget my visit here," he said, "although the two things I came down for didn't really turn out as I hoped. One was to see you," he continued with a smile, turning towards me, "and the other was to persuade George to go into a play in a part after his own heart, but he wouldn't even consider it. I don't want you to think me impertinent or unduly curious, but I hope Miss Reynolds' departure doesn't mean that things aren't progressing as favourably as they might."

There was no point in concealing the facts from him, as he had been closely associated with George for more than ten years, and had conducted his business, and in some cases his private affairs for him for nearly as long. I told him briefly that as far as one could see things were not progressing at all, and no more was said, although I pondered deeply over the affair as we walked homewards and from Mr. Mill's silence and absorbed air, I judged that he, too was commiserating with George on the hitch in his hitherto smooth and untangled existence.

The empty place at lunch was a reminder to us all that though we might eat and drink, an unhappy member of our company strode hungry among the hills — or so we presumed.

Mr. Mill proved very good company, and Brian expressed a hope that he would stay at Rushing at least until after the wedding.

"It's a little informal," he added, "but

we shall be very happy to see you."

"I had set my heart on coming," said Mr. Mill with obvious sincerity, "and now that I'm formally on the list of guests, may I ask if my car would be of any use — or have you already arranged cars and so on?"

Aunt Flora looked at him gratefully. "Nothing at all was arranged," she said. "I was counting on asking the Wheelers, who have the only car in Rushing — the only car one could use for a wedding, that is — but they're to be away until after the wedding. Brian," she added, "probably intended walking round to the church with Phyl on his arm."

"Why not?" demanded Brian. "A nice little bit of exercise before the ceremony. It takes exactly seven minutes to walk there — even Phyl can manage the distance."

"It's the look of the thing," said Aunt Flora, "and you're not going to haul your bride into the church by yourself. It won't really matter how Brian gets there," she went on, turning to Mr. Mill, "but if you could drive George and Phyl round it would make the thing look a little more — well, more legal than it does at present."

"God knows," said Brian gloomily, "whether we'll manage to get married at all. George is giving the bride away and he's also best man, and he's in no state to be trusted with a wedding ring — that is if he turns up at all. I think he's forgotten all about the whole show. If only I'd foreseen this I'd never have let that girl get as far as Rushing the first time I saw her. Practically wrecked my nuptials, and got George into such a state he'll never be able to act anything in future except Hamlet's ghost."

"Is the outlook as gloomy as all that?" asked Mr. Mill in genuine concern.

"Speaking entirely for myself," said Aunt Flora, "I would say not. But I'm afraid this is a matter in which one can only stand by and refrain from interference."

I looked at her and noted with astonishment and relief that she had lost the look of strain she had worn lately. I wondered whether Angela had telephoned or written, and wished fervently that we had been alone so that I might have put the question to her.

"Well, if you feel the car will be useful," said Mr. Mill, coming back to practical matters, "it's at your disposal. I'll bring it round early in the morning and I shall be happy to drive the bride to church — and the bridegroom too, and any of you who — "

"Want to arrive in style," said Brian. "It's very decent of you and we'll be grateful. I think that's everything now, isn't it?" he asked Aunt Flora. "Special licence, day and time, bridal equipage — can you think of anything else?"

Aunt Flora couldn't, and Phyl, who had been studying Brian closely while he spoke, now voiced the result of her scrutiny.

"Darling, you're getting fat," she said.

"Nonsense," replied Brian. "A fellow of my age always gets a little bit wider here and there. I was never what you might call emaciated, you know."

"Well, you're getting fat," repeated Phyl.

"It's happiness and a sense of well-being," explained Brian. "And pride and a feeling of elation — that blows you out more than anything."

"So does lack of exercise," commented Aunt Flora. "Don't you do any physical jerks?"

Brian looked hurt. "Of course I do," he said. "I bend down and touch my knees several times every morning. When I've been married to Phyl a few years and tuned myself in to her wave-length and got accustomed to her ceaseless activity, I'll be so enormous that they'll have to hoist me on to the bridge with a pulley."

"Well, you've got some exercise to do to-morrow," promised Aunt Flora. "There's a pile of unopened wedding presents to be looked at — you've got to get them all out and arrange them somewhere."

"We're not going to display them, are we?" asked Brian.

"I think so," said Aunt Flora. "People like to see them and they'll be a reassurance to the guests that this really is a wedding. Sometimes I wonder whether it is myself."

Before Mr. Mill left it was arranged that he and Brian would ask Mrs. Exley for the loan of the four children the next day, to tackle the really stupendous task of sorting, listing and arranging the wedding presents, which lay in the hall as Mr. Stebbing had delivered them, and which Aunt Flora and I and even Phyl, now seriously sorting clothes, had had no time to deal with.

Mr. Mill promised to come over soon after breakfast and put himself at our disposal, and I was relieved at the thought of having a responsible person to take a little of the extra work off our hands.

There was no opportunity to engage Aunt Flora in talk until bedtime, and before going to my room I knocked on her door and found her inside with Phyl. On her bed was spread the exquisite frock in which Phyl was to be married — she called it ice blue, and I could think of no other name to describe the soft yet definite, satisfying colour. I held it against Phyl and smiled at her over its lovely folds.

"It's perfect," I said, "and you'll look lovely."

I laid it carefully on the back of the sofa.

"I know what you came in for," said Aunt Flora, "and it wasn't to see Phyl's frock."

"No," I admitted. "It was the remark you made at lunch about Angela. It sounded rather definite and you look different and I wondered if you'd heard anything."

"I'm sorry I said anything that sounded definite," said Aunt Flora, "because I've absolutely nothing to go on except her letter this morning. There's nothing in it to make one rush to conclusions, but" — she paused thoughtfully, and then continued — "there's no rubbish in it about phobias, for one thing, and it sounds sane and collected and not at all like the jingle-jangle she talked in here."

"That doesn't mean she's changed her mind," argued Phyl.

"No, it doesn't," said Aunt Flora, "but it means she has done some thinking, and is feeling calmer."

"I don't see how thinking about him calmly will make her like him any more," said Phyl.

"Perhaps it won't," agreed Aunt Flora,

"but she's a sensible girl and she didn't take long to realize that she'd made a great deal of fuss over saying 'No' to an honest proposal. If she can own herself wrong in her method of refusal — which she does frankly in her letter — she can go a step further and decide that her reasons for her refusal were equally foolish. There it is, and now go to bed, both of you. I'm sure nobody made silly speeches about phobias and complexes in my young days. A girl nowadays gets an offer from a clean, healthy fellow like George and turns it down because it doesn't fit in with some God-forsaken idea she had when she was eleven."

She sat down with what was almost a flounce and began to unpin her hair. "Phsaw," she ended. "Stuff and utter nonsense. I've no patience with it."

We kissed her quietly and left her muttering maledictions against foolish virgins, or it might have been prayers for George's happiness.

19

THE day before the wedding of Phyl and Brian stands out in my memory in the same way as I imagine the journey in the tossing, overcrowded Ark did in Noah's when he looked back upon it after the waters had subsided and their roaring was no longer in his ears.

No doubt Noah managed to keep his mind on his navigation while the monkeys chattered and the elephants trumpeted. So did I proceed with the preparations for an unknown number of guests, setting out tables, helping Phyl with her packing, preparing wedding finery for Paul, Polly, Diana and myself supervising Carrie and Mrs. Watt in the kitchen and making the house look as lovely and flower-decked as possible, while the telephone shrilled ceaselessly and my attention was claimed constantly to answer problems which arose from every quarter.

All the parcels had been carried into the drawing-room, and the children waded waist-high in packages and wrappings, while Brian sat perched precariously on a chair set on a table, like a tennis umpire, list in hand, calling in strident auctioneer fashion the particulars of the presents and the names of the donors, while Mr. Mill laid the gifts artistically on tables round the room and gave orders to the children. I was used to a slightly-modified form of this kind of noise and chatter, and could work in spite of it, but I was quite unprepared for the stream of visitors who came, presents in hand, to wish Phyl luck and happiness. These were our friends, and I had to pause and speak at least a few words to each, and they proved the most serious hindrance throughout the day.

The Colonel came early, and I led him to the door of the drawing-room, where we were brought up short by an impassable pile of wrappings. We stood waiting for a pause in the proceedings before we could make our presence known.

"Salt cellar," shouted Brian, "salt

cellar, silver, Mrs. Bruce Manning. Salt cellar — dammit, I've got that down once already."

"But there are two," said Polly, holding them up for his inspection and then passing them on to Mr. Mill.

"Salt cellars, two, next please, here we have a — what on earth is it?" asked Brian, peering down from his precarious perch.

"I've no idea," said the bewildered Diana. "Do you know?" she asked, appealing to Paul.

Paul looked round to pass the inquiry on, and saw us in the doorway. "Whoa," he called up to Brian, "wait a minute."

Brian waited, and greetings were exchanged, and I led the Colonel on to the verandah, which I decided was the only place in which anybody would be able to talk and be heard.

"You're awfully busy, and I'm not going to stay," he said, "but I'd like to wish Phyl the best of luck if she can spare a moment."

I brought Phyl down and went back to the drawing-room to find out whether the wedding presents could be dealt with in a slightly less deafening way.

"We're not making any noise," protested Brian. "I can't stay down in that welter of packages, and they've got to call up the names. Shut the door, Jonny, and nobody'll hear us and we'll get the job done some time. Who asked everybody to send us all this stuff?" he went on wrathfully. "You're only going to have the job of packing it all up again and chucking the whole lot into a trunk. Oh well, let's get on with it. Decanter, one, decanter, Mr. Bruce Manning — here, wait a minute that can't be right — they sent salt cellars — "

"That was *Mrs.*," said Polly, "this is Uncle Bruce separately."

"Why the devil," demanded Brian, "couldn't he have thrown in a third salt cellar and left it at that? all right, decanter, Uncle Bruce — your Uncle Bruce and from to-morrow, my Uncle Bruce, too," he said wagging his pencil at Polly. "Now proceed — are there any little Bruces?"

"Yes," said Polly, "but I haven't seen anything from them."

"Well, we won't give up hope," said

369

Brian, "there'll be a couple of little pepper-pots coming along soon. Next please — "

I shut the door and went upstairs to hang Polly's and Diana's newly-pressed dresses out of harm's way in my wardrobe, and Ivan called to me from below. Aunt Flora had commandeered his services and he had cut and brought in several bunches of flowers and was now waiting for me to relieve him of yet another fragrant armful.

"It's going to rain, Miss Manning says, and we're going down to the church to arrange the flowers there."

"Thank you, Ivan," I said. "Your mother has rung up to say she's expecting all you children back to lunch, so you mustn't be long."

Miss Peel arrived just before the rain fell, and I took her into the amazing scene in the drawing-room, one half of which now looked like a West End silversmith's, with a shining array tastefully laid on small tables, while the other half was still a welter of open and unopened packages.

Brian waved a hearty welcome from his

perch, and Phyl picked her way across some parcels.

"How nice to see you," he called, "you must walk round the tables and tell me if you approve of the display."

"A private view," said Miss Peel, with satisfaction. "You all look extremely busy. Perhaps I can do something?"

Without the slightest hesitation I filled her arms with flowers and indicated vases, and another helper was added to the growing list. She worked faithfully until Aunt Flora returned and she realized it was almost lunch time. She refused an invitation to stay, and made preparations for departure.

"See you to-morrow," sang Brian cheerfully.

"I shall see you," said Miss Peel, "but I very much doubt whether you'll have eyes for me."

"Then I'll have ears," said Brian, suddenly remembering that she had something to do with the organ. "I shall hear you playing your twiddly bits."

Miss Peel hesitated and looked appealingly at Phyl. "You didn't say anything about the organ," she faltered.

"I thought perhaps — "

"We have left undone all those things which — you know," said Phyl. "If you will play for us, we shall love it."

Miss Peel's homely features were irradiated with happiness as she departed, and Phyl came back into the room and looked reproachfully at Brian.

"There," she said, "you went and asked her."

"I went and what?" demanded Brian, pausing in the act of turning over a page in his notebook.

"You asked her to play," said Phyl.

Brian looked astounded, and looked at the children for corroboration of this accusation. They nodded their heads in agreement, and his gaze returned to the upturned face of Phyl.

"You did," she said, "and now we'll have those wails and they do sound so mournful."

"Did I really say 'Come and play at my wedding'?" asked Brian. "I must have been talking in my sleep."

"You didn't exactly put it into those words," said Mr. Mill, "but you gave a general impression."

"He's been giving general impressions to everyone he met in London," said Aunt Flora, "and we ought to have held the reception in the Albert Hall."

"Well, I rather like the Wedding March," said Brian philosophically. "I wonder whether she'll play the Da dee dee-da one or the Da da dee-da da day doh one."

"You mean the Mendelssohn or the Wagner," said Mr. Mill.

"Do I?" asked Brian, surprised. "I've been neglecting my practice shockingly lately. My music's going to pieces."

Phyl pulled me outside and shut the door behind us. "Come upstairs with me, Jonny," she said. "I'm feeling depressed."

"Depressed!" I exclaimed. "At such a time?"

Phyl went up the stairs, her hand still in mine, and led me into her room. "It's George," she explained, sinking on to the bed and resting her chin disconsolately on the bed rail. "Do you think he's forgotten all about the wedding, or will he appear at the last moment looking like a death's head and upsetting Brian?"

I hadn't the faintest idea what George

would do, and I looked helplessly at Phyl and thought hard thoughts of her brother.

"Don't worry, Phyl," I said at last. "He'll turn up, I think. If he doesn't feel sociable it's better for him to stay away — it would be dreadful if he mooned about and damped everybody's spirits."

"Do you suppose *she'll* come to-morrow?" asked Phyl.

There was no need to ask who she was, and again I was quite unable to find an answer.

"I'm being foolish," murmured Phyl, half to herself, "but I keep forgetting Brian and the wedding and concentrating on George and his misery. It oughtn't to have happened — we were all having such a nice time."

Carrie sounded the gong for lunch and Phyl sat up and looked round at the preparations for her wedding and departure.

"You can't do anything for George," I said, "but you can make sure that Brian doesn't see you're worried. It would be mean to upset him."

Phyl promised to try and put George

completely out of her mind, and we went down to lunch, and, in the dining-room, looking round calmly at the evidences of wedding preparations in the shape of extra tables and masses of flowers, stood George with Aunt Flora.

"Hello," he greeted Phyl unemotionally. "I heard you were being married — how's everything going?"

Phyl assured him that everything was going well, and Brian and Mr. Mill came in to complete the party.

"Where are all the hordes of children?" inquired their uncle.

It was explained that they were being taken off our hands by the kind Mrs. Exley, and George thought this an excellent idea and wondered why I did not arrange it more often.

The party was a little constrained at the beginning of lunch, as it was felt that the wedding, which was the subject uppermost in all our minds, might make painful listening for George. He sensed this, and after sitting in silence for some time, listening with a slightly sardonic expression to our efforts at easy, general conversation, gathered the party into his hands and led the talk into the channel we had been carefully avoiding.

"What," he asked Phyl, "do you want me to do tomorrow? Do I stand next to Brian at the altar while you come up the aisle by yourself, or do I leave Brian and devote myself to you?"

"Well, there's been a lot of planning," confessed Phyl. "but I don't really know what's going on. Ask Brian."

"It's all absolutely set," said Brian. "Aunt Flora goes ahead to see that everybody behaves nicely in the church, and I go next in the car of your friend Robert here — he's going to stand at the altar with me until you come and take over."

"And I do what?" inquired George.

"You come with us to drive the car back," said Brian, "and you come back for Phyl — oh, I forgot you, Jonny — what happens to you? Oh, you stay with the bride until the last moment, seeing she's nice and tidy, and leave her just as George takes her up the aisle."

"Well, do you mind if I get it straight?" said George. "I drive you and Robert to the church and come back for Phyl and

Jonny — is that it?"

"That's it," said Brian. "And you're best man and you're giving Phyl away and after that your time is your own."

"And the guests all go straight to the church and then come back here afterwards?" said George.

"It depends," said Aunt Flora, "on how many thousands there are. I'm trying not to think about it — I shall let Brian cope with the crowds of strangers he was so good as to invite."

"They're not strangers," protested Brian. "They won't turn up, but they were all people with some kind of family look about them — fourth cousins and so on." He took a large mouthful of food and seemed anxious to say something more, so we waited patiently until he swallowed the last piece. "I may say," he went on, "that the list of presents made me feel a bit apprehensive — there's a lot of stuff there from people who can have had no reason to send anything unless they intended to get back the value off the wedding breakfast. Why would Aunt Whatshername, for instance — the one living in the purlieus of

Kensington — why would she hand over a perfectly good biscuit box which she's had for years unless she had ulterior motives?"

"I'm sure you asked her," said Phyl, "but don't worry — a lot of them will turn back when they get to Felling and see the bus."

Brian looked more cheerful at this thought. "Of course," he said, "if old Duff had one of his stop-no-go turns, everything would be all right and we could have a really nice wedding by ourselves."

"It isn't quite in order, is it," asked George, "for the bridegroom to be falling round our feet on the day before the wedding — not to mention the day itself."

"Oh — all that stuff," said Brian airily. "Do you mind, darling," he asked Phyl, "if I come to-morrow before the actual kick-off."

Phyl didn't. She was looking a picture of quiet content. George had remembered, George had come back and was behaving charmingly, and it was going to be a lovely wedding.

George was indeed behaving very well. He joined the working party in the drawing-room after lunch, and in a very short time the children, back from the Exley lunch, had folded neat stacks of paper and rolled large balls of string. The presents were ready and assembled after tea, and made a good show, and when the room was ready George sought out Phyl and found her with me in the final stages of packing.

"I think it wouldn't be a bad idea," he said, "if I took Robert and your rather excited fiancé out to dinner. Bachelor stuff — you know."

"Where on earth," Phyl inquired, "would you get dinner?"

"I didn't mean anything metropolitan, of course," said George, "but I think a quiet evening wouldn't do you women any harm, and a change wouldn't hurt Brian either — but if you want him, I won't make the suggestion."

"It's sweet of you," said Phyl, "and I think they ought to go. Don't bring them back too late, and don't — " she hesitated.

"Don't let Robert drive too far or too

fast, don't let Brian have more than two at the very most and don't forget to be at the ceremony to-morrow — is that it?" asked George.

"Well, something like it," said Phyl, going to him and slipping her arms round his neck. "Oh, George," she said softly, "I do wish you all the happiness in the world."

"Thanks," said George briefly, and disengaged himself gently. "See you to-morrow." He went out and left Phyl looking after him anxiously.

She turned to me with a worried frown.

"It makes me feel worse when I see him behaving so well," she said.

"It makes me feel worse too," I admitted. "I keep expecting the normal George to reappear, and this Spartan-boy attitude makes me dreadfully uneasy — I don't mean to be unkind," I added hastily, "but don't you remember when we were young and Aunt Flora sometimes lectured him about being more polite to us — he used to open doors for me and make sweeping bows and courtly speeches and drive me mad until he got tired of it and became his awful self again. The suspense was worse than the reality."

"You're never satisfied," said Phyl in amusement. "You don't like his rudeness and you find his politeness too great a strain — which way do you want him?"

"I don't want him any way," I replied. "The only way I really appreciate him is far away. Was that funny?" I asked in surprise.

"Not very, but at least it was clear and concise," said Phyl kindly. She studied me with affection for a few moments. "Oh, Jonny," she burst out, "I am going to miss you so dreadfully."

"Not nearly as much as I'll miss you," I said, "but I'm glad I'm going to be here always — I can't explain — "

"Oh, don't say it," begged Phyl. "I know what it is and it sounds terribly selfish, but I'm glad too."

We said no more, but the same thought filled both our minds. She had experienced one shipwreck and so had I, but we both knew that not the wreck itself, but the subsequent hopeless time of drifting, had been the hardest of all to bear. This time she might founder, but Rushing was our home and to Rushing she would return and find healing and comfort.

20

EVERYBODY came down to breakfast on Phyl's wedding day clad in a variety of bath robes and dressing-gowns, and changed into wedding garments immediately afterwards. The telephone seemed to ring every time anyone put down the receiver. Sometimes it rang continuously while everyone left someone else to answer it, and at other times several of us rushed into the hall at the same moment and reached for the receiver. This became so irritating that Paul volunteered to deal with the problem, and stationed himself at the hall table with a sheaf of writing paper, writing down telegrams and messages. These he called up the stairs during his free moments, and Polly and Diana, leaning perilously over the banisters, echoed his information and then went in to tell Phyl. This was a serious hindrance to their dressing, and after walking backwards and forwards between

Polly's room, the stairs and Phyl's room hooking dresses and tying ribbons, I gave up in despair and went to attend to my own dressing.

"Do you want any help?" I asked at Aunt Flora's door.

"Come in," she called. "No — I'm almost done and I'm going in to Phyl in a moment. Do I look my best?"

I assured her in all sincerity that she looked beautiful, and looked her over with pride and love.

"What's the day doing?" she asked, looking anxiously out of the window.

"It's doing nothing," I said, "and I think we'll have to be content with it as it is. No sun, but no rain and no sign of any."

Aunt Flora went into Phyl's room, and Polly stopped me at the top of the stairs. "Paul says please go down," she said. "There's a message he can't answer."

I took the receiver from Paul and heard the voice of a man in trouble. The station master at Felling had on his platform a large number of persons who wished to get to Rushing, and what, he inquired, had we arranged in the way of transport?

384

"Nothing whatsoever," I told him. "We weren't expecting a large number, and Duff was told to meet all the London trains."

Duff, I was informed, was there, and so was the bus.

"Well, what's the trouble?" I asked impatiently.

The trouble, it appeared, was the bus. There was a rooted conviction in the minds of the waiting guests that the stationmaster was mistaken in his statement that the waiting vehicle was licensed to carry human passengers.

"They're a bit dressed-up like," added Mr. Reed in explanation.

"Well, Mr. Reed," I said desperately. "It's Duff or nothing, and I think the best thing to do is to tell them that the transport arrangements have broken down and they must either come on the bus or go back on the next train."

I rang off, snatched the receiver up again with a sudden recollection that I had forgotten to ask how many there were, and put it down again.

"What's the matter?" called Aunt Flora from upstairs.

"Felling station swarming with guests," I said briefly, "all shirking the ride in Duff's chariot — and do you wonder!"

"How many are there?" asked Aunt Flora apprehensively.

"He didn't tell me," said I. "Go on dressing Phyl, and don't worry."

"Will you please to hook this up," said Carrie, emerging from the kitchen in a bewitching toilette composed mainly of lace flounces the colour of strong tea. "Why can't they put pops on dresses instead of 'ooks?"

I could have told her that no pop could have stood the strain of holding together the yawning breach between her brawny shoulders. I forced the hook side across to the eye side, and with much labour effected a junction. Carrie and I had been up before six and Aunt Flora since half-past, and the kitchen was a sight from which we felt it wise to exclude the ever-hungry children.

"Mummy," screamed Polly, "come upstairs and look at the bride."

I went up to Phyl's room and stopped in the doorway, gazing at the lovely, cool, fair vision that was going out of our lives once more. I found it difficult to speak, but I thought she looked as lovely, in a more poised, more serene way, as when she stood years ago in her white bridal dress and veil. It was not to be wondered at that Brian had found it impossible to forget her.

I was recalled to more practical matters by a summons from Paul at the telephone.

"Same man, same problem," he announced, handing me the receiver.

"It's the second train," said Mr. Reed, "I got the first lot off and this lot's waiting for the bus. Duff's a long time — I was wanting to know whether he's coming back — this is the slow train and he perhaps didn't expect anybody on it."

"I said *all* London trains," I answered, "but I'll send one of the children round to see where he is and remind him."

"I'll go, if you mean Duff," said Ivan. He went towards the front door, and stopped with bulging eyes at the magnificent sight coming down the drive. Brian in all his glory was a very grand figure indeed, and Ivan was plainly unable to proceed on his errand until he had got the dazzle out of his eyes.

"I," said Brian, striking an attitude in the hall, "am the bridegroom, and don't I look a fine fellow?"

He looked so fine that I had hardly noticed that George and Mr. Mill were both with him, George having walked over after breakfast to see that Brian finished his packing, paid his bill and got his luggage over to the house before the wedding.

"Aunt Flora," yelled Polly, rushing up the stairs, "they've come and Brian looks terribly pretty."

This caused a minor sensation in the hall, and I answered another telephone call while Brian rallied from the shock.

"Do you want to hear the messages?" I asked. "And there," I added, pointing to a pile of telegrams, "are a few more."

"I can't see the written word — I'm a bit shaky," said Brian, "and the messages can wait until my next leave, when I won't be so busy. Has that telephone," he inquired, as it sounded yet again, "been doing that all the morning?"

"It has," I said, "but I'm afraid to leave the receiver off in case anything important comes through."

There was a stir and we looked up to see Aunt Flora and Phyl coming down the stairs. Brian went forward and held out a hand to his lovely, blue-gowned bride, and kissed the smiling face under the small blue hat.

"Don't touch her, anybody," ordered Aunt Flora. "I'm going off now with the children and Carrie. There's only one more train due."

"And there it is," I said, as the telephone rang.

Mr. Reed sounded almost happy this time. "I've got the Upper Rosing bus to do a run into Rushing," he informed me triumphantly. "I'm afraid you'll have to pay him a good deal, but it was good of him to do it."

I thanked him sincerely, and could almost see him mopping his brow with relief as he reminded me that there were now no further trains from London before the wedding.

I put the receiver back with thankfulness, and went into the drawing-room to stay quietly with Phyl for a few minutes before we had to leave for the church.

It was cool and peaceful and quiet, and we were silent and thoughtful. Phyl and Brian stood at a window hand in hand, looking out into the garden; Mr. Mill wandered in and out of the tables and paused now and then to change the position of one or other of the presents. George was obeying Aunt Flora's last instructions and carrying the chairs from the drawing-room into the dining-room, to leave more space for people looking at the presents. I wandered into the hall and looked round to see that all was in order. The telephone rang and I looked at it with loathing. "Go on, George," I entreated.

"Go on yourself," said George kindly, going into the drawing-room to get the last chair.

I picked up the receiver wearily and nearly dropped it again as I heard Angela's voice.

"Oh, Mrs. Manning," she wailed, "I'm here and now I can't get to the wedding. Oh — do please do something."

"But all the London people came in on

the bus," I said in bewilderment. "Why didn't you?"

"I didn't come from London," cried Angela. "I've only just got here and they say Duff isn't coming back and it's no use getting a bicycle because I shan't get there in time and oh — oh, please," she ended desperately, "do something quickly."

George paused in the doorway of the drawing-room, a chair in his arms, and looked with amusement at my stricken face.

"But, Angela," I began in despair, "I can't — "

There was a crash as the chair hit the floor, and I had the presence of mind to bound aside and avoid by a hair's-breadth the impact of George's arrival. I looked anxiously at my fingers and was relieved to find he had not snatched any of them away with the receiver.

"Where are you?" he said abruptly, and then: "Stay exactly where you are — I'll be there in three minutes."

Phyl and Brian and Mr. Mill had appeared in the hall with as much celerity as George had dropped the chair, and

Phyl made a little sound which George interpreted as protest. He stopped at the front door and swung round.

"If you move a step while I'm gone," he said menacingly, advancing towards her, "I'll break your silly little neck. And yours too," he snarled, swinging round and fixing Brian with a brief but terrible glare.

He vanished through the doorway and the car came to life almost the same second; there was a grinding of gears that made Mr. Mill turn pale, and a scream of brakes as George reached the road and turned towards Felling; then a roar that gradually died away, and finally a frozen silence.

Phyl sat down slowly and carefully on the chair dropped by George, and folded her hands.

"We're marooned," said His Majesty's Navy. "Sunk, in fact. What do we do now? I suppose we go back to my original suggestion and walk."

"He won't be long," said Phyl calmly. "After all, Angela's in a hurry to get to the wedding."

"And do you think they'll remember

the wedding?" demanded Brian.

"I think they will," I said. "I think Angela will. Let's wait until they *ought* to be back, and then go."

The minutes went by, and nobody felt like speaking. George had the bridal equipage with all Brian's luggage, and perhaps he would come back and perhaps he wouldn't. Brian was plainly of the opinion that he wouldn't, and after watching the clock, made his decision.

"Look, my sweet," he said to Phyl, "Mill and I are going to walk. There'd better be one half of the wedding ingredients there anyhow. You and Jonny can come on in exactly ten minutes — you can't wait longer than that, Phyl."

"All right, darling," said Phyl. "I promise if he isn't here by that time I'll walk with Jonny."

Brian dropped a light kiss on her hat and went out with the sorrowful-looking Mr. Mill, and the party now consisted of one placid and one extremely worried woman.

We watched the clock steadily, and I thought more than once that there was a distant buzz of an engine, but at last the buzz persisted and swelled until Phyl and I both got to our feet and ran through the hall and out of the house.

The car came to a screeching stop and George, without a pause in the speech he was making to Angela, reached his arm backwards and fumbled for the door-handle.

Angela made a faint sound of greeting, but George's voice became even more urgent and she turned back and resumed her listening pose.

"You see what I mean," said George in continuation, "You can't argue about it — it's so *clear* — get in, you two," he ordered in parenthesis.

I began to explain that we were already in, but before I had spoken two words the car shot forward, backed and turned with murderous effect on the gravel and flowering borders, and shot down the drive and out of the gate.

"And another thing," continued George, half an eye on the road and the other one and a half fixed on Angela, "you're wrong in your second surmise and if I weren't a patient fellow I'd — "

I leaned forward and pounded as hard as I could on his back.

"The church," I shouted, "the church — not Felling!"

"Blast!" said George, bringing the car to an abrupt stop, so that I hit his back again, this time with my nose.

He executed a rapid half-circle and headed back towards Rushing.

"And if I weren't a patient fellow," he went on, "I'd shake you until your teeth rattled. How on earth do you suppose I would — "

The car came to a stop in response to my urgent prods, and George frowned at the building in front of us and apparently recognized the church. He got out and opened our door politely and held it open for three seconds, and then, apparently under the impression that we had alighted, banged it again.

Phyl and I sank back on the seat and I groped desperately for the handle on the other side. We got out and Phyl turned to her brother. He had come round to Angela's side and was leaning against the car and pursuing his conversation with her through the window. There were, fortunately, no spectators outside the church; Rushing felt that this was a family affair, and had assembled inside to view the whole proceeding.

The bride waited a moment for her escort to come to himself, and looked helplessly at me. I was feeling a little dizzy, and discovered that my nose was bleeding from its violent thump on George's back. I put my handkerchief to it, and the sight of the blood roused me to a shaking and unaccustomed fury. I discovered an unsuspected strength and, seizing George by the arm, I hauled him round to face Phyl.

"Take her inside, you — you — " I choked with sheer rage, and he looked at me in surprise and displeasure.

"Get out, Angela," I ordered.

She got out and looked at me apologetically.

"I'm sorry," she began.

"Not now," I said abruptly, and turned back to George.

"Take Phyl in, you selfish beast," I said.

"He isn't," said Phyl hotly.

"He is," said Angela, "and so am

I — go on in, George."

George looked from me to Angela and back again, his face registering swift changes from loathing to longing as he did so. Words quivered on his tongue, but he choked them back, drew Phyl's hand through his arm and turned towards the door of the church. He reached it and paused, looking back at me.

"Don't you bully Angela," he said in guarded but menacing tones.

"Self-centred pig," I hissed, mopping my aching nose.

They vanished into the gloom of the interior, and in no mood for conversation, I led Angela into the church and found a few inches of space at the end of one of the back rows. I could see nothing of the ceremony for a sea of hats, and as the service proceeded and my nose ceased to bleed, I began to feel ashamed of my exhibition, and prayed that I had not upset Phyl. Angela, by my side, looked thoughtful. She was no doubt, I reflected, deep in dreams of another wedding in which she and George would be united. Well, she was welcome to him, and only hoped that somebody would put her in a car on her wedding day and drive her wildly round the countryside and keep George in an agony of suspense at the altar. We were lucky to be here now with only one injured nose between us.

I forgot my nose presently as I calmed down, and I began to look round the crowded church and count the number of guests we might expect at the house after the wedding. My eyes roamed round the pews separating Rushing from visitors, and when I had counted up to thirty, I stopped out of sheer pity for the remainder, who would, I hoped, be able to get a meal immediately on returning to their homes. I wondered whether Aunt Flora had counted them, and whether Brian, conscious of vast throngs as he went up the aisle, had felt uneasy.

The organ, which had been giving out curious little tunes in a whisper, suddenly broke into the Wedding March, and I noticed with interest that it was the Da dee dee-da one.

I slipped out quickly, closely followed by George and Mr. Mill. The latter got into the driving seat of the car, and George held the door open as Brian and

Phyl came through the church door.

There was a great deal of confusion and laughter, and I felt a pinch on my arm and found Aunt Flora beside me.

"Come home quickly for goodness sake, Jonny," she besought me urgently. "And try and prevent me from doing Brian an injury before he goes off and leaves us with the starving mob."

21

MY instinct on reaching home was to rush upstairs and lock myself in my room until the last guest had departed, but this was unfortunately impossible, and I did the next best thing and entrenched myself behind a serving table, where I filled glasses and plates in comparative privacy and peace. Phyl and Brian stood at the foot of the verandah steps greeting guests as they arrived, and the rather bewildered Aunt Flora moved about doing what she could to make conversation with anonymous aunts and cousins. George and Angela, once more in their respective roles of lecturer and listener, were rather absently putting full glasses on to trays and Mr. Mill, going round with the trays, was being a most magnificent butler.

"Can I do anything?" asked Miss Peel's soft little voice beside me.

"It's sweet of you," I said gratefully, "but I don't think anybody can do much until Brian is free to identify a few of his relations."

"Well, I can do what you're doing, while you go out there and talk to them," suggested Miss Peel.

This was very similar to the noises which my uneasy conscience had been making for the past quarter of an hour, and my resistance broke down. I summoned my resolution and walked into the garden and decided that the solitary gentleman who had been walking slowly round and round the beech tree for some time would need some refreshment after his exercise. I missed him on his next round and waited for him to make his reappearance.

"How d'you do?" I said. "I'm Mrs. Manning — won't you come and get something to eat and drink?"

He looked at me with rather sour interest.

"I'd like to meet Miss Manning," he said abruptly. "Had old Edward on her hands for years, I understand. Fine old feller — went to school with him."

"I'll take you to Aunt Flora," I offered.

"No hurry," answered the aged stranger.

"You might sit here a moment" — he tapped the bench with his stick — "and tell me who some of these people are."

Here, I felt, was something in common.

"I can tell you who the local people are, if it interests you," I said, "but perhaps you'll know a few of the others — Brian's relations."

"Don't you know 'em?" he inquired.

"Not one," I confessed. "It would be nice to get a few names." I hesitated. "You're an uncle, aren't you?" I hazarded.

"Great-uncle," he corrected. "Name of Lionel."

"Oh, but I thought — " I began, and stopped abruptly, but not before he had seen my eyes searching his face for the vanished whiskers. I selected a stranger at random and nodded towards her. "Do you know who that is?" I asked.

"No — don't know half of 'em," grunted Lionel. "That woman decked up in the abominable carrot colour is my wife. She's been following Miss Manning round trying to get in a word about Edward." He studied Aunt Flora, now partially engulfed by a wave of guests.

"Damn' fine woman, your aunt," he continued. "That woman near her with bits of ostrich on her hat is Brian's Aunt Cecilia. Ever heard of her?"

I hadn't.

"Real name's Chrissie," he snorted with contempt and scorn. "On the musical side, so changed it to Cecilia. Keeps givin' recitals and God-knows-what — can't go to dinner there without having to listen to screechin' and bawlin' afterwards. Pah!"

I leaned back more comfortably, prepared to enjoy the trickle of acid information. My social sense, such as it was, recognized that I ought by this time to have led Uncle Lionel to the refreshments and there disposed of him, and dealt similarly with half a dozen other guests, but I was more interested in the caustic commentator by my side. I was, however, to hear no more, for toasts and speeches were now beginning, and immediately these were over I had to go upstairs and help Phyl to change into her travelling clothes.

"How many of those people out there do you know?" I asked her as I put the last things into the suitcase.

"I know a lot of faces," said Phyl, "but I couldn't put a name to a single one — is it going to be frightful for you after we've left?"

"I don't think so," I said. "I've got as far as Lionel and his wife and Cecilia already."

"Lionel? — he's harmless, but he's not quite what Brian calls fully assembled, you know," said Phyl.

"Isn't he?" I asked in surprise. "I didn't notice anything missing except the whiskers, and I liked his comments."

We went downstairs and found Aunt Flora and Brian in the hall, and slipped into the dining-room for our brief farewells. Phyl kissed Aunt Flora lingeringly and Brian took me into a fervent embrace.

"You've been sweet, Jonny," he said, "and I don't know how to say thank you."

"Well, look after Phyl," I said.

"I love you with all my heart," he said to Aunt Flora, with genuine affection, "and I am very proud indeed to be your nephew."

"One of your nephews," corrected George, joining us. "Robert says if you don't go now he won't guarantee to get you to Felling in time for your train. You're going with them to Felling, aren't you?" he asked Aunt Flora.

Aunt Flora was, and the little party prepared to run the gauntlet of the guests, now lined up waiting for the departure.

"Look here, George," said Brian urgently, "if there's anything going on, remember I want to know about it."

"You keep your mind on the British Navy," replied George coldly. "Did I ever interfere in your affairs?"

"No, but I'm a brother now," pointed out Brian, "and I want to know everything that goes on."

"All right, you shall," promised Aunt Flora, urging him through the door.

Brian went reluctantly. His own affairs were now in excellent order, and it was a pity to be leaving without any clear idea of the state of George's.

"Don't you let him keep you in the dark," he warned Aunt Flora, as they went out. "You've got to be a reporter on a first-class paper before you get anything out of that oyster."

I drew Aunt Flora aside for a moment. "There's an Uncle Lionel outside who wants to talk to you about Uncle Edward."

Aunt Flora looked aghast. "I hope you told him," she said, "that this is not an occasion on which I should dream of mentioning poor Edward." She grasped my arm firmly. "If he mentions it again, Jonny, tell him he's out of his mind."

"That's what Phyl said — "

"And another thing," went on Aunt Flora hurriedly, "you might try and control that tall affected woman who's going about making disparaging remarks about her betters. She must be suppressed, and if you haven't done anything by the time I come back, I'll look into it myself — Phyl, my dearest, do come on."

When the car was out of sight I slipped through the waving and cheering crush and hurried on to the verandah to make a hasty survey of food and drink. George detached himself from the returning guests and ran towards

406

the house, taking the verandah steps at a bound.

"I'm awfully sorry about this morning, Jonny," he said, coming across to me. "I was a selfish swine."

"I'm sorry, too," I acknowledged. "I went quite mad because you made my nose bleed when you stopped the car so suddenly."

"Was that it!" he exclaimed. "I remembered in the middle of the service that I'd seen blood and I wondered whether you'd broken a blood vessel in your wrath."

"I probably did," I said, "but it wasn't in my nose."

"Look here," he said urgently, as the crowd began to close in. "If you can help a bit with the Rushing lot, Angela and I will take over the rest. Do you know who any of them are?"

"Only two or three," I said, "and only their first names."

"Well, I'm going to mix them up a bit," said George. "Watch me go to work."

I watched with interest and admiration as he went quietly, unobtrusively and skilfully among the guests, reassembling and re-arranging, merging and separating, until they became a well-assorted company, enjoying themselves and finding interest and amusement in one another.

Nobody could have told George that Cecilia was the musical one, but he led her over to Miss Peel, and though no two women could have been a greater contrast outwardly, it was clear that their souls had met over a keyboard and were blending harmoniously. Uncle Lionel watched anxiously for Aunt Flora and stayed as near the drive as possible. He looked with interest and distaste at the children, his glance lingering on Ivan with something of triumph in it, as though he felt that here at last was a boy who could not disguise, under a human exterior, the fact that he, like all his kind, was a monkey and up to monkey tricks. I missed Nobby, who to his rage and grief had been compelled to attend school as usual. The school at Felling had opened and absorbed many of the small forms which would otherwise have been there to grace the wedding.

George had almost finished his task,

and the party was going with gratifying success. There was no doubt, I thought, that he had faults, but there were some things which he did surpassingly well. Like all work done by an expert, it had an effortless look, and I felt that I might do my small share in welding the guests into small and happy groups. I looked round but saw very few isolated units left to work on. My efforts would no doubt have had the effect of neutralizing much of George's work, but I was, as it happened, prevented from making any efforts at all, by the sight of Claudia, obviously in distress, hurrying by me to seek refuge in the dining-room. I followed in alarm, and found her mopping her eyes and looking very dismal indeed.

"Are you feeling ill?" I asked anxiously. "Do come upstairs and rest."

"No, thank you," she replied. "I'm just being foolish. I shall — I shall so miss your sister-in-law!"

I led her upstairs to my room, feeling a little foolish myself. I felt that our positions ought to have been reversed; I should have been shedding tears for Phyl. I tried to say as much to Claudia to bring a smile to her woebegone countenance. "I don't quite know why I don't feel more sad," I confessed. "I think it's probably because Phyl and I have parted so many times before — and never for long. We were never very far apart even when Hugh and Tommie — her first husband — were alive. You see, Phyl doesn't make many new friends — she's too — well, too lazy. Everybody likes her and tries to draw her into their circles but somehow Phyl never really merges. Do you see what I mean?" I asked, and Claudia nodded.

"Yes," she said. "We all really love her here, and yet what you say is true — she doesn't make many contacts outside the family. We've always come to her."

"Whenever she's near enough," I said, "or free enough, she comes to Aunt Flora or to me — and now I know it'll be the same. She'll be with Brian whenever she can, and when he's moved somewhere she can't follow, she'll be here — sitting on her long chair on the verandah as though she'd never left it, doing nothing, and looking as though she would never go away any more. I miss her, but in the same way as I miss Paul when he's at school — he must go, but this is home and he'll come back, and even when he's back, I know that he has to go again. I'm awfully bad at putting things into words," I confessed, "but perhaps you see why there's no reason to mourn Phyl as a total loss."

Claudia sat on my sofa, dry-eyed now, but still thoughtful.

"You must think it odd," she said slowly, "to have an old spinster in no way connected with your family weeping because one of you has left. Most things," she continued bitterly, "that old spinsters do are considered odd. I love Phyl because — I think because she's the only lovely woman I ever met who was truly kind — truly gentle. She was never hurried or impatient or bored, and in talking to her I always felt a two-fold pleasure — three-fold, because I had the selfish pleasure of talking to a wonderfully good listener; the joy of watching her quietly and for long peaceful, uninterrupted spells, and the happiness — and I can't tell you, Mrs. Manning, what a rare happiness it was for me — to know that someone was actually listening without being irritated or bored!"

I felt that if this went on I would soon be having a good cry myself, and Claudia must have seen me preparing for one, for she rose and smiled with real amusement.

"This," she said, "is a good way to behave at a wedding — take the hostess into the bedroom and make a dreadful scene! But I'm very grateful to you — I feel better for having told you. If I had been quite myself," she added apologetically, "I wouldn't have been so foolish, but I'm not really recovered yet."

I took her hand and stroked it rather awkwardly. "If you want to come and talk to me, do, at any time," I begged. "Only I can't sit on the verandah — I love to listen, but I love to work too! If you'll follow me about — "

We laughed and prepared to go downstairs, Claudia peering into my glass to see if the little storm had left any traces on her face.

"I'm glad you brought me out of

412

the dining-room," she said gratefully, as we went down, "the house is full of people."

Everybody seemed to be indoors looking at wedding presents, and it was a pity Mr. Mill was not present to hear the compliments paid to the excellent arrangements he had made. I made my way across to Angela, and in a brief sentence explained Claudia's sense of loss and asked her to keep an eye on her.

She held my arm for a moment and detained me.

"Can I borrow pyjamas for to-night?" she asked. "I didn't bring anything with me but I'm staying at the Trotters and going back with George in Mr. Mill's car to-morrow."

"But of course you'll stay in Phyl's room," I said. "Don't talk nonsense about going to the Trotters."

Angela protested, but I told her that Diana would be pleased to have her on the last night of the holidays, and it was settled.

I looked into the garden — Uncle Lionel was still stationed as near the gate as possible, and I wondered why

Paul, Polly and Ivan were all standing and watching a small group of women on the lawn. The faces of all three were intent and innocent, but I had an uneasy feeling and moved towards them.

"Oughtn't you to be helping George?" I asked "There's a great deal to be done."

There was no reply from the absorbed trio, and the next moment a tall figure detached itself from the group and came towards me, and as she spoke I knew that here was what had acted as a magnet to the children and an irritant to Aunt Flora.

"You must be Mrs. Manning," drawled the stranger in so affected a voice that I thought for a moment it must be what Polly called a pretend one. "Are all these" — she waved a hand at the children and left it dangling elegantly in the air — "your own?"

"I get a little mixed up sometimes," I said smiling at Ivan, "but I think only two of them are mine."

"I'm Brian's cousin Brenda — ever heard him speak of me?" inquired the lady languidly.

I was certain that if Brian had ever given an impression of Cousin Brenda it would have remained firmly in my mind, and said as politely as possible that I had never heard of her.

"Charming place you've got," she said kindly. Her glance round the lawn took in the Exleys, Miss Peel, the Trotters and several more of our friends. "I suppose," she said in sympathetic tones, "you have to see a good deal of the villagahs?"

I was quite unequal to this, and wished I had listened more carefully to Aunt Flora's warning. I was aware that every gesture and every word was impressed for ever on the minds of the children, and that Cousin Brenda would appear in many disguises whenever we were treated to impersonations by the children for years to come.

Rescue came from a strange quarter, and in the form of a poke in the back from Uncle Lionel's stick. I turned round in amazement and found him beckoning me urgently. I went reluctantly, but he was better than Brenda.

"No sign of your aunt," he growled. "Want to talk to her about old Edward."

This was obviously the time to deliver Aunt Flora's message, but I could think of no inoffensive way of informing him that he was out of his mind, and I was relieved to see the car enter the drive. Lionel helped Aunt Flora out with eagerness.

"You remember me," he asserted rather than asked "Want to talk — "

"Of course I remember you," said Aunt Flora. "All those years ago. I've acquired a great-nephew and niece since then — you must come and see them." Before the horrified and outraged man could protest, he found himself once again face to face with the children, while Aunt Flora, with a pleasant introduction and an airy instruction to them to "have a nice chat", had vanished once more.

The children retreated hastily under the ferocious glare turned upon them, and I sought refuge on the verandah, where Aunt Flora approached me.

"I don't suppose you'd know where George and Angela are?" she said in rather cold tones.

"Why, yes," I said. "George is being awfully good and looking after everybody, and Angela is helping him."

Aunt Flora gave me a sour and scornful glance.

"Very fine work indeed," she congratulated me. "Excellent. Lionel at my heels for his chat, Brenda let loose among the villagahs, and George and Angela making an exhibition of themselves — look!"

I looked and saw the pair at a cosy table for two at the far end of the lawn, and it was obvious that they had forgotten the company and resumed the apparently endless discussion which had begun in Mr. Mill's car that morning.

I rallied my drooping spirits. "Well, if you'll tell me what to do now," I said meekly, "I'll do it."

"There is fortunately no need for you to exercise your magnificent social gifts any longer," said Aunt Flora, "because, thank God, everyone has got to go home fairly soon."

This was undoubtedly a great relief, and I watched the preparations for departure with what I hoped was concealed pleasure. Mr. Mill proved himself once again a very good friend.

"If you don't think the children will

417

be too tired," he said, "we can get all those presents packed up and put away as soon as the foreigners have gone."

I thanked him wholeheartedly, and went forward to say good-bye to the visitors, asking Mr. Mill to rouse George and Angela from their abstraction and ask them to come back to the party. George appeared shortly afterwards, almost as eager to see the last of the guests as I myself was, and we walked slowly and with much noise and chatter to where Duff waited with his bus.

Uncle Lionel stopped short and looked at the vehicle in complete amazement.

"What's that thing?" he inquired of George.

"That," replied George, directing his glance towards it and assuming an almost tender expression, "is our bus — our only bus."

"Rubbish," said Lionel. "Didn't come down in that disgustin' thing."

"Perhaps not," said George. "We managed to borrow a local one this morning."

"Borrow it again," ordered Lionel.

"Not goin' in that. Never saw such a thing in m'life."

We looked towards his wife for guidance, and she met the situation exactly as I would have done, and clambered hastily into the bus and out of our reach.

George braced himself.

"You're like Aunt Flora," he said, in gentle and pleasant tones. "She always refuses to ride inside, and insists on sitting with the driver. She's the only one, as a matter of fact, he'll ever allow to ride beside him."

Uncle Lionel responded to this challenge by striding up to the front of the bus and climbing stiffly up into the seat beside the driver. Mr. Duff stood waiting to swing the starting handle, and gazed at the old gentleman with rather bleary interest.

"Fellow's half tight," announced Lionel, after a brief but expert glance.

Those passengers who heard the remark were not unnaturally a little uneasy, and Duff became the focus of anxious glances.

"What are we waitin' for?" roared Lionel, losing patience and banging his stick on the floor. "Get in — get in and let the fellow get off. If he can't drive, damme I'll do it m'self."

A horrified murmur of protest and alarm rose from the interior, and Lionel turned purple.

"Come on — you!" he roared at Duff, and Duff, turning the handle with spirit and energy, brought the bus to life, sprang to his place at the wheel and turned the vehicle towards Felling.

"God knows," said Aunt Flora piously, "whether they'll ever get there."

"Perhaps I should have taken the old fellow over in Robert's car," said George, "but it's too late now. If he wrecks them all perhaps we'll get a new bus."

Everyone felt brighter at this thought, and we turned toward the house.

"You go straight up to your room and rest," I advised Aunt Flora, "and the rest of us will have things straightened out in no time."

"I don't want to rest," said Aunt Flora. "I want to look and see what they've done to my garden."

With Aunt Flora in the garden, Carrie and Mrs. Watt and myself in the kitchen, and Mr. Mill with George and Angela and the children in the drawing-room, all clearing and cleansing energetically, the rest of the day passed quickly. We all sat down to a substantial tea-supper, feeling tired but glad to know that the house was once more in fairly good order. After supper came the sad business of saying good-bye to Ivan, who, like Diana, was to return to school the following day. The farewells lost much of their gloom by being conducted in the Brenda manner, and Master Exley departed with mincing steps, assuring his playmates in the most refined accents that he would soon be back among them, villagahs though they were.

"'Bye, Mrs. Manning — thank you for all the fun," he said with a return to his normal manner. "'Bye, Miss Manning." He bowed elegantly to George and Angela, and backed skilfully down the verandah steps. "Ta, ta, my deah friends," he ended in character. "Ta, ta, till Christmas."

I urged Diana and Polly upstairs, and they went with less reluctance than usual, for it had been a full day. George handed

Polly up the first stair with a low bow.

"I'm sorry you can't have Angela yet," he said. "She promised the Trotters she'd go and see them after supper."

Polly assumed an air of profound boredom. "Trotters?" she asked in supercilious tones. "Ah — villagahs, no doubt." She trailed up a few stairs and looked at George over her shoulder with disdainful interest. "*Do* they eat?" she drawled.

★ ★ ★

At last the children were asleep and the house had resumed almost its normal aspect. I sat on the verandah with Aunt Flora, Mr. Mill making a restful and welcome third, and with only a word now and then we remained until it was almost dark and the footsteps of George and Angela were heard on the drive. George drew a chair close to Aunt Flora's and looked at her affectionately.

"You don't look very bereaved," he complained. "You know that I am leaving you to-morrow?"

"Of course I know," she replied, "and

you mustn't come back for a long time. Jonny and I have had a very busy summer and we're going to take it easy until we recover our strength. Of course, I shall miss you," she added. "All those screechings and shoutings you do — it's rather the same as having that drilling thing at the dentist's — it's a shocking noise but when it's over it certainly leaves a hole."

George bowed.

"How do you think he looks?" Aunt Flora asked Mr. Mill. "Don't you think we've made a good job of the repair?"

"An excellent job," said Mr. Mill, "but although you've put the machine in order, it still refuses to work."

"Not at all," denied George. "I merely refuse to go straight back to work — I'm going to concentrate on my private life for a few weeks."

"Well, you must concentrate somewhere else," said Aunt Flora. "Although where, I don't know. A week of you pursuing Angela like a cyclone round her old lady, and the poor old thing will be dead."

"Isn't the centre of a cyclone quite quiet and still?" I asked.

"That's what I said," answered Aunt Flora. "She'd be quiet and still, quite dead."

"I suppose I'm correct in assuming," said George, "that you don't want to hear the word wedding mentioned for quite a while?"

"Perfectly correct," replied Aunt Flora firmly. "If your plans include the word wedding, I don't want to hear anything about them. You can come down at Christmas" she added kindly, "and bring Angela — Diana will be here — and I shan't be busy in the garden so I shall be able to listen to you. Go to bed, Angela," she ordered. "You're almost asleep."

"I'm not asleep," said Angela. "I'm dreaming lovely dreams about — "

"About me and that house at Smallfish," said George.

"About Christmas and Rushing and snow-fights and things like that," said Angela. "I didn't know that you and the house at Smallfish were just a dream."

George rose and drew her to her feet, and kissed her lightly.

"Go to bed," he ordered gently, "and Aunt Flora will tuck you up presently when she's passing. And I hope sleeping in Phyl's bed won't mean that you have to dream of Brian."

"That reminds me," said Aunt Flora. "He sent a telegram from King's Cross."

"What did he say?" I asked.

"He said," replied Aunt Flora, "that he'd been married this morning and was very happy."

THE END

Other titles in the
Ulverscroft Large Print Series:

TO FIGHT THE WILD
Rod Ansell and Rachel Percy

Lost in uncharted Australian bush, Rod Ansell survived by hunting and trapping wild animals, improvising shelter and using all the bushman's skills he knew.

COROMANDEL
Pat Barr

India in the 1830s is a hot, uncomfortable place, where the East India Company still rules. Amelia and her new husband find themselves caught up in the animosities which seethe between the old order and the new.

THE SMALL PARTY
Lillian Beckwith

A frightening journey to safety begins for Ruth and her small party as their island is caught up in the dangers of armed insurrection.

NURSE ALICE IN LOVE
Theresa Charles

Accepting the post of nurse to little Fernie Sherrod, Alice Everton could not guess at the romance, suspense and danger which lay ahead at the Sherrod's isolated estate.

POIROT INVESTIGATES
Agatha Christie

Two things bind these eleven stories together — the brilliance and uncanny skill of the diminutive Belgian detective, and the stupidity of his Watson-like partner, Captain Hastings.

LET LOOSE THE TIGERS
Josephine Cox

Queenie promised to find the long-lost son of the frail, elderly murderess, Hannah Jason. But her enquiries threatened to unlock the cage where crucial secrets had long been held captive.

TIGER TIGER
Frank Ryan

A young man involved in drugs is found murdered. This is the first event which will draw Detective Inspector Sandy Woodings into a whirlpool of murder and deceit.

CAROLINE MINUSCULE
Andrew Taylor

Caroline Minuscule, a medieval script, is the first clue to the whereabouts of a cache of diamonds. The search becomes a deadly kind of fairy story in which several murders have an other-worldly quality.

LONG CHAIN OF DEATH
Sarah Wolf

During the Second World War four American teenagers from the same town join the Army together. Forty-two years later, the son of one of the soldiers realises that someone is systematically wiping out the families of the four men.

THE LISTERDALE MYSTERY
Agatha Christie

Twelve short stories ranging from the light-hearted to the macabre, diverse mysteries ingeniously and plausibly contrived and convincingly unravelled.

TO BE LOVED
Lynne Collins

Andrew married the woman he had always loved despite the knowledge that Sarah married him for reasons of her own. So much heartache could have been avoided if only he had known how vital it was to be loved.

ACCUSED NURSE
Jane Converse

Paula found herself accused of a crime which could cost her her job, her nurse's reputation, and even the man she loved, unless the truth came to light.

THE PLEASURES OF AGE
Robert Morley

The author, British stage and screen star, now eighty, is enjoying the pleasures of age. He has drawn on his experiences to write this witty, entertaining and informative book.

THE VINEGAR SEED
Maureen Peters

The first book in a trilogy which follows the exploits of two sisters who leave Ireland in 1861 to seek their fortune in England.

A VERY PAROCHIAL MURDER
John Wainwright

A mugging in the genteel seaside town turned to murder when the victim died. Then the body of a young tearaway is washed ashore and Detective Inspector Lyle is determined that a second killing will not go unpunished.

DEATH ON A HOT SUMMER NIGHT
Anne Infante

Micky Douglas is either accident-prone or someone is trying to kill him. He finds himself caught in a desperate race to save his ex-wife and others from a ruthless gang.

HOLD DOWN A SHADOW
Geoffrey Jenkins

Maluti Rider, with the help of four of the world's most wanted men, is determined to destroy the Katse Dam and release a killer flood.

THAT NICE MISS SMITH
Nigel Morland

A reconstruction and reassessment of the trial in 1857 of Madeleine Smith, who was acquitted by a verdict of Not Proven of poisoning her lover, Emile L'Angelier.

SEASONS OF MY LIFE
Hannah Hauxwell
and Barry Cockcroft

The story of Hannah Hauxwell's struggle to survive on a desolate farm in the Yorkshire Dales with little money, no electricity and no running water.

TAKING OVER
Shirley Lowe and Angela Ince

A witty insight into what happens when women take over in the boardroom and their husbands take over chores, children and chickenpox.

AFTER MIDNIGHT STORIES,
The Fourth Book Of

A collection of sixteen of the best of today's ghost stories, all different in style and approach but all combining to give the reader that special midnight shiver.

DEATH TRAIN
Robert Byrne

The tale of a freight train out of control and leaking a paralytic nerve gas that turns America's West into a scene of chemical catastrophe in which whole towns are rendered helpless.

THE ADVENTURE OF THE CHRISTMAS PUDDING
Agatha Christie

In the introduction to this short story collection the author wrote "This book of Christmas fare may be described as 'The Chef's Selection'. I am the Chef!"

RETURN TO BALANDRA
Grace Driver

Returning to her Caribbean island home, Suzanne looks forward to being with her parents again, but most of all she longs to see Wim van Branden, a coffee planter she has known all her life.

SKINWALKERS
Tony Hillerman

The peace of the land between the sacred mountains is shattered by three murders. Is a 'skinwalker', one who has rejected the harmony of the Navajo way, the murderer?

A PARTICULAR PLACE
Mary Hocking

How is Michael Hoath, newly arrived vicar of St. Hilary's, to meet the demands of his flock and his strained marriage? Further complications follow when he falls hopelessly in love with a married parishioner.

A MATTER OF MISCHIEF
Evelyn Hood

A saga of the weaving folk in 18th century Scotland. Physician Gavin Knox was desperately seeking a cure for the pox that ravaged the slums of Glasgow and Paisley, but his adored wife, Margaret, stood in the way.

DEAD SPIT
Janet Edmonds

Government vet Linus Rintoul attempts to solve a mystery which plunges him into the esoteric world of pedigree dogs, murder and terrorism, and Crufts Dog Show proves to be far more exciting than he had bargained for . . .

A BARROW IN THE BROADWAY
Pamela Evans

Adopted by the Gordillo family, Rosie Goodson watched their business grow from a street barrow to a chain of supermarkets. But passion, bitterness and her unhappy marriage aliented her from them.

THE GOLD AND THE DROSS
Eleanor Farnes

Lorna found it hard to make ends meet for herself and her mother and then by chance she met two men — one a famous author and one a rich banker. But could she really expect to be happy with either man?

THE SONG OF THE PINES
Christina Green

Taken to a Greek island as substitute for David Nicholas's secretary, Annie quickly falls prey to the island's charms and to the charms of both Marcus, the Greek, and David himself.

GOODBYE DOCTOR GARLAND
Marjorie Harte

The story of a woman doctor who gave too much to her profession and almost lost her personal happiness.

DIGBY
Pamela Hill

Welcomed at courts throughout Europe, Kenelm Digby was the particular favourite of the Queen of France, who wanted him to be her lover, but the beautiful Venetia was the mainspring of his life.

PREJUDICED WITNESS
Dilys Gater

Fleur Rowley finds when she leaves London for her 'author's retreat' in the wilds of North Wales that she is drawn, in spite of herself, into an old tragedy.

GENTLE TYRANT
Lucy Gillen

Working as Ross McAdam's secretary, Laura couldn't imagine why his bitchy ex-wife should see her as a rival.

DEAR CAPRICE
Juliet Gray

Clifford Fortune married Caprice but his brother, Luke, knew the marriage was a mistake. He could allow himself to love Caprice blindly but that would be betraying his own brother.

IN PALE BATTALIONS
Robert Goddard

Leonora Galloway has waited all her life to learn the truth about her father, slain on the Somme before she was born, the truth about the death of her mother and the mystery of an unsolved wartime murder.

A DREAM FOR TOMORROW
Grace Goodwin

In her new position as resident nurse at Coombe Magna, Karen Stevens has to bear the emnity of the beautiful Lisa, secretary to the doctor-on-call.

AFTER EMMA
Sheila Hocken

Following the author's previous auto-biographies — EMMA & I, and EMMA & Co., she relates more of the hilarious (and sometimes despairing) antics of her guide dogs.

LEAVE IT TO THE HANGMAN
Bill Knox

Dope, dynamite, guns, currency — whatever it was John Kilburn and his son Pat had known how to get it in or out of England, if the price was right. But their luck changed when one of them killed a cop.

A VIOLENT END
Emma Page

To Chief Inspector Kelsey there was no shortage of suspects when Karen Boland was murdered, and that was before he discovered that she stood to inherit substantially at twenty-one.

SILENCE IN HANOVER CLOSE
Anne Perry

In 1884 Robert York is found brutally murdered at his home in Hanover Close. When, three years later, Inspector Pitt is asked to investigate, the murder remains unsolved.

A RARE BENEDICTINE
Ellis Peters

Three vintage tales of medieval intrigue and treachery featuring the author's monastic sleuth Brother Cadfael.

POIROT'S EARLY CASES
Agatha Christie

In this collection of eighteen stories, Hercule Poirot begins his celebrated career in crime.

THE SILVER LINK
— THE SILKEN LIE
Lynn Granger

Elspeth is determined to preserve her Scottish heritage and the Elliot name, but running Everanlea, a large hill farm, presents problems.

Love is
a time of enchantment:
in it all days are fair and all fields
green. Youth is blest by it,
old age made benign:
the eyes of love see
roses blooming in December,
and sunshine through rain. Verily
is the time of true-love
a time of enchantment — and
Oh! how eager is woman
to be bewitched!